What the

MW00737608

"In *Red Leopard*, national multi-award-winning, multi-published author Tracy Cooper-Posey, has produced an untamed, wildly exciting story of love and raw sexual desire. With steamy, pant-provoking sex scenes and a love to rival the most notorious forbidden affairs in history, Red Leopard will leave the reader in a state of arousal that will require a Tarzan-like beast of the jungle to sate! Tracy Cooper-Posey receives the highest rating for her great writing, intricate plotting and tasteful yet extremely erotic sex scenes." - *Titania Ladley, Women on Writing*

Five Stars!
"This is a great suspense story. ... If you love those movies where you don't know who's side the hero is really on until the end, then you'll love the intrigue of Red Leopard." - *Angel Brewer, TRS Blue*

4 Stars!
"Red Leopard ... keeps the reader glued from beginning to end. The romance between Nick and Calli is spell-binding. The mixture of romance and sexual ecstasy made this book worth reading over and over. This reviewer found herself drawn to the mysterious sexy red leopard, wanting to find out more about him. The whole romantic country and words that are used take you deep inside the book and you find yourself there. It takes you from an ongoing war to a romantic get away back to the war. It just goes to prove two people from different countries can fall in love and be together even when the countries don't want them to be." - *Ruby, Love Romances*

"Pros: Fresh new idea. Cons: none. The Bottom Line: Calli Munro, an American, arrives in Vistaria during LaFiesta le La Luna, a combination of Mardi Gras and Carnival. Red Leopard is a strong sensual story that deals with irresistible attractions and the forces that stand in the way of love. This has both romance and action throughout the story. Reading about the political climate of Vistaria, and the unfolding of romance between Nicolas and Calli will keep you on the edge of your chair. For Romantica this is something new and fresh." - *Pat McGrew, About Romance.com*

"Tracy Cooper-Posey weaves this tale in a delightfully exotic setting. The people on the isle of Vistaria are sensual and the descriptions of the landscape are beautiful. The characters are well developed and have great sensual chemistry together. The love scenes are well written and very hot! The plot moves along at a nice pace and is filled with sexuality. I really enjoyed the suspense of wanting them together intimately. I really enjoyed this and I would recommend Red Leopard to other people who love romanticas." - *Maria Desrosiers, eBook Reviews Weekly*

"In RED LEOPARD, Ms. Cooper-Posey has written a spellbinding, adventurous novel. The sexual tension between Nick and Calli is compelling. I could not see how it would be possible for Calli and Nick to have a future together and worried that there might not be a happy ending. I hope that there will be a sequel to RED LEOPARD as there are a few unanswered questions at the end. I am anxiously waiting to see what comes next from Ms. Cooper-Posey's talented pen!" - *Denise Powers, Sensual Romance Reviews*

Discover for yourself why readers can't get enough of the multiple award-winning publisher Ellora's Cave. Whether you prefer e-books or paperbacks, be sure to visit EC on the web at www.ellorascave.com for an erotic reading experience that will leave you breathless.

www.ellorascave.com

RED LEOPARD
An Ellora's Cave publication, 2003

Ellora's Cave Publishing, Inc.
PO Box 787
Hudson, OH 44236-0787

ISBN # 1843607476

ISBN MS Reader (LIT) ISBN # 1-84360-424-8
Other available formats (no ISBNs are assigned):
Adobe (PDF), Rocketbook (RB), Mobipocket (PRC) & HTML

RED LEOPARD © 2003 TRACY COOPER-POSEY

ALL RIGHTS RESERVED. This book may not be reproduced in whole or in part without permission.

This book is a work of fiction and any resemblance to persons living or dead, or places, events or locales is purely coincidental. They are productions of the authors' imaginations and used fictitiously.

RED LEOPARD edited by Allie Sawyer.
Cover art by Scott Carpenter.

RED LEOPARD

Tracy Cooper-Posey

DEDICATION
To Julie,
who started it all.

ACKNOWLEDGEMENTS
Thank you to the whole Ellora's Cave team — it's so nice to be a person! Special thanks to Allie, whip-wielding editor extraordinaire, and to MamaZuca, for correcting my Spanish. And of course, thanks to my family for putting up with me;

Mark, Terry, Matthew and Kate.

AUTHOR'S NOTE
This novel is set in a fictional country, featuring fictional characters, and it is a romantic fantasy first and foremost — please practice safe sex in your own life.

Chapter One

Calli gripped the prison bars and looked out upon the carefree people celebrating the festival fifteen feet below her, all of them totally ignorant of her plight. It was *La Fiesta de la Luna*, which Vistarian citizens celebrated for the three nights of the first summer full moon. Calli was not Vistarian, she was American, and twenty-four hours ago she had been sitting in her apartment in Butte, Montana. The glorious republic of Vistaria had welcomed her onto the main island a scant five hours ago, and for the last three hours and twenty-five minutes she had been in this jail.

She turned back to face the bars of the dingy cell she stood in. It wasn't really a cell at all. Two short walls of bars keeping her penned in a cramped corner of the room — it was really a cage, not a cell. But when she looked out at the rest of the room, she welcomed the bars.

The dingy holding cells of the Lozano Colinas city police barracks were on the second floor of an adobe building on a large public square. The walls of the room, once white, showed a dirty yellow-gray now, with the combined effects of years of dirt and smoke brushing against them.

Five men occupied the room, all wearing army green uniform pants with red stripes up the legs and white collarless dress shirts — their uniform jackets hung over the backs of chairs. Clearly they resented being on duty during the first night of the festival, for they were holding their own party.

Bottles of whiskey and black rum with colorful labels dotted the big round table with the battered wooden top. Between the bottles laid half a dozen old tobacco tins being used as ashtrays for the cigars and thin yellow cigarettes with the harsh tobacco they smoked.

Four of them sat at the table playing cards, laughing and talking in loud voices. From their gestures and expressions Calli guessed their conversation was ribald. Many times the comments were about her. They would speak, glance at her in her corner, then comment in the bastardized Spanish that was common here. A deep belly laugh would follow. Their thick cigarette smoke fogged the air, and the big multi-colored Vistarian currency liberally covered the table.

In the opposite corner to her cell the leader of the group, possibly a sergeant, sat on a stool with a woman on his knee, his big hands about her waist, as he whispered things into her ear. She was dressed like many of the women had been dressed that Calli had seen in the few short minutes she had been on the public streets tonight: a white off-the-shoulder blouse, a dark cummerbund about the waist and yards and yards of long skirt in panels of glowing, gloriously colored silk that floated about their legs. With their dark straight hair tied in buns low on the back of their necks, a spray of the odd blue-colored wisteria she had seen everywhere tucked behind one ear and hoop earrings, the women looked wonderful. They moved with the sophisticated confidence of sensual, mature women, their hips swinging invitingly. It was an art Calli had never mastered, that confident poise.

The soldier's hand slipped inside the neck of the woman's blouse, and beneath the cotton Calli could see the shape of his hand cup her breast, the thumb moving as if he stroked the nipple. The woman gave a small low laugh, her shoulders arching back a bit, easing his access to her breast.

Calli swallowed dryly. It seemed *La Fiesta de la Luna* shared Mardi Gras's lack of inhibitions.

Then the thought struck her like a gun shot: *Is that why the soldiers are staring at me that way?* She looked back at the table again. Another furtive glance towards her. Another comment and the chuckle that moved around the table.

Yes, she decided reluctantly. That's what they were doing. Sizing her up.

She brushed at the jeans she wore, wishing mightily she had chosen to wear sackcloth for the journey. The jeans and tee shirt had felt perfectly respectable in Montana—the low rise waist-band that sat around her hips was far more conservative than the pants some of her students wore.

But now she was uncomfortably conscious of the band of flesh that sometimes appeared between her tee shirt and the jeans, and that the tee shirt, even though it remained her favorite, fit a little snugly from too many washings.

She turned back to the tiny window with the bars, willing to watch the endless carousing on the street for hours if it meant she didn't have to look at the soldiers around the table. She didn't know anything about Latin American countries except what she had read in books, but she knew in her gut that watching the soldiers would be inviting trouble.

How the hell was she going to get out of this mess? They certainly hadn't offered her a phone call before they'd thrown her in here, and she hadn't seen a single sheet of paperwork. Would anyone—Minnie, Uncle Josh—know she was even here? Surely some sort of alarm must have gone up when she didn't show up on schedule. With the festival in full swing would they be able to trace her movements?

For a long while she watched the dancing and merriment down below. The heart of the festival appeared to be in the square itself. The hundreds of people down there appeared to be ready to party all night.

At least she would have something to look at while she idled her night away here. She certainly wouldn't be sleeping.

He entered the room so quietly that at first she didn't notice him. It must have caught the soldiers off guard, too, for the first hint she got was an overly loud "*¡Atención!*" followed by the sound of men scrambling to their feet, knocking over their stools in their haste. Grunts of effort and an alarmed cry sounded.

She turned, alert.

He wasn't in uniform. He didn't even look Latino. Dark red hair and midnight blue eyes, with the pale skin that went with that coloring. He looked more Irish than her great-grandmother, who came from county Kildare.

American? she wondered. Help, at last?

But no, they stood rigid, waiting. The sergeant, the big soldier in the corner, now stood with his hand locked into a salute, quivering with perfect attention. The woman next to him leisurely pulled her blouse into place.

The man looked about the room, sizing the men up. What had the soldiers called him? It had sounded, amongst the gibberish of mongrel Spanish, like the name "Roger" had been spoken.

He looked at the woman, and gave a little shake of his head. "Rosali…" and he spoke to her.

She gave a shrug and a smile and moved slowly to the door behind the man. He patted her shoulder as she went. She shut the door behind her while the man looked around again.

Not one of the soldiers had moved an inch. He spoke a quiet word, and they relaxed, but none of them sat down again.

He spoke to the sergeant then, in the same quiet, understated way. He didn't use his hands, either. In this land of flamboyant gestures and uninhibited volume, he was icily contained, controlled. His hands stayed relaxed at the sides of his dark, modern suit.

The sergeant rattled off a stream of words. Explanations, she realized.

They had been royally busted…so who was this guy?

When the sergeant had run out of words and fallen silent, the man studied him for a pregnant moment. Then he spoke a few words.

The sergeant quailed and nodded eagerly. He spoke to the other men, who scurried to clear the table and go about their business.

The man in the dark suit turned then, finally, to look at Calli for the first time.

It felt like being pinned down by lasers. His direct gaze, the unflinching eyes, locked onto her face. The blue seemed almost black when he stared at her directly that way—as if a trick of the light made them appear that dark indigo blue only when reflected correctly.

He slid a hand into his pants pocket. "You have been in the country for less than five hours, Miss Munro, and already you are in trouble. It does not augur well for the remainder of your stay here, does it?"

His English was flawless. His voice had a gravelly quality that reached out and caressed the back of her neck. Calli shivered.

"It's not my fault I'm here. There were three of them, and I kept saying no…"

He considered this. "Then you very forcefully backed up your 'no' by breaking one nose and leaving various cuts and bruises for them to remember you by."

"How many times do I have to say no before it sticks?" she asked, trying to keep her voice sweet and reasonable.

Again she got the thoughtful silence. "This is not Montana, Miss Munro. This is Vistaria, in South America, during the Luna festival. Americans here are treated with suspicion and prejudice. You should make allowances."

"Like they did for me?" she asked, appalled to realize her voice was rising. What allowances had the men who had come up to her tonight made? They had appeared out of a dark side street as she had been making her way towards lights and civilization and scared her silly. They had been in the mood to have some fun, and now she thought about it, she recalled that "*Americana*" had dotted their talk as they had surrounded her, laughing and pushing playfully. She had shaken her head, repeated "no" a few times while trying to slip out of their little circle. When one hand had briefly cupped her buttock, she had reacted. Three years of karate had paid off…sort of.

But the man did not appear to agree with her point of view.

"You are a visitor, Miss Munro. Things are different here. You cannot demand the same rights that you are used to in the States."

"You're not American," she judged.

He seemed a little amused at that one, for his mouth curled up at one corner. Just a little. "No, I'm not American."

"Don't I at least get a phone call?" she asked.

He once again appeared to consider her request seriously, carefully. He took a step or two closer to the cage. Calli already stood close to the bars and his paces brought him much too close to her for comfort — she didn't like to have to tilt her head up to look someone in the eyes. But she held her ground, unwilling to show him by stepping backwards just how much he had disturbed her.

His gaze dropped to the ground. He spoke barely above a whisper, but each word reached her with crystal clarity.

"Miss Munro, you are an American, and your nationality is declared by your hair, your skin, your very demeanor. You come to my country dressed in provocative clothes, during the festival when inhibitions are loosened, and complain when you are subjected to unwanted attention."

She pushed at stray locks of hair that had fallen around her face, suddenly conscious of their golden wheat color and their wild disarray. Somewhere along the way they had escaped the long braid she normally wore. "I didn't go looking for trouble," she said, in the same whisper. The whisper seemed appropriate.

"I know."

"Then — ?"

"You have to understand this country, Miss Munro, if you are to have a peaceful stay here. Americans are not loved. They are looked upon with suspicion and dread, and you have been subject to some of the prejudice that fear engenders. You would do better to spend your time here being as insignificant as possible. The political situation in Vistaria verges on explosive—we have guerillas in the mountains just waiting for an excuse to swoop down on the capital, and an...incident would be all the excuse they would need."

She licked her lips. "You mean rebels, don't you? They are rebels in the mountains."

He smiled a little and looked at her with that same direct glance. "*Touché*, Miss Munro. You have revealed my own prejudice." The smile was deprecating, with a touch of wry humor. It reminded her that he was only a man, after all. A man with weaknesses...and passions.

He stood much too close, she decided. Despite the bars barely two feet separated them. She could almost feel the heat of him washing against her. A masculine, strong scent curled around her, evoking a sense memory of being wrapped in a man's arms, his warm long body against hers. A picture flashed into her mind—firm flesh, heat, moisture, the caress of a hand along her bare hip.

The man stared at her through the bars of the cage, not moving, his gaze as fixed as a hunter's.

The pit of her stomach rolled over slowly and the old familiar ache awoke.

"Do you know me?" she asked, her voice husky.

"Yes." The answer was low, a verbal caress as beguiling as his scent.

Her heart gave a little leap and thudded hard against her chest. "I mean..." She cleared her throat a little. "You know my name."

"I know all about you, Miss Callida Munro." He pulled his hand out of his pocket. Her passport was in it. He pushed it through the bars towards her. "Take this. Keep it safe. Keep it on you. In a while, after I'm gone, you will be released. Your uncle, Joshua Benning, will be waiting for you downstairs."

She took the passport with a small sigh of relief, and pushed it into the back pocket of her jeans. It was warm — from his body heat.

His hand had returned to the pocket.

"Do you have anything else of mine in there?" she asked, nodding towards his pocket.

"Should I have?" He seemed surprised.

"They took my handbag, my luggage..."

"They?"

"The soldiers. The police. The men who arrested me."

"This country is run under a military junta," he said politely, as if he informed her of the weather.

"I'm sorry. I'm woefully ignorant of your country and I feel like I'm insulting you."

"You are no worse than most tourists here," he said.

"But I'm usually much better prepared. I'm a college professor, for god's sake, and you're making me feel like a big ugly American blundering around and tripping over her own ignorance. I came in a hurry — that's my only explanation."

"Just as I have asked you, I too, am making allowances." He gave that same little lift to the corner of his mouth. "And you are not a college professor quite yet."

"How on earth do you know that?"

"The internet is available in Vistaria, too, Miss Munro. I looked up your college website."

"Dry reading for a festival night."

"On the contrary." He took his hand out of the pocket. "You may or may not get your belongings back. I will see what I can arrange. Count yourself lucky regardless of what is returned. Good night, Miss Munro."

She grabbed the bars. "Wait a minute," she said quickly.

He swiveled a little to look at her, and one brow lifted in query.

"Are you going to tell me who you are?"

He barely paused. "No."

"No name? Nothing?"

"No."

"No, wait!" she said, lifting her voice a little more.

He turned back to face her, stoic patience in every line of his body.

She swallowed dryly. "This is wildly inappropriate, and I don't know how to do this in a way that doesn't sound totally forward...but...can we...can I...hell..." She cleared her throat again.

Curiosity show on his face, then dawning understanding. She recognized it as clearly as if he had spoken, for her whole body took an internal leap and suddenly her heart really *was* in her throat, choking her. Throughout their short interview, the expression in his eyes had not changed from the cool assessing look. But now she saw heat flicker there, just for a moment.

"You have not had your fill of Vistarian men?" he asked softly.

The look in his eyes, the knowledge, made her heart hurt. Her whole body tingled in response, and it killed any finesse she might have used under normal circumstances. She had run out of time, anyway. He wanted to leave. She shook her head. "Not you," she said, just as softly.

"Ahh..."

An entire world of conversation lived in that breathed response, and Calli knew she caught only part of it. She heard understanding, pleasure...and regret.

His hand lifted to where hers clutched at the bars, the right hand hidden from the soldiers by his body. The long fingers rested against hers, and the touch thrilled her. The tip of one finger slid against the very tender flesh at the side of hers, and she shivered as a little ripple of pleasure swept through her.

He watched her, recording every minute reaction. When she focused on his face again, he gave another of those little half smiles. The regret lingered in his eyes. Moving his head by only a fraction, he shook it.

She let her hands fall away, and this time when he turned to leave she did not stop him.

Chapter Two

An hour or so later Calli was escorted down the narrow steep stairs to the front office of the police station by a sullen soldier—one of those who had been chastised by *him*, as she had begun to think of the stranger who had churned up her insides so much that she still felt a lingering throbbing need. The soldier led her to the desk in the corner, and dug beneath it. Finally he lifted a single sheet of paper to the top of it and handed her a disposable pen, tapping the sheet.

She turned the sheet around. "What's it say?" she asked him, although she suspected the document was some sort of release or waiver.

He shook his head a little. "*No Ingles,*" he muttered.

"Callida! Thank god!"

She turned toward the front door where the shout had come from. Her uncle Josh, his curly brown hair rumpled agreeably, strode toward her looking very sweaty despite his tropical weight suit. He hugged her, squeezing tight. "We've been worried sick!" he declared.

"We?" she asked, looking behind him.

"Minnie and I—" He looked behind, too, and frowned. "She was right there. Now where on earth did that girl get to? I swear she will be the death..." He started back to the door.

"Uncle Josh, wait up. Can you tell me what this says? They want me to sign it."

He came back to the desk, muttering a little, clearly distracted by the absence of his daughter. He pulled reading glasses out of his breast pocket and slipped them on his nose, then lifted the sheet up and peered over the top of them to read it, dropping his chin down to his chest for a better view. "Hmmmm…doesn't seem to be too intimidating. You're attesting to the fact that you were treated well and given fair consideration during your incarceration." He glanced at her, then leaned forward and lowered his voice. "I'd sign it," he said. "They're very big on due process here, even if it doesn't match ours at home."

"That surprises the hell out of me," Calli raged. "Do you know where they've been holding me?"

He nodded his head vigorously. "Yes, yes. But you'd better sign it anyway. We don't want them to get annoyed now you're so close to the front door."

He had a good point. Calli sighed and signed on the blank line at the bottom. The soldier smiled broadly at her. "*Gracias. Muchas gracias,*" he said, putting the sheet away again.

Uncle Josh tucked his hand under her elbow. "Let's go," he said.

"Hang on." She looked at the soldier. "My bags," she said flatly. "I want them back."

His big smile faded. "*¿Qué?*"

"Uncle Josh, you tell him. My luggage, my stuff. They have it somewhere."

He cleared his throat and said something in Spanish that sounded distinctly English and awkward, even to Calli's uneducated ears.

The soldier shrugged and spoke briefly.

"Okaaaay," her uncle said, and blew his breath out. He pursed his lips, then tried another slow sentence in Spanish.

This time the soldier threw him a dirty look and went back up the stairs, treading heavily.

"Is he coming back?" Calli asked.

"He might. Let's give it a minute," Uncle Josh said.

After a few moments the soldier did return, this time with Calli's shoulder bag in his hand. He put it on the desk and shoved it toward her.

Calli took the bag. "Wow, what did you tell him?" she asked Uncle Josh.

He shrugged a little. "I said I would call on the same people I called on last time if he didn't give you your things. I think. My Spanish is pretty horrible."

"I gotta tell you about that too," Calli said, looking through her bag. The wallet was missing. "And the rest of my stuff?" she asked the soldier.

He looked her square in the eyes, and crossed his arms. "*No.*"

"Even I understand that one," Calli murmured. She recalled what the red-headed man had said: *Count yourself lucky no matter what is returned.* But it was hard to give up a suitcase of clothes and personal items and just walk away.

"You got your handbag, Calli. I'd say call it quits and let's go," Uncle Josh said. He took her arm again and tugged. "Come on, let's get you home. Minnie will be able to dig up spare clothes from that monstrous great collection of hers. And I'll take you on a shopping trip tomorrow."

Calli studied the soldier a little longer, not breaking his stare, not willing to let him think he'd got the better of her by walking away with her tail between her legs. Even though he professed to speak no English, she knew he understood enough to get her intent, so she shook her head and said, "I wish you well of my clothes, soldier, and whatever else you took out of my bag. I know you have them. I'm only dropping it because you've got the advantage of home turf, but I will remember this."

Then she let Uncle Josh pull her back towards the front door, and they stepped out into the busy, lantern-lit square. The night air refreshed her—she could smell the ocean—but still nicely warm that she didn't feel the need for a sweater. Just as well, as she no longer had one to put on.

Josh looked around, frowning again. "Where *is* she?" he sighed. "I tell you, Calli, I'm so glad you decided to come after all."

"You want me to play watchdog, Uncle Josh? Is that why you flew me here?"

He pushed his hand through his hair, and she realized then why it looked so rumpled. "I don't know what else to do," he confessed. "I'm worried about her in this place. Beryl's not well, and I've got my hands full with the set up of the mine—we're starting from scratch, for god's sake." He swung his head from side to side, scanning the street for a sight of his daughter. "Where *is* she?"

Calli looked around for a petite brunette and realized she might be hard to pick out from the thick swirls of people dancing and moving around the big square. Over in the far corner musicians with guitars, flutes and drums stood on a low platform. Their music was heady, infectious. The beat made Calli's foot tap, and her hips sway in time to the languorous melody. That's what most of the people in the square seemed to be doing. Many of the women had their hands up, weaving them in the air with incredibly graceful motions. Their hips swayed as they turned, dipping and whirling, helped here and there by men who would spin them, sometimes dance along with them for a few steps, their hands on the women's hips, before the woman would move along to another man and dance beguilingly in front of him. Some couples, hips locked together, spun as a pair, their attention solely on each other.

The men, in contrast to the glowing colors the women wore, dressed almost completely in black — tight black pants, short black jackets, and white shirts beneath. Some of them wore the very Spanish looking flat-brimmed black hat, and nearly all of them wore well-heeled boots. Some had discarded their jackets while they danced. Calli could see a pair, not far away from her, dancing together in a shadowy corner created by the big statue in the middle of the square. She'd draped her arm around his neck, and he had one arm tight around her waist. She watched him bend his partner over his arm; as she arched back, her head dropping low, his hand smoothed its way up her torso in a long, loving caress that ended at her breast.

She smiled as he lifted her back up, his hand still at her breast, and they began turning slowly together again, looking deep into each other's eyes. Then their mouths met, and their steps slowed even more. His hand lifted to her blouse, snagged the gathered top edge of it and slid the cotton even further down her arm, revealing the top of her breast.

Calli licked her suddenly dry lips and looked away, which brought her gaze swinging around to the dark shadows on the edges of the square. The movement of something white caught her eye—a group, not far away, with a woman in the middle. Then her eyes adjusted to the dim light, and she realized that one woman danced in the middle of a circle of perhaps five men, holding their rapt attention. As well she might, for she also held Calli's attention. Calli's mind hazed with astonishment as she watched the woman turn in languorous circles, hands on her thighs slowly raising her skirts, showing more and more long, slender leg with each gyration of her hips. Her blouse rode so low around her shoulders it revealed the start of the underside of her arms, along with most of her breasts. The elegant, sinuous curve of the breasts from the armpit down beneath the top of her blouse promised firm, full bounty beneath.

As she moved, one of the men stepped up behind her, mirroring her moves. His hands slowly settled on her hips, as if he tested her response. She smiled and pushed back into him, encouraging him. His hand spread across her abdomen, possessive fingers spreading, laying claim to her. The other lifted to her blouse and pushed the fabric down, exposing first one breast, then the other. His big hand cupped the full, lush globes, while his mouth kissed her neck and bare shoulder. The couple's lazy circles had almost ceased. The other men smiled. One slid his hands beneath the hem of her skirt. Each hand circled her ankle. He slid his palms up along her legs, bringing the silk skirt with them.

The other men moved in closer and blocked Calli's view.

She blinked and cleared her throat. "They call this a *fiesta?*" she asked Uncle Josh. "This is more like...a carnival," she remarked.

Uncle Josh, still busy scanning the square, answered with a little shrug. "It's a religious festival all right, but I don't know what religion celebrates the moon except for the older pagan ones."

"Isn't Vistaria Catholic?"

"Nominally. There's pockets of this and that everywhere. Vistaria's been invaded by a dozen different cultures throughout its history. Maybe that's where the carnival atmosphere comes from. They're certainly not inhibited, are they?"

"No," Calli murmured. Then she saw Minnie and realized why they had not seen her straight away.

The wall of the police station building was in shadows — the light from the paper lanterns didn't reach that far. Minnie leaned back against the wall, laughing up at a soldier who stood over her, his hand against the wall by her head.

"There she is," Calli said.

The soldier's head hovered close to Minnie's, and as Calli skipped down the steps, heading in her direction, his finger slid down the side of her face. He was tall, as tall as Uncle Josh, with wide shoulders and small hips, and he'd pulled his dark glossy hair back into a short ponytail, revealing the olive skin and dark features of a typical Vistarian. He was, frankly, gorgeous. Even as Calli made her way towards them, she marveled over Minnie's almost magical ability to find and draw the sexiest man in the area to her side. Minnie had a quality Calli had never been able to pin down precisely; attitude, walk, body — perhaps the whole damned package, who knew? But almost without exception, any warm-blooded male in her vicinity would respond to that mysterious element in her.

In Vistaria, during *Fiesta*, it could cause trouble. Minnie didn't always know when enough was enough. Calli had had a tiny taste of the different attitudes here, and her gut clenched. No wonder Uncle Josh looked harried.

She hurried over to her cousin. "Minnie, for heaven's sake. There you are."

Minnie smiled up at the soldier before looking at Calli. "Just having a chat," she said with another big smile. "Dad said it might take a while, so I stayed outside to listen to the music. Calli, this is Eduardo...right?" she asked the soldier. He had straightened up.

"Friends call me Duardo. I insist. *Eduardo*, I like not," he said, his voice low. His eyes almost twinkled, as if he laughed mentally. He held out his hand to Calli.

Not one of the men that had been in the holding cell room. Good.

She took the offered hand and disguised her surprise when he turned hers a little and brought the back of it up to his lips. They felt hot against her skin. He watched her over the back of her hand.

"My pleasure to meet you, Miss Calli," he purred. His slow smile showed off white teeth.

"...er...thank you," Calli murmured, and pulled her hand away the moment he released it. His old-fashioned courtesy had completely bamboozled her, she realized with a touch of amusement. And she couldn't help feel a little more feminine and appreciated as a result. No wonder Minnie had succumbed so quickly.

She grabbed Minnie's arm. "Say goodnight, Minnie."

"Yeah, course. Okay. Duardo, it has been a blast."

"Most certainly, Minnie," he replied, his smile widening.

Calli yanked on her cousin's arm, just as Uncle Josh reached them.

"Minnie, when are you ever going to remember you just can't go wandering off by yourself here?" he said.

"*¡Adios!*" she called out to Duardo as he walked away, then looked at Josh. "Dad, I was just talking! I didn't wander. I'm ten feet from the door."

He pushed his hand through his hair again. "Okay, can we please leave now?" he asked, sounding very tired. "The car is on a side street. No parking here tonight. Come on. I don't know about you two, but I need a good stiff belt of scotch."

"Me, too," Calli agreed with feeling.

* * * * *

The scotch and soda slid down her throat, hissing all the way. Calli sighed. She put the heavy crystal glass down on the coffee table and sat back to look around the apartment the Bennings had rented in a very old but well-maintained building in the hilly section southwest of the city center. It had taken barely ten minutes to reach here by car, despite the slow drive through narrow, winding streets. Josh had ushered them inside, checked on her aunt, who dozed in their bedroom recovering from a bad migraine, while Minnie headed for her room to 'scare up' some clothes and essentials for Calli. When Josh reemerged from the bedroom he'd gone straight for the silver tray and decanters on the sideboard and poured them both the promised stiff belt of scotch, then dropped onto the sofa opposite Calli's with a heavy sigh.

In the quiet room, she could still hear music from the streets, filtered and distant.

The apartment had white adobe walls, hung with Vistarian art and interesting textiles in the same jewel colors the women had been wearing tonight. Rooms led off from this central room, but the big kitchen area adjoined the central room at the back, separated only by a huge chopping block island. Terracotta tiles covered the floor throughout, including the big balcony beyond the sliding doors. Blue wisteria-like flowers hung in big clusters from the tangle of vines that climbed up the adobe walls arching over the balcony.

"What *are* those flowers?" she asked as Josh gulped back half his glassful in two big swallows. "They almost look like wisteria. I've been seeing them everywhere."

"Yes, they're wisteria," he said, without looking.

"They're blue, though."

He nodded. "It's some sort of tropical variant that grows wild here. It's the national flower of Vistaria, of course."

That would be why so many women had been wearing it. "Why *of course*?" she asked.

He rubbed his eyes with thumb and forefinger and let his arm drop across the back of the sofa. "*Vistaria* is Spanish for wisteria. That's what this country is called. *La Vistaria de Escobedo*. The wisteria of Escobedo. Escobedo's Wisteria. Escobedo's country, for all the difference it makes, too."

Calli frowned and shook her head a little.

"I have thrown you in the deep end, haven't I?" Uncle Josh said. "The Escobedo family have been virtually the royal family here since forever, seems like. José Escobedo y

Castaños is the current president and supreme commander of the Vistarian Army."

"The military junta," Calli murmured.

"A damned benign one, let me tell you. It's thanks to Escobedo's moderate policies that we're here at all."

"Is that who you called to get me out of jail? Someone high up in the government?"

"Nothing so impressive, I'm afraid," Josh confessed. "I phoned the government liaison that has been assigned to work with us opening up the silver mine and asked him who I should call. He never got back to me. But I must have sounded a bit upset, because he obviously did something. I'm sorry we didn't get there to pick you up in time, Calli. We were on our way, but I hadn't planned on traffic grinding to a halt because of the fiesta. By the time we got there, you had disappeared. People remembered seeing you, though Customs wouldn't tell me a damned thing. That's when I phoned the government guy. What happened, anyway?"

"I hung around for a while, waiting. Even tried phoning here and when I got no answer I figured something had happened to you. So I thought I'd find a cab, point to your address on the email you sent me, and get him to take me there. The information desk told me there were no taxis at the airport because of fiesta, but if I walked up the street I could hail one. So I walked up the street, dragging my case and watching out for a cab when five men came around."

She explained what had happened, the jostling and the grope that had caused her to react. "The man at the jail told me I'd broken at least one nose and handed out a few bruises. If they'd been feeling less generous I think they might have charged me for assault or something, but the man—he knew why I had reacted that way. He understood."

"What man?"

"I have no idea who he is, but he carries a lot of weight. I've never seen men scramble to attention so fast as these guys did when he walked into the room. We talked a bit, then he said I'd be released shortly, and that you'd be waiting for me."

"They phoned me, said to come and get you."

"Who did?"

"The police station." He frowned. "So you explained to this man what had happened to you?"

"I didn't get a chance to explain too much. He seemed to know all about it. All about me."

"A general?"

"He wasn't wearing a uniform. He had red hair, and they called him Roger."

"*Red hair?*" Josh paused from rubbing his eyes again, startled. "Roger?" He thought about it. "For a minute I thought...but no, if they called him Roger..." He shrugged. "I have no idea who it is."

She frowned. "Who did you think it might have been?"

Joshua shook his head. "No one. A passing idea, but far too ridiculous to consider."

Minnie emerged from her bedroom carrying an armful of clothes, which she dumped on the coffee table. "I don't have all that much you could wear, Calli. You've got at least six inches on me, so all the pants will be high-waters. But there's a skirt and some tee shirts, and something for bed, if you really wear anything to bed." She held up a pair of diaphanous pink baby-doll pajamas and winked at Calli, her pixie-like features filled with mischief.

"Minnie, do you have to talk like that?" Josh asked.

"Dad, it's Calli. She knows me." She dropped the pajamas on the pile and patted the collection. "Tomorrow I'm taking you shopping. I know exactly where to go."

"Of course you do," Calli said. "You would've had it figured out twenty-four hours after landing here."

"No, in one hour. I met a woman lawyer in the customs and immigration lounge at the airport and asked her where she got her suit and, *voila*, insider information on the best shopping spots on *la colina*."

"'In', you mean," Calli suggested.

"*On*," Minnie said firmly. "*Colina* is 'hill'. The city is *Lozano Colinas*, and the locals shorten it down to 'the hill', coz good ol' Lozano lost claim to his hill when he kicked the bucket."

"It sounds so much prettier in Spanish. You'd better add a Spanish-English dictionary to the shopping list," Calli added with a sigh.

* * * * *

She danced, whirled, dipped—her silk skirt brushed her legs with cool light caresses. She was as free as a bird, her heart light, bursting with elation, tingling with joy. She lifted her hands up to the stars above, the music encouraging her to swing and turn. Hands settled on her hips and a warm weight pressed up behind her. Blood warm. *Hot*. She laughed out loud, the contact fizzing through her blood. She let him feel the sway of her hips. He pressed himself against her, and a silvery thrill ran through her as she felt the thick hardness of his cock against her ass. He wanted her. *He wants me.*

They swayed together, their feet moving in gentle spirals as they turned. His hand rested low on her abdomen. His fingers spread out and pushed against her, driving her hips back into him. The hand slid a little lower, the fingers sliding over her mound. She could feel her nakedness beneath the silk for the heat of his hand seemed to brand her. Her clit, her whole cleft, throbbed in reaction. Lower. She wanted his hand lower, deeper.

His other hand had lifted to her shoulder and gave a tug on the blouse. With the misty insubstantial magic of dreams, the blouse slipped down her arms, lower, lower, until it rested against her tight hard nipples.

He tugged again.

With a silent flutter, the shirt dropped to her waist, baring her aching breasts. She couldn't stop her shoulders from pulling back, lifting the breasts up, offering them. She wanted them caressed. *Touched.*

The hot hand cupped her breast, while the other pushed between her legs. And she realized then that not only her blouse had fluttered away, but her silky skirt had melted away to nothing. She was naked, quivering with a hot need that had not been met for far too long. But the hand between her legs did not caress her clit or slide into her vagina as she longed for.

Instead, the hands smoothed their way back up to her hips and turned her around to face him. She looked upon a broad chest, a white shirt, but a common business shirt, not the full white cotton shirt she had expected.

When she tried to look up at his face she found her view blocked by the brim of a black hat, bent low. Determined, she twisted and ducked her head to look under the brim. He dropped his head lower, matching her movements, and she had to move her head backwards to avoid a collision. His motion forced her into a curve backwards over his arm.

She caught her breath, as she leaned back. Her whole body leapt to the alert. Every part of her was exposed, open. Her bare breasts pushed up into the air, and her pelvis thrust forward, her mound, her clit, forced against his hip with a hard, luscious pressure. She knew what came next, and ached for his touch, for the hand to rest on her waist and swoop up to her breast.

The expected hand settled on her waist, and she drew in a sharp breath as it slid along her torso, but the specific touch, the cupping of her aching breast, did not happen. She lifted herself up with a small, frustrated sigh, and he helped her, bringing her to her feet with a power and speed that made her dizzy. He brought her to an abrupt standstill, her hips against his, her breasts pushed against his chest. He was hot against her, and she could feel his heart beating under her hand. He looked at her now.

It was *him*. His dark red hair, thick and shining in the evening glow. He studied her with the same speculative gaze as before, but she could feel his arousal against her stomach, hot and hard.

She stared at him, willing him to kiss her, her hand moving in restless little strokes against his hard chest and shoulder, the silk warm under her fingers. She could feel the desire for his mouth to touch hers building like a scream inside her.

But he shook his head a little.

Her disappointment was so acute it stabbed at her chest like a knife. She gave a cry—her throat hurt with the strength of it, but no sound emerged. He let her fall back again and she held out her hands, unwilling to lose contact with the heat and hardness of him. But she fell too hard and too fast...

Calli awoke with a whole-body jerk and a soundless cry that strained her throat. Within a second she realized she had been dreaming, and fell back on her pillow with a shuddering sob of relief.

It had been so intense!

She rolled over on her side, hugging her still throbbing body, trying to claw back any fragments of the intensely erotic visions and feelings of the dream. That was when she saw him. She drew in a sharp, startled breath, her already taxed heart leaping in her chest. Fright tore through her like cold water through her veins, but at the same time her aroused, prepared body went to high alert.

He sat in Uncle Josh's leather office chair, one hand on his bent knee, the other elbow propped against the arm of the chair, his long forefinger resting against his temple.

And he watched her, the same measuring stare as before.

Calli sat up, bringing the damp sheet with her. "What are you *doing* here?" she whispered furiously.

"You are a restless sleeper, Miss Munro," he said, just as quietly.

"Are you *crazy*? You have to leave. Right now."

"I'm not crazy," he said, getting to his feet. "If I were, I would not have understood what you were telling me in the holding cell this evening." He walked over to the bed, and Calli shrank back against the headboard, pulling the sheet with her. But he did not touch the mattress. Instead, he lowered himself so he could look her in the eye. The blue of his eyes seemed to glow in the light coming from the wide windows. Full moon, she remembered... *Fiesta de la Luna.*

"I know you," he said, very quietly, the low voice rumbling in her mind, her heart.

Yes, yes, you do. You see my soul. You see I want you. My heart locks when you're near. I can think of nothing but how much I want you to touch me.

"You have to go," she said aloud.

"Do you want me to go?"

She couldn't bring herself to lie when the truth pushed at her conscious mind so insistently. She said nothing. Instead she scrambled from the bed and headed towards the door, intending to shepherd him from the apartment. She was three steps from the bed when she heard a little noise behind her, and whirled.

He straightened up, staring at her. "My god, look at you," he breathed. "You are...magnificent."

She couldn't help but look down at herself, at the fragile chiffon of the baby doll pajamas, and the tiny matching panties with their satin bows. And her cheeks grew warm in reaction.

"Your legs, such endless legs." He moved towards her. "Athlete's muscles. Callida, you are more beautiful than I suspected. Your hair is glowing in the moonlight." He halted just in front of her, so close she could feel his body heat. He brushed a thick lock of her hair back over her shoulder. His hand whispered across her skin, a fleeting touch that sent a shudder through her. She couldn't move now, couldn't resist the primal urges strumming through her and send him away—not when she wanted him to wreak havoc upon her, to turn her inside-out with delight. Her cleft throbbed, slick with her juices.

He reached for the satin bow between her breasts, the only thing holding the triangular pieces of lace together. She felt the little tug and the chiffon and lace fell away, revealing her breasts. In the silvery moonlight they were pale, luminescent globes, and the nipples and areolas dark points of focus. Her nipples crinkled hard at the touch of air.

He drew a slow, deep breath. Let it out. Moving slowly, his hands reached for the satin bows over each of her hips. He watched her…waiting for her to protest. But she could not find her voice. She did not want to speak, for she knew that a protest might emerge. So she remained a silent witness to her own seduction, letting it happen.

Two more small tugs and the panties fluttered to the floor between her feet. He stepped closer, and his hand, hot and large, slid between her thighs, up into the moist folds of flesh, pressing against her clitoris and making her groan. His fingers dipped into the entrance of her vagina, just as his mouth touched hers. The kiss was fleeting, not nearly satisfying enough, nor was the gentle pressure of his hand.

His touch had opened a floodgate.

Take me. Now! She wanted to beg, but she didn't speak the words for he controlled the moment.

Her body throbbed, heavy with expectation. She wanted him to drag her to the floor, to push inside her with rough, frantic movements, his body a heavy weight on top of her. She anticipated, longed for, the sweet-sour mini-satisfaction of penetration. She wanted to feel him thrusting in her—hard and demanding. She wanted to be held and stroked.

"What do you want?" he whispered against her lips.

She opened her mouth, but nothing emerged. She could say no words, no sound, although the words were there, ready to tumble out. She fought to speak them and failed.

His hands dropped away from her. He stepped around her and began to walk away, and she lifted her hand toward him, pleading, but still the words would not emerge, until he had left, and then the cry of frustration and despair came back to her throat.

Calli sat bolt upright in her borrowed bed, her heart and head pounding with the pressure of dream induced horror, and a sexual excitement more intense than anything she had ever experienced in her life. Not just her genitals throbbed—her whole body pulsated with the coursing arousal. Her chest heaved beneath the pink chiffon, and her nipples could feel every little rub of the fabric. They were tight, taut and almost painfully sensitive.

She opened her mouth and took deep measured breaths, bringing her pulse down, working for calm. It took several minutes, for her mind was a jumble of dream images, still fresh, still able to arouse.

Chief amongst them, the feel of him holding her up against him. Soft, warm silk beneath her fingers. Underneath the silk, the hard wall of chest muscles. His mouth mere inches from hers. His knowing gaze. And the waves of sexual tension pouring from him, washing over her. The pressure of his hips against hers. The powerful, arousing pressure.

"Ah, shit," Calli murmured to herself in the dark. Playing back the dream memories wasn't doing a thing to help steady her pulse. She reached over for the glass of water on the edge of the desk beside the bed. The desk would be removed from the bedroom tomorrow, along with the empty leather chair beside it. Her uncle had intended to use the third bedroom as his study, but the demands of the job on-site were enough that he had barely used the room—he spent all his time at the mine, instead. So the room would revert back to its designed use as a bedroom.

She groped for her watch until she remembered it was one of the items that had been stripped from her and not returned. It was still dark outside the window, though—excuse enough for her to lie down again and try to find sleep.

Add a watch to the list, Calli, she reminded herself.

The throbbing arousal was slowly subsiding, but still strong enough for her to slide her fingers between her thighs in a restless unconscious movement intended to address the ache. Then she stopped, realizing what she was doing. She moved her hands, and slid them under the pillow, away from temptation.

She would not be dictated to by a figment of her imagination. She was Callida Munro, soon-to-be professor of economics, a thirty-something single-by-choice woman with a career, a house, a life, thank you very much.

But his eyes, the feel of his body against her, followed her down into an uneasy sleep, along with writhing shame, for even if she had resisted his dream image, she had not resisted the lure of him in person. She had virtually begged him for a boon. That was something she would never tell another living soul. Not even Minnie, who might understand.

And thank god she would never see him again and have to look him in the face.

Chapter Three

"Calli, you're not really paying attention, are you?" Minnie said, looking over the top of the shimmering dress she held up for Calli's inspection.

Calli blinked away the sense memory of last night's persistent dream images for the tenth time that morning and struggled to stay in the moment. She looked at the bright patterns, the predominance of red in the abstract swirls of the dress. "Not my color at all," she said.

"Not you. Me." Minnie held it against herself.

"You, certainly," Calli agreed.

"For tonight, do you think?"

"Tonight? What's on tonight?"

Minnie rolled her eyes. "Great, Calli. I only told you about twenty minutes ago. You agreed, don't you remember?"

"I did? To what?"

"Tonight. The party. Duardo. And his friends."

"Duardo?" Suddenly Calli's scattered thoughts congealed into a cold whole. "You mean the *soldier* Duardo? From last night?" Horror filled her. "Minnie, did you give him your phone number or...or...?"

"God, relax Calli. Sometimes you treat me like I'm still eighteen and wet behind the ears. He invited me last night — actually, me and a friend because I said I wouldn't meet him somewhere alone."

"Well, that sounds a little more sane. But Minnie, I've only been here twelve hours and I've already heard how little Americans are liked here. Do you know how close Vistaria is to outright revolution? What if this Duardo is part of some rebel faction?"

Minnie gave a low peal of laughter, shoved the dress back on the rack and flipped through more hangers. "Not Duardo," she said with complete certainty. Her voice held the same firmness as when she had explained the local use of *las colinas*.

"Okay, so you know more than me about the way things really work here. But what makes you so certain he's not into something dire and nasty? You have no idea who he is at all."

"I know he's an admirer of the Red Leopard, so of course he's not a rebel."

Calli shoved the dress she had been inspecting back onto the rack impatiently. "Who the hell is the Red Leopard?" she demanded.

"Why are you getting so angry?" Minnie asked sweetly.

Calli cast about for a reasonable answer to her reasonable question. She had to dig hard. "I'm so sick of not knowing what's going on," she muttered.

Minnie smiled a little. "You've been too long on that campus, Calli. So you're out of your comfort zone. So what?"

"I like my comfort zone."

"Dull, boring. Deadly."

"Shut up." Calli's demand was a token one. She couldn't think of a better answer.

Minnie laughed again and came around and tucked her hand into Calli's elbow. "You need a long, cool margarita under a shady patio with a view of the ocean," she declared.

"I need sleep, is what I need."

"Siesta. That I can arrange, too. But first the drink." Minnie tugged on her arm. "Come on."

* * * * *

The patio *was* shady, and faced the deep blue Pacific ocean. A cool breeze, laden with salt, flapped the spice-colored tablecloth and Calli turned her face into it, enjoying the moist wind. They had climbed a dozen stairs to reach the patio, and consequently, the buildings across the road didn't hide the view of the ocean. The ground here sloped sharply down towards the sea.

"The ocean looks wonderful," Calli confessed. "I wish we were going down there afterwards, but it seems like all we've done today is climb."

"The city is built right next to mountains. What else did you expect?"

"To go down at least fifty percent of the time."

Minnie grinned. "They say here that if you get tired climbing the hills, you can always lean against them."

A huge margarita for each of them arrived at the table, along with a platter of rolled tortillas surrounded by tomato slices, sour cream and green salsa.

"We didn't order this," Calli said.

Minnie looked up at the waiter. "What's this?" she asked. Then she pointed at the tortillas. "*¿Qué?*" she repeated.

The waiter nodded. "*Sí.*" He turned and pointed to a table at the far end of the patio, where three men sat with a bottle of tequila between them. There was a woman at the table too, wearing a very modern, quite short business skirt and a silky blouse. The man next to her had his hand on her tanned, glowing thigh, stroking the flesh along the inside of it while she leaned back, a dreamy expression on her face. One of the other men—young, and with bright, happy eyes—lifted his shot glass toward them.

Minnie smiled at him and shook her head regretfully, a hand over her heart. "Please take them back," she told the waiter. "We just want to have a quiet drink."

The waiter looked at the man at the other table, shrugged and picked up the platter.

The man shook his head and called out something. Then he motioned that the waiter should put the platter down again. He got to his feet and bowed from the waist toward them, then with deliberate, almost exaggerated, motions, he turned his chair to face the table of men, his back to them. He would leave them alone, despite his gift.

"Oh, the darling," Minnie breathed.

"How do you *do* that?" Calli asked, rubbing her temple. She took a sip of the margarita. Delicious, and with just the right amount of kick—featherweight—for this heat.

"Do what?"

"Get them to leave you alone after you've hooked them and drawn them in?"

"No idea," Minnie admitted. "They just seem to understand."

"Even here?"

Minnie waved towards the table where they talked together busily, not taking the slightest notice of them now. "Apparently."

"I wish I'd had you with me last night," Calli muttered.

"It didn't occur to you that the men last night just wanted some fun?" Minnie asked.

"Groping constitutes fun?"

"Groping is virtually a compliment. The men here, they see, they like, they do something about it. It's refreshing. You know where you stand."

The image from her dream came zinging back into Calli's mind. It had faded now, losing its edge, but it still had the power to catch her breath, make her pause. She remembered to breathe again, and picked up one of the tortilla wraps. "I bet you do," she said, and took a bite.

Minnie tilted her head inquiringly. "Calli, when are you going to forgive the race of men for what that bastard did to you? They're not all tarred with the same brush, you know."

Calli choked on the mouthful of tortilla as the spice hit the back of her mouth, her tongue, her lips. Afraid to take a breath in case her mouth burst into flames, she sat with the morsel on her tongue, not sure if she could swallow it. What would it do to her stomach? Tears watered her eyes.

"Swallow, then suck on the tomato," Minnie advised, passing her a napkin.

Calli swallowed, then reached for the margarita.

"No, the tomato. Trust me," Minnie said, grabbing the glass from her. "That'll make it worse."

She grabbed a slice of the tomato and stuffed it into her mouth, and was astonished at the instant relief it brought. "Ohmigod!" she said, when at last she could draw breath. "Do Vistarians have cast iron stomachs?

Metal linings in their mouths? I think my lips have gone numb..." She prodded them experimentally.

Minnie smiled and took the remainder of the tortilla from her. "Excuse fingers," she said and unrolled it. Along the row of spicy meat and vegetables inside she dabbed big dollops of sour cream and a line of the green salsa. Then she rolled up the tortilla again and handed it to Calli. "Try that."

"Is it safe?"

Minnie merely sipped her drink with a smile.

Calli took a bite. This time the cream and the salsa, which had almost a fruity flavor, dulled the fire of the meat and vegetables a little. Enough to allow her to enjoy the flavor and chew before swallowing. But she still reached for some tomato anyway.

"Why are you doing this, Calli?" Minnie asked as she unrolled a tortilla of her own and added the fillings. "Robert's already wasted the first half of your life for you. Why let him destroy the rest of it by hanging onto a grudge that stops you from enjoying yourself?"

Calli carefully avoided answering. She took another bite of her tortilla, beginning to enjoy the sharp flavor of the spices. She'd had Mexican food before, but these spices had a slightly different flavor. Fresh, or green, or something. After mulling over the differences for a while, she took another sip of her drink, then said to Minnie, "Tell me about the Red Leopard."

Minnie pursed her lips, then sighed. "Okay. Serves me right." She ran her hands through her short hair, ruffling it and patting it into order again. "I don't know who he is," she admitted.

"You said—" Calli began.

"I said," Minnie overrode her, "That I don't know who he is. And I don't. But I do know all about him."

"Give. Why does Duardo admire him? And why does that mean Duardo couldn't possibly be a rebel?" She shook her head. "*The Red Leopard*," she quoted. "Isn't it just a tad ridiculous? The name? Honestly, who outside the movies goes around with a name like that?"

"He doesn't call himself that. He doesn't call himself anything at all. All the soldiers that like him do. Because that's what he's like."

"He's in the army?"

"Don't think so. I think that's part of why they like him. He's no man's servant. And master of none. He's got no official position anywhere. But he has influence. Power. He gets things done. He is everywhere at once. Watching them, keeping them on their toes. He's very, very sharp, doesn't miss anything."

"It still sounds like a fairytale," Calli muttered.

"Yeah, it does a bit, but Duardo didn't think so. He said he has seen him a few times and wanted to see him again. That's why he hurried to the police station, but by the time he'd got there, *el leopardo* had gone — *poof*! He'd prowled in and slinked out before Duardo got there."

Calli almost knocked her drink over as Minnie spoke and now she gripped Minnie's arm. "He was there last night?" She rubbed her temple, trying to recall the muttered Spanish she'd heard just before she'd whirled to confront the man with the red hair. "What did you just call him?" she said to Minnie.

"*¿El leopardo?*"

"Yes. That's 'the leopard', but red…" She dived for her newly purchased dictionary.

"*Rojo*," Minnie supplied. "*El leopardo rojo.*"

Calli laughed. "*Rojo*...Roger. *That's* what they said last night, and I thought they'd called him Roger."

Minnie's eyes shone. "You met him? The Red Leopard?"

Calli could feel another huge bubble of mirth welling up inside her. "No wonder the soldier at the desk went back and got my bag. He didn't want Uncle Josh to bring the Red Leopard down on him again. I *knew* the guy had power, but I didn't suspect..."

"So who *is* he?" Minnie begged. "Duardo wouldn't tell me. They say it's a mark of respect not to speak of his real identity, even though they all know. He wouldn't tell me no matter how I asked. But you will, won't you? You'll tell me who he is."

Calli shrugged. "I don't know. He didn't tell me either. He refused."

Minnie banged the table with her tiny fist. "Damn! This thing is driving me crazy. I've been trying to find out who he is for days, but all the soldiers are the same. El zippo on his real name."

"God, Minnie, how many soldiers have you been talking to about this?" Calli asked, alarmed.

"A few. Any of them that would talk to me."

"You can't go around bugging them about this. If this Red Leopard man really wants his identity kept quiet, then they won't appreciate you, an American, trying to dig it up. Promise me you won't do it any more."

"Don't be silly. It's just casual chat."

"To you. Not to them. Promise me," Calli insisted.

Minnie looked at her, as if trying to judge how serious she was. Then she sighed and dropped her napkin on the table. "Oh, all right, already. No more questions." She planted her chin on her fist and pouted for a moment, although Calli knew the pout was more for effect than a genuine sulkiness. Minnie was too even tempered to ever truly sulk. Pouting was how she teased Calli for being, in Minnie's opinion, a stick-in-the-mud. Then, true to form, she visibly brightened and sat up in her chair. "We'll be surrounded by the military tonight," she said. "Maybe we won't have to talk. Maybe we can just keep our ears pricked and we'll hear something."

"In that mashed Spanish they use?" Calli pointed out.

"Okay, *see* something then," Minnie amended. "Come on, let's go get that dress we saw. It's just the thing for tonight." She pulled the big Vistarian bills out of her bag, counted off enough to cover the drinks and dropped them on the table.

Calli willingly picked up her bag and followed Minnie down the steps to the road and the walk back to the shopping area, feeling a little of the weight drop from her shoulders and her mind. She was learning, making connections, figuring out the lay of the land. And with her new knowledge came the reassurance that she would never see *him* again. No one who worked to keep his identity a secret would move freely around the city, out in the public.

"Can we find *me* a dress, too?" she complained to Minnie as she strode to catch up with her cousin.

* * * * *

The problem with allowing Minnie to help with clothes shopping, Calli realized five hours later, was that you ended up with something you wouldn't have considered buying if you'd been on your own.

But her lack of wardrobe meant she had to wear the aquamarine gown regardless of the wisdom of her choice. Oh, she had been fine about the dress when they had been in the store. Minnie had pounced on it on the hanger and insisted it would be perfect for her and as usual, Minnie had been right. It had fit well, the color intensified the green of her eyes, and the layers of chiffon gave the whole outfit a delicate appearance that offset her height. She had liked the effect in the mirror. But that had been before they had reached *el Hotel Imperial*.

Duardo had been waiting in the cavernous foyer with its white stone walls and gorgeous Persian carpets and heavy mahogany furniture. He wore what Calli could only assume was the formal uniform of the Vistarian army — very dark green pants, a white dress shirt and waist-length jacket. The cut reminded her of the black costumes the men had been wearing last evening, and she had seen hundreds of them again this evening on their way to the hotel. At the neck Duardo wore a green and red ribbon in a flat, formalized knot, with a gold pin through the middle. The breast of his jacket had a row of medals and ribbons, and black stripes on the sleeves of the jacket replicated the red ones he'd worn when she saw him the previous evening, talking to Minnie.

When he saw them enter the foyer, he straightened and walked towards them, and Minnie sighed, coming to a halt. "Now isn't that the sexiest man alive?" she murmured to Calli.

Duardo smiled at them both. "My pleasure it is to see you again this evening," he told them. He came to formal attention in front of them and bowed from the waist in greeting to Calli. He did the same to Minnie, then reached into his jacket and withdrew a single blood-red carnation and presented it to her.

"Oh, how lovely!" she declared.

He lifted a finger a little towards her hair. "For your hair."

She laughed and ran her fingers through her hair. "It's not long enough to hold a flower."

He laughed too. "I forgot. I only remembered your eyes and that red is your color."

"Never mind," she said. "I know just where to put it." She broke off all but a couple of inches of stem, and pushed the flower into her cleavage, so that it nestled between her breasts and the top of the low vee of her gown. The flower matched the color of the swirls on her dress.

"Perfection," Duardo declared, studying the effect with close attention.

Calli hid her smile and surveyed the hotel. It seemed to be an older building, but well-maintained and reeking of money. The few women in the foyer glittered with jewels and costly dresses. Every man there, with the exception of hotel staff, wore military dress — not a single civilian male in sight.

"What is the party for tonight?" she asked Duardo.

"Tonight is the birthday party for our beloved General Maxim Blanco Alonso," Duardo answered with pride.

"Nothing to do with the fiesta then?"

"Most certainly not. General Blanco is very…correct. Very…" He tugged on the bottom of his jacket. "*Un perfecto caballero.*"

Calli got the sense of his meaning from the tug of his jacket and the squaring of his shoulders. Upright, dignified. Proper. A gentleman.

"Best bibs and tuckers and all that?" she asked with a mock English accent.

"*¿Qué?*" Duardo asked.

"Nothing," she assured him. "Forget it. I'm teasing." But Calli was suddenly glad Minnie had insisted on buying the gown she wore. Minnie had assured her Vistarians were very formal in the evenings, and she hadn't quite understood what she meant. Now she did.

"Shall we?" Duardo asked, holding out his arms to them.

Calli let her fingers rest inside his elbow as they walked around the islands of low, heavy furniture in the center of the foyer towards a grand archway that framed a sweeping staircase of stone stairs. Many more people ascended the stairs ahead of them. Most of them wore uniforms and seemed to know each other.

They climbed the staircase a step at a time, for progress at the top of the stairs seemed slow. Duardo and Minnie chatted in low voices, laughing a little, taking no notice of their surroundings. Duardo had his hand on Minnie's waist. Calli looked behind her when they paused for a longer moment, halfway up the flight. The stairs were thick with dark-haired, olive-skinned men and a few Vistarian women. Calli glanced at Minnie. Despite her dark hair and petite stature, Minnie stood out in sharp contrast to everyone there. Her skin was pale in comparison, and her pixie-like features and huge eyes with their pale brown coloring marked her as foreign. A stranger. The only non-Vistarian standing on the staircase except for Calli herself.

Then Calli grew aware of the effect of her own gown and coloring. Straw-blonde hair, white skin, green eyes and a gown that added to the effect of insubstantial lightness. She licked her lips, her heart giving a little flutter. She must stand out like a sore thumb amongst these people.

The idea made her uncomfortable. She worried it over as they ascended the last few stairs and finally arrived at the top, standing before the big double doors that were apparently their destination. In her heels, Calli stood at least as tall as many of the men and could see between heads to the doorway—a formal greeting line had caused the delay.

Beyond the line she saw a large ballroom, with decorations in red and green, and the blue wisteria color that must be Vistaria's national color. More people waited inside. More soldiers. More dark-eyed, sultry Vistarian women.

Calli leaned forward a little to catch Minnie's eye. "What have you got us into?" she demanded.

"Only the party of the *year*," Minnie assured her.

"Screw that," Calli shot back. "Do you realize we're the only Americans here?"

Minnie looked puzzled. "And?"

Duardo patted Calli's fingers where they rested on the inside of his arm. "It will be all right," he assured her quietly. "You are with me."

"Duardo, no offense, but I got chucked in jail last night because your fellow Vistarians took exception to me being in their country. And we're stepping inside a room full of patriotic Vistarians."

"These are *good* Vistarians," he said, and frowned. "They know Americans help us. They would not be rude."

Only slightly mollified, Calli allowed herself to be drawn forward, through the double doors and into the line of guests being received. Duardo, perhaps sensing her distress, did not chat with Minnie and leave Calli to her thoughts. Instead, he spoke to them both.

"General Blanco is a great man. He has been leading the army under President Escobedo's direction for twelve years. Every year he has a big birthday party. Officers who have been honored throughout the year come and celebrate with him. It is a very important evening. Soldiers work hard to be chosen, so that they will get to come here."

"That's you, right, Duardo?" Minnie asked. "You were honored?"

"Yes. I am chosen."

"What did you do?" Calli asked.

For the first time she saw his upbeat mood slip. His smile faded just a little. "It was small. Nothing."

She didn't need a neon sign to know Duardo did not want to talk about it. "Okay," she murmured.

"What's nothing?" Minnie persisted. "What did you do?"

"I helped defend Vistaria. A little thing. You would be bored with the talk of it," he assured her with his smile turned to full incandescence.

The smile dazzled her as he had clearly intended it to do, for Minnie smiled back. "You're a hero, then, " she said, just as they reached the beginning of the formal greeting line.

Duardo stood ramrod straight and held out his hand to shake it with the first officer in the line. "Captain Eduardo Peña y Santos, *señor*."

The officer shook his hand and spoke—formal Spanish, Calli realized, pleased her ear could already distinguish between the day-to-day mongrel they used and true Spanish.

Duardo pulled her forward a little. "Major, may I present Miss Callida Munro, and Miss Minerva Benning. Miss Benning's father, and Miss Munro's uncle, Joshua Benning, is the project manager of the Garrido Silver Mine on *Las Piedras Grandes*. Calli, Minnie, this is Major Alvarez, my commanding officer."

"Miss Munro, Miss Benning," the major murmured, dipping his head forward in a short little bow. He did not smile, and Calli guessed he was displeased to see his junior officer with two American women on his arms. Nor did he offer his hand, but men here did not usually shake hands with women.

She smiled and murmured hello, then Duardo stepped up to the next person in line, a stout man in his fifties with a chest full of ribbons and gold braid everywhere. Undoubtedly, this must be the beloved General Blanco. Then she looked ahead to the next person in the line. Her thoughts scattered to the four winds and her heart seized in her chest.

Dark red hair, indigo eyes. He spoke to the person whose hand he shook, a small polite smile on his face. *Him.*

Her hearing seemed to fade, the noise around her blanketed to a dull far-off sound. Her heart beat, hard and heavy, and her breathing was overly loud. Excitement gripped her, even as dismay settled into her bones. This was the man she had beggared herself in front of last night. Despite her shame, she studied him hungrily: The black tuxedo, and a white shirt. *Is it silk?* her treacherous mind whispered and her hand itched to investigate for itself. One small step and she could lean forward a little and touch him. Barely five feet separated them.

Had he seen her yet?

"...Miss Callida Munro, General," Duardo finished, and Calli dragged, ripped, pummeled her attention back the man standing before her. The general favored her with a beaming smile and took her hand and bowed a little over it. "You are most welcome in my country, Miss Munro," he said.

"Thank you," she said, but her concern about being a hated American here had fled, scattered under the onslaught of heady exhilaration. Almost breathlessly she anticipated the next few seconds when he would turn to greet her and see it was she. What would he do?

Duardo moved along, they were done with the General. *His* turn next.

She began to tremble.

Remember this is not the man from your dreams. They're not the same. But it was no good—he *had* been in her dreams. He had prompted the dreams and they had haunted her all day. She was helpless to prevent her response now.

But even Duardo squared his shoulders, lifting his chest. They stood in front of him now, but his head remained turned, while he spoke to the officer in front of them in the line. In a second he would turn to them.

He turned, smiled at Duardo. His glance did not even flicker towards her.

"Captain Peña...you made it. All the way from Pascuallita and during fiesta, too. I am sure General Blanco appreciates your efforts."

Her heart leapt a little. He spoke English! He would only do that if he had noticed her. Had he seen her long before she had seen him?

"Señor, I would not miss this night for Chinese tea," Duardo answered. He indicated Minnie on his left. "May I present to you Miss Minerva Benning, a friend of mine."

Calli watched his hand encase Minnie's tiny one, the long fingers curling right around it.

"Minnie, this is Señor Nicolás Escobedo."

Escobedo. The name throbbed in Calli's mind. She recalled Uncle Josh's words: *Escobedo's country.*

"Hi there, señor," Minnie offered in response as he shook her hand gently.

He smiled a little, good humor lighting his face. "Hi there yourself, Miss Benning. You have made an effective assault upon Vistaria's military, I see." His gravelly voice was low, pleasant. "Are you enjoying your stay here?"

Minnie glanced up at Duardo. "I am now," she said.

Duardo glowed with pride and excitement, his gaze never leaving the man standing before him. Calli caught her breath, remembering now what Minnie had said: "*He wanted to see him again. That's why he had hurried to the police station, but by the time he'd got there*, el leopardo *had gone.*"

The Red Leopard. Nicolás Escobedo.

Calli's mind, the analytical mind that had always driven Robert mad, but had delighted professors with its clarity and precision, that grappled with slippery economic equations on a daily basis, analyzed the facts now. His name, the fact that he stood here in the receiving line consisting of the top military personnel of the country could only mean he was a member of the presidential family. That would make him…untouchable.

All her delight cooled and dispersed, as the chill of reality touched her. She remembered the miniscule shake of his head, his rejection. He had known then what she realized now.

Duardo presented her. *He* was looking at her now and he gave not a single hint they had met before. He took her hand, gave the same bow over it as the general had. His warm fingers smoothed their way over the back of her hand, sliding across the flesh there. Despite the cold, lead weight in her stomach she felt a ripple of pleasure from that tiny, unconscious caress. She took a deep breath and looked him in the eye.

"Señor Escobedo," she said.

"Miss Munro. When I studied in your country, people called me Nick. It would please me if you would do so, for Vistarians do not say it the same way as Americans."

"What did you study?" Minnie asked.

"Philosophy," he supplied, and glanced at Calli. She thought she saw a flicker of humor in his eyes. "I minored in Economics," he added, and then they had to move along. "Enjoy yourselves," he said in parting.

* * * * *

Duardo escorted them to a large round table, where half a dozen fellow officers and three women already sat. He knew them and introduced Calli and Minnie around. Calli saw no sign of hesitation or discomfort in their welcomes, and they ensured both she and Minnie had glasses of champagne within minutes of being seated. The women spoke no English, except for the one called Elvira, and her English was disjointed, hesitant, and her accent thick. The other soldiers had varying degrees of broken English, but their smiles seemed friendly enough.

Soon a band began to play. Not the sort of visceral, compelling music the small band had been playing last night, for this was a big ensemble. The noise level spiraled upwards. Couples began dancing as soon as the music began—no modest three or four sets before someone shyly broke the ice on the dance floor; they scrambled for the floor as soon as the first bars of music sounded. But it was a long time before Calli got the opportunity she waited for: Duardo on his own at the table, with only Minnie as witness. They sat looking at each other, and Minnie smiled a little.

"Duardo, you know Nicolás Escobedo?"

He shrugged. "Everyone does."

"I don't. He is related to the President?"

"He is *el Presidente*'s half-brother."

"*Half*-brother?" Calli repeated sharply. She thought about that. "That would explain the red hair, those eyes."

Duardo watched her warily. He knew where she took the conversation then.

"He has no formal role in the government?" she asked.

"No."

"I see." She glanced across the room where the general and his party sat at the long head table. Nicolás Escobedo sat there, too. He bent his head, listening to the general with deep concentration. As far as Calli could tell, he had not so much as glanced her way all evening.

She looked at Duardo, who still watched her. "I know who he is," she said.

He shook his head. "Do not speak it," he warned.

"Speak what?" Minnie asked.

It was a measure of Duardo's preoccupation with the subject matter that he picked up Minnie's hand absently in his and kissed it, like a man soothing a fretful child. "It is nothing," he assured her.

"You keep telling me that," Minnie complained.

He stirred, and Calli saw him mentally shake off his mood and look down at Minnie. "We dance, yes?"

"Mmm, yes," she agreed with a smile.

He glanced at her. "Excuse me, Miss Calli," he said, and stood to lead Minnie to the dance floor.

Calli sighed as they left her alone at the table, and stole one more glance at Nicolás Escobedo. He stood now, talking to an officer who stood behind the General's chair, one hand in his pocket again.

She reached for the champagne and sipped, trying to quell the stupid schoolgirl leap of joy because she knew his secret. He had warned her at the police station: this country was three steps away from violent revolution, and Americans were not welcomed. Good reasons existed for secrecy, for quiet manipulations behind the scenes, for maintaining appearances, and none of them had anything to do with the rush of pleasure she had felt on the two occasions he had looked at her.

To think he felt anything but passing irritation for her was a fantasy more foolhardy than Minnie's infatuation with an honorable soldier in the Vistarian army. Had Uncle Josh really thought Calli capable of watching out for his daughter?

Chapter Four

Supper was a long, multi-course meal served on silver platters by dozens of waiters, and finished off with a standing toast for the general's birthday. Then the hotel staff wheeled a massive six foot high cake out onto the middle of the dance floor.

Big enough for a pretty girl to jump out of the middle, Calli thought.

And with a fanfare of trumpets, the top of the cake did pop off, but what emerged was not a pretty, scantily clad girl. Rather, a mature woman rose up with a Spanish hat in her hand and a rose between her teeth, dressed in a traditional Flamenco costume that encased her bountiful figure in red satin. She paused at the top, a hand in the air, for effect.

And the room full of soldiers went wild. She heard a low chant; "Conchita, Conchita!"

Four men rushed to help her to the floor, and the staff rolled the cake away while someone escorted General Blanco to a chair on the dance floor. Conchita shimmied her way across the floor to drop the hat on his head, a kiss on his cheek, and the rose in his hand. He laughed, playing up to her. With a toss of her head, at the rumble of Spanish guitar chords, she went into a wild dance in front of him.

The soldiers in the room remained on their feet, clapping to the music, stamping, their hips moving in time to the music. Their backs hid most of the dance floor from Calli, but the lead weight that had been in her stomach since she had learned Nicolás Escobedo's identity gave her no enthusiasm for the floor show, and therefore no reason to get to her feet and strain to see.

Instead she found her attention wandering upwards, above the heads of the soldiers in front of her, and she looked up at the gallery that ran around three sides of the room. A stone balustrade edged the balcony, and tall columns supported arches that framed the top of the gallery. There was very little light up there, and the balcony seemed virtually deserted. If she could find her way there, she would be alone for a while, and she would be able to see the dance floor.

Better than sitting here alone.

She got to her feet and slipped between the ranks of soldiers to the side of the room. Their table had been on the edge of the room anyway, and close to the door — as far from the head table and the dance floor as possible, but Duardo and his friends were junior officers, so it was appropriate.

She found the stairs to the balcony easily enough, and she climbed slowly, tiredness seeping through her. She had not slept on the plane here, and last night her dreams had robbed her sleep of any restfulness. The last few hours had been thick with action, events that took her attention away from the growing weariness, but now that she found herself in a pocket of stillness, she could feel it as an ache in her bones, gnawing at her.

She emerged at the top of the stairs through a doorway onto the balcony. The doorway was hidden by a wall that jutted along the front of the gallery for about six feet, before the stone balustrade began. She walked along the balcony for a few feet until she had passed the wall and could look down upon the ballroom. It was a sea of military uniforms. The round tables with their pristine white tablecloths stood in stark contrast to the uniforms' darker hues. Shadows covered most of the room, while on the gallery on the far side of the room a single operator trained a spotlight on Conchita on the dance floor. To Calli's right was the huge double-doored entrance to the ballroom. Their arched tops reached up almost as high as she stood, fifteen feet from the floor of the ballroom.

The slender columns that held up the arches over the balcony were not so miniscule this close—they were at least five foot in diameter, solid granite, and designed to last generations. The smooth stone of the closest column felt cool against her bare shoulder. She sighed and relaxed against the support. The noise dropped a little up this high. She hadn't realized how loud it had become.

"Your cousin has found herself some interesting friends." The words, low and quiet, came from her right, close by.

Calli jerked around, startled.

Nicolás Escobedo leaned against the wall next to the stairwell door, hidden from below. He stood barely four feet from her. As she spun to face him he lifted a hand and made a small calming motion.

"Jesus Christ!" she breathed. "Did you follow me up here?"

"Yes."

"I'm surprised you even know where I sat."

He did not smile. "You underestimate yourself."

"I think I have a pretty good grasp of my place in the grand scheme of things in Vistaria. And yours, too," she said.

He smiled a little. "You've been listening to Duardo."

"And a lot of other people." She took a breath, trying to still her heart from its frantic pattering. "Why did you come up here?"

He straightened from his lean. "There are things that...must be said."

"Now that I know who you are," she added dryly. "Why didn't you tell me? Why did you...why did you let me..." She grimaced. "Never mind."

"You think your offer foolish because there is no chance that I, being who I am, would ever consider it seriously. So you feel shame for beggaring yourself that way."

She swallowed with a throat gone dry. "Yes," she breathed.

She couldn't look away from his eyes. He held her gaze, not letting her go. "I saw the light go out of your eyes when you heard my name, tonight," he said. "I saw you recall what you said at the police station. That is why I stand here now. I did not like watching that spirit in you die as you put it all together. Calli, do you not know how refreshing it feels to be made such an offer from a woman who had no idea who I am?"

Her mouth opened a little as her jaw sagged. "No," she said honestly. "I could only think that you have women throw themselves at you every day, and I was just one of dozens—of no passing concern. A moment's amusement."

He nodded. "So you squirm with shame for responding to a natural impulse."

She gave a dry laugh. "It's not *natural* for me. Not since Robert—" She clamped her jaw tight, suddenly realizing what she had been about to say, to no less than the president of Vistaria's half-brother.

"You just remembered who am I, didn't you?" he said softly.

She looked down at the stone balcony rail where her hands rested. "Yes." She couldn't look him in the eye while her cheeks burned with embarrassment. "Did you come up here simply to watch me squirm while you reminded me of my foolishness, Señor Escobedo?"

He did not answer at once, but when he did, his rasping voice was even lower. "I dreamed of you, Calli."

Her whole body seemed to leap at the quietly spoken confession. She looked at him, her pulse skittering.

He nodded. "Yes. I dreamed of you, of running my hands all over that pale, soft skin of yours. Your long legs wrapped about my hips — I spent hours simply savoring the taste of your flesh, pleasuring you."

She shuddered as a wave of pure silver excitement rippled through her, brought to life by the low, sensual sound of his voice, his words. She licked her lips, remembering the knowing expression she had seen in his eyes. There *had* been regret there, and something else…

"Then, in the cell, I didn't imagine — "

"No, you did not." His voice seemed to reach directly into her mind and throb inside her bones.

She turned to face him properly, but did not move towards him. She feared to hope, to make any movement that might indicate that foolish hope.

"That is what you had to tell me?" she breathed.

He shook his head, the same tiny movement he had made in the cell, and she almost cried out her dismay, for she knew what would come next.

"I wanted you to know, to understand how...dangerous it would be for me...for us. You've been here twenty-four hours now, and I know your uncle will have brought you up to date on the politics of Vistaria. My brother, José, is a moderate, just as I am. We know that we need American help to keep Vistaria whole and alive, but there are factions out there who would tear this country apart than allow a single American to have any influence here."

"Why are we hated so much?" Calli whispered.

"It is a hatred born out of fear. For generations Vistaria has watched other South American nations fall under the might of the American economy and know-how, their identities, their culture be swallowed whole by the U.S.A. And they tremble knowing how easily it could happen here. Radical factions have played on that fear, whipping it up into hatred, bigotry, worse."

The tiredness crept back into her bones. "I see," she said with a sigh.

"Calli, I am a bastard who cannot use his mother's name as any Vistarian does by right." She heard a surprising amount of bitterness in his voice. "But no one forgets who my half-brother is, and I have some power here as a result. If any hint escaped of a foreign woman in my life, if it was thought for a moment that I might be influenced by an American, then what little power I have here would be gone in that instant."

"And you want to keep that power so you can help Vistaria," she finished.

"No, I *must* keep that power, or the precarious balance here will be lost and Vistaria will crumble into civil war and worse."

She felt her eyes widen. "Is it that…critical?"

He sighed and pushed his hand into his pocket. "You're used to thinking in terms of billions, Calli. This is a very small country, with barely a million people on four islands. There are perhaps half a dozen key people, and I'd be a fool if I didn't know I was one of them. The army, for undisclosed reasons of its own, extends its loyalty to me. For as long as the army stays loyal to me, and by extension, my brother, then the country can be held against the rebels. If I lost that loyalty, if they had any reason to think I had betrayed them, then their sympathies would swing to the rebels. The civilian population would have no choice but to support the army. And Vistaria would be lost."

"You have a tiger by the tail, don't you?" she said. "You can't let go now."

"You understand, then."

She nodded. "But you did not have to tell me this at all. You could have left me—"

"Squirming?" he supplied.

"Ignorant of how you feel," she amended.

His silence gave her the answer.

"You wanted me to know?" she said.

"Yes."

"Why? If nothing will come of it, *why*?"

"Because I could not stay away," he ground out. "I want to live in your mind, at the very least."

Far down on the dance floor, the show had ended. "I have to go," she said. "They will be looking for me now." She moved towards the stairs, and as she passed him, his hand touched her wrist. It halted her. She looked at him as he straightened up from his lean. He stood very close to her now…she could feel his body heat radiating from him. The blue eyes looked totally black in this light.

"I must go," she said. "They are waiting for me down there." But she couldn't get her feet to move. With him standing this close, her whole body prickled with anticipation. He swayed a little, and she felt his hot breath on the nape of her neck. His fingers stroked the inside of her wrist, slowly, almost as if he did it unconsciously. He seemed to taste her with his fingertips. A shiver rippled through her in response, and she turned her head to look at him.

"If it is so dangerous, Nicolás, then I must go now, before my delay is noted." She couldn't help adding bitterly, "This is the point you wanted to emphasize, I believe?"

"I want to hear you call me Nick, like any other man you know," he said.

"You're not any other man," she whispered. She could feel the flesh between her legs throbbing—not simply her clitoris, but the whole sensitive saddle of flesh pulsed. Her breasts were almost painfully tight and erect. She wanted nothing more than for him to slide the straps of her dress from her shoulders and take her breasts in his hands. Her body remained perfectly still but her mind urged him to follow his instincts.

For sure, Nicolás Escobedo beckoned her like no other man she had ever met. She had never felt this rush of wantonness before.

He moved a little, and she could feel the brush of his jacket against her bare shoulder. His voice sounded in her ear. "I regret what cannot be."

And just because he had taunted her with the knowledge that he wanted her after all, only to snatch it away with the next breath, she lifted her chin to look him in the eye. "I dreamed of you, Nick. I dreamed of us making love."

She paused long enough to watch his eyes widen, for the knowledge to spear him, before she moved away, through the doorway to the stairs that would take her back down to the ballroom and the safety of a room full of soldiers.

And the thought made her laugh a little. She had been frightened of them all when she had first arrived here, wary and braced for trouble. Trouble had come, but from an entirely unexpected quarter.

Perhaps she could convince Minnie to go home now. She needed peace and time to think.

But when she got to the table, it was completely empty. She spotted some of the occupants on the dance floor. Elvira, with her upswept hair and black crepe dress, waltzed sedately with one of Duardo's men. Calli couldn't see Minnie or Duardo anywhere.

* * * * *

Nick stood for a long time in the gallery alcove with his head down, his eyes closed, listening to the sound of the party below, while tension clamped his body into stillness. He could still smell a hint of her perfume, something light and clean. When he had stood next to her, her warm scent and the touch of perfume had wreathed his head, making him giddy with the explosive arousal that had gripped him.

The need to touch her had been almost overwhelming. Only the knowledge of how unfair it would be to indulge himself had stopped him.

I dreamed of you, Nick, she had said, in a voice smooth and mellow like brandy.

At least he had wiped that look of desperate shame from her eyes. He'd managed something constructive. True, anger had replaced it, but he could live with anger. Better that she be filled with fury—it might give him the edge he needed to hold on to his sanity. While he clung to sanity, he could avoid any lethal decisions.

As long as she hated him, he could stay away from her.

* * * * *

Calli had done a tour of the upper floors and was searching the service rooms on the lower floor when she found them in a small, unused kitchen, tucked away on a back hallway. She paused, her hand on the swing doors, one pushed a few inches aside. She had no intention of interrupting them, but she had frozen completely and could not move, either, for the first glimpse she had of them had caught at her heart and throat.

If she had been asked to find a phrase to describe that first astonishing sight, she would have said without thinking: *pure, driven passion.* The image would stay with her forever— Minnie, her dress fallen down around her waist, lying on the wide steel counter, her back and hips a taut curve, offering herself as Duardo took one creamy brown nipple into his mouth and lapped at it with his tongue. Her hands were in his hair, encouraging him, as she gave a low groan. He stood with his thighs against the table. His jacket had gone. His shirt was unbuttoned and half off, revealing smooth brown shoulders. Firm rounded muscles bunched and moved under his flesh as he slid his hand up Minnie's thigh, pushing the dress up with it. He gathered the fabric around her waist, revealing garters and stockings, smooth bare skin and nothing else. No panties, not a glimmer of hair, just the smooth slit between her legs. Duardo made a deep rumbling sound of appreciation.

Calli couldn't pull her gaze away. Their hunger for each other hammered at her heart and body. The small, eager movements they made, the little noises, sighs, groans of pleasure...the pure eroticism grabbed her throat and held her there to watch, breathless.

Minnie lifted herself a little, reached for the buttons on his pants, and Duardo straightened, giving her access. He held her hips, thumbs moving in restless circles, as she nimbly released each button. She pushed the cloth aside, and his cock sprung free, thick and visibly pulsing with excitement.

Minnie gave a little laugh, low and throaty. She stroked him, her hand curling around his cock and sliding up to the tip.

Duardo's eyes narrowed in response to her touch. "No more," he growled. "It must be at once."

"Yes," she agreed.

He drew her closer to him, and she guided the head of his cock between her legs. He pushed inside her, and Minnie's head rolled back in ecstasy, even as Duardo groaned aloud. He thrust. Hard.

Her legs folded around his waist, drawing him closer, and he lifted her hips with each thrust. He gazed down upon her, his eyes narrowed, his expression almost one of bliss, of fierce satisfaction.

Minnie reached up a hand towards him and he kissed her palm.

Their movements grew more frantic as the excitement spiraled upwards. Calli could feel her heart picking up speed to move along with them. She was caught up in the spell, mentally a part of their pleasure, her own body responding. Slick heat grew between her legs, and her breath quickened.

To be loved like that...to be the subject of such longing...oh, she wanted it! Her body trembled with the imaginary joy of taking a man. Each time Duardo thrust, Calli felt the heavy, hard pressure as if it were her own body he pounded into.

Her breasts seemed to swell a little, to grow heavy inside her dress. Her clitoris throbbed behind the chiffon.

She held her breath, until the moment Duardo gasped and shuddered and grew still.

As Minnie sat up and reached for him, her breasts gleaming in the darkened kitchen, Calli at last forced herself to turn away. Her heart trip-hammering, she took a step on legs that seemed weak.

Behind her she heard Duardo's voice, thick and slow. "One sip of you is not enough."

"Drink your fill, if you dare," Minnie said, very low.

Calli hurried up her pace, heading back for the ballroom.

When Minnie and Duardo returned to the table fifteen minutes later, she had herself back under control. She made no comment about their absence and they gave no hint of what they had been doing. Duardo treated Minnie with utmost deference, bowing over her hand when Calli said they had to go, and uttering polite expressions of regret and gratitude for their company this evening. Not a single hint was given of the passion that had gripped him moments before.

He's a·soldier and used to staying in control. Just like Nicolás Escobedo.

The comparison rankled. For Duardo had chosen to take the moments he wanted, unlike Nicolás.

* * * * *

"You going to tell me what's eating you?" Minnie asked as she carefully steered the car around another group of fiesta-goers wending their way home.

Calli stirred, her attention drawn from her dark reflection on the side window. "No," she said, as gently as she could.

"Duardo thought he had upset you."

"He did? I'm sorry, I didn't intend that."

"Then you do like him?"

Calli roused herself, trying for Minnie's sake to give an honest answer. "He's an honorable and loyal officer. But Minnie, he's in the army. They lead such…precarious lives—especially now. There's danger for him, being with you. Are you aware of that?" The echo of Nicolás's words set up a pang of sadness in her.

"The army people don't mind Americans," Minnie said. "No one was rude to us tonight, just as Duardo said."

"There is more to Vistaria than the army," Calli pointed out.

"Lots of civilians work at the mine Dad is setting up. They don't hold grudges either."

Calli shook her head. "It's not that simple."

Minnie gave the steering wheel a little thump. "Damn it, Calli, I have to live here too. For as long as Dad is working the mine, I have to live amongst these people. I have to find acceptance where I can. Do you think I'm so thick and stupid I don't know what some of them think of us? But I can't do anything about how they feel about me, because they don't know me. So the only thing I can do is ignore them, and find the few who do not think I'm some sort of…disease or parasite that will suck the life out of them. So quit trying to depress me, because I just don't want to hear about it, okay?"

"Okay," Calli agreed. "I'm sorry, Minnie. You just seem to move through life with so little concern."

"I get concerned," Minnie muttered.

"About the latest dress length."

"Well, that's something I can do something about!"

"Okay." Calli held up her hand, motioning for peace, and realized the gesture echoed Nicolás Escobedo's motion, too. Quickly, she dropped her hand back to her lap and held it with the other. "God I need sleep," she muttered.

* * * * *

Something warm and soft supported her back. A hand, warmer still, pressed against the back of her shoulder, holding her. His hot heavy body moved against her restlessly. She felt the touch of skin upon hot skin and the moisture building between them. Sweat. And a softness of flesh over unyielding bones.

The pressure of his body against her was good. Welcome. It'd been far too long since she had last enjoyed the sensation of a man laying over her...and it had never felt like this. Not this feeling of being overwhelmed by his size and weight...of being smaller, weaker, more feminine.

He looked into her eyes. His hand was on her waist. It slid down along her hip. The muscles there quivered as his thumb stroked across the little dip by her hipbone. He cupped her thigh, and brought her leg up around his waist. The good, hard pressure of his thigh between her legs pushed against her. His cock, thick and large, throbbed against her pelvis.

He dipped his head, and his hair tickled her chest, then his mouth fastened upon her breast, around her nipple, and she let her head fall back with a sigh. But his mouth did not give the sharp jolt of pleasure she expected. It felt ghostly, distant. She tried to look at him, to protest, but she could not speak, no matter how she struggled to get the words out...

* * * * *

Calli wiped the sleep from her eyes and let her hand fall back on the pillow with a sigh. Her body zinged with arousal. Her throbbing clit kept time with her slowing heartbeat. Sweat had gathered between her breasts and now trickled down to her stomach.

She swallowed, wishing she had put a glass of water by the bed.

Why could she not speak in these dreams? What held her mute? The inability to talk had shadowed both nights' dreams, along with the thundering sexual arousal.

And that arousal was another novelty. She had not had a sexy dream since before she had met Robert, and never this explicit, this stimulating.

The hand along the hip... Of all the images and sensations in the dream, this one burned in her mind. The possessive sweep of his hand against her hip had felt *real* in the dream, more real than the other ghostly, unsatisfying sensations.

She sighed again, and turned over, bringing the sheet up and over her shoulder, burying beneath the cotton. The ache was worse now that she knew he wanted her, too.

Why him? Why, after five years since Robert had left did she now suddenly yearn for sex? And with someone so impossibly out of reach?

Just before she fell asleep the solution occurred to her, and astounded her with its simplicity. Sex was the issue. So go get some. Problem solved. Life back on track.

Chapter Five

"Everything takes longer here," Uncle Josh explained, pouring Calli another cup of coffee. "You just have to go with the flow."

"But my credit card company isn't *here*. It's in Montana, and it's —" she looked at her new watch and added two hours, "— ten in the morning. They've at least had two coffees and a doughnut by now, so they can't plead that they're asleep."

Josh smiled a little. "Is that a comment about my breakfast-making skills?" he asked, picking up the huge big broadsheet newspaper that covered the remains of his breakfast plate, piled high with blackened toast crusts. "You could always phone the competition and tell them they can have your business if they will give you a card sooner than your replacement will get here." He buried himself behind the newspaper.

"There's a thought," Calli said.

"You're late today, Dad," Minnie said from the door to her room. She belted closed an apricot satin robe, her hair spiky from sleep, and her eyes still half shut. She looked as though she had slept soundly.

"Speak for yourself," Joshua returned. "I'm meeting some people in the city for lunch. Actually, Calli, I meant to mention something and that reminds me. There's a man on my staff, single, American. From Wisconsin. A lawyer —"

"Well, no one's perfect," Minnie said, pouring herself a coffee.

Calli smiled a little. "Are you setting me up on a blind date, Uncle Josh?"

He lowered his paper a little, considering it. "I suppose I am," he admitted. "Although it didn't feel like that when Peter first proposed it."

"Peter?" Minnie asked. "You're talking about Peter *Kaestner*? He's a creep."

"He's perfectly normal," Joshua said calmly. "That he told you to grow up simply emphasizes he has the necessary maturity for a man who holds the responsibilities he does. You know, there aren't all that many Americans in Vistaria, and most of them are with the company. Single women are unusual...I think he's lonely."

"Or horny," Minnie added.

Joshua glared at her.

"What?" she asked, spreading her hand. "Am I wrong?"

He chose to ignore that and looked at Calli instead. "What about dinner tonight?"

Calli nodded. "Yes, I'd love to," she said, without pausing to consider it. She knew if she allowed herself to think about it, she would find a reason to say no.

"Good." Joshua folded up the newspaper and plopped it onto the middle of the table, then stretched. "I should get going, anyway. There's stuff to do at the palace. I'll talk to Peter at lunch and call you with details, okay?"

"Sure," Calli said briefly, but she stared at the front page of the newspaper which now faced her. The picture was grainy, but unmistakable. A wide shot of the head table at last night's dinner. The general sat front and center in the photo, but Nicolás Escobedo's features were clear too. The headlines screamed something in huge type, exclamation marks either side, the first one upside-down.

Uncle Josh picked up his briefcase, jiggling his pocket for keys.

"I'll walk you to the car," Calli told him, getting to her feet.

"'kay," he said without hesitation.

When they were outside he raised his eyebrow. "Something in the paper spook you?" he asked.

"A little. What did that headline say?"

"Congratulations to Blanco for his excellent leadership and his birthday."

"Oh."

"It's *El Liberalé*, which is a conservative newspaper despite the name. What were you hoping for? Disclosure of a conspiracy?"

She shook her head. "It was the man a couple of seats to the right of Blanco."

"Nicolás Escobedo?" Joshua said, a little sharply. "What of him?"

"He's the man who helped me at the jail."

Joshua rested his briefcase on the hood of the silver Chevy Cavalier, and leaned on it, as if thinking hard. "You're sure?" he asked quietly.

"Positive."

Another thoughtful silence. "*Jesus Maria…*" Joshua breathed. "He really *does* have feelers out everywhere."

"He's the man the army calls *el leopardo rojo*."

"Yes, I just made the connection," Joshua said, frowning. "Although I wouldn't go around blurting that out to just anyone, Calli."

His brow smoothed. "Well, it's good to know we have friends in high places," he said. "This really does confirm they're working to support us here. With the problems I get handed every day I sometimes wondered."

He patted her shoulder. "Thanks for telling me." He got into the car and drove away.

Calli stood on the narrow cobbled street, watching the Chevy twist around the hairpin bend twenty yards down the hill, and disappear.

The conversation had cheered Josh immensely, but Calli, perversely, felt more uneasy than ever.

I want to live in your mind, at least. His voice curled through her thoughts.

Had he honestly thought she would be able to dismiss him with his face plastered on the front page of the daily national newspaper? But...gut instinct told her his intention had been to linger in her memories at a far more personal level.

The image from her dream, her thigh over his hip, his hand on her skin, hot and demanding, slipped into her thoughts. *That* was what he had meant.

Why her? Why? When no other man had raised so much as an eyebrow in her direction for five years? More? She was a dusty, ill-used thirty-something woman well on her way to becoming a rusty, disused old spinster set in her ways, entrenched in academia and teaching dry economic theory until she retired.

Why me? And why him?

It was beyond comprehension.

And it was all theory, anyway. He had made that clear last night. Nothing would ever come of it. He was as untouchable as she had suspected.

She went back inside, blinking in the dimness of the apartment after the brilliant sunshine outside, and asked Minnie to take her shopping again. She would need something sexy to wear tonight if she was going to get herself laid.

* * * * *

"You know, you really are a knockout," Peter said. "Joshua said you scrubbed up well, but I think he was being conservative."

Calli smiled mechanically and swallowed another mouthful of the dry, overcooked steak. Peter had told her three times already what a knockout she was, and it didn't sound any better on the third repetition. But his need to please her added points in his favor.

She had surreptitiously checked off other criteria throughout the evening. His breath smelled sweet; he had no discernable body odor. Clean hands, a nice white smile, and a small bonus: tight buttocks beneath the dark business suit. He stood perhaps half an inch shorter than her, which she could overlook for now. In bed, the height difference would be no difference at all.

The absolute lack of any appeal he had for her *was* a drawback, however. He had light brown hair, light brown eyes, nicely tanned skin to go with the white smile, and he obviously worked to maintain his body. Nothing wrong with him at all. But nothing sparked her interest.

He had picked her up at the apartment right on time. She had walked out the door knowing she looked as beddable as it was possible to look. Minnie had worked all afternoon to ensure Peter got the right impression.

Minnie had somehow intuited Calli's intentions for she had rapidly discarded various options, settling on a look that she pronounced with her arms crossed, "totally fuckable, honey."

She wore a dress made of stretch lace. The halter top had a v-neck that ended low between her breasts. Virtually backless, the dress dipped down to the point where the indentation of Calli's spine flattened out over the back of her hips. It had no lining—her skin showed clearly through the mesh of the lace, except for a virtually invisible flesh-colored panel of elastic that covered her breasts and supported them. The skirt hugged her hips— the elastic fabric gave her flexibility, but the dress clung to her. The hem stopped several inches short of her knees.

Minnie had insisted she wear the tallest shoes they could find, a black pair with ankle straps. All her hair had been piled on top of her head and held down with dozens of hair clips. Wisps fell around her face. Minnie also directed the application of her makeup. Red lips, red toenails, and gold hoop earrings. But Minnie could do nothing about Calli's work-worn fingernails other than file them neatly and paint them.

Calli had looked in the mirror and frowned. "Don't you think it's a bit subtle?" she asked Minnie. "I should be wearing a mini skirt and thigh high leather boots or something. This looks…"

"Sensual," Minnie declared.

"I want to say 'sex' not 'sensual'."

"Do you want good sex or 'wham, bam, thank you ma'am'?" Minnie asked.

Calli pursed her lips. Minnie did know more about this than her, after all. Yet Calli didn't want to play a slow game of subtle seduction. She wanted to be fucked, and then she could move on with her life.

"Believe me, sensual will get you good sex," Minnie added. "If a man understands the difference between the two then he knows how to please a woman in bed. And if Peter doesn't understand it, he doesn't deserve you. Besides, if you did walk into Ashcroft's wearing a mini skirt and leather boots you'd be arrested for prostitution. They're very conservative here."

"Not from what I saw the first night of *La Fiesta*."

"That's the festival for you. People let off steam during the fiesta. It's condoned. But only then."

Calli studied her. "You *have* been taking notice, haven't you?"

"Told you I had," Minnie returned. The phone rang and she almost jumped across the room to pick it up. "Duardo!" she said happily, turning away, leaving Calli to wait for Peter to arrive.

Ashcroft's, one of the best restaurants in the city, served what they optimistically titled "international cuisine". Peter had been proud to show her the menu that featured Texas beef, and insisted she indulge herself. Calli had been curious to try some of the local dishes, but in order to keep Peter happy, had ordered the beef. It had been a mistake.

She put her knife and fork down and sat back, looking around. The cavernous restaurant had a high ceiling and dark wood paneling on the walls. It felt very Victorian, with large potted palms and ferns in collections throughout the room, which managed to provide each table a small measure of privacy.

"It feels like one of those mens' clubs they used to have in London," Calli said.

"Very observant," Peter said with a grin. "It used to be exactly that, way back when. The British had a small colonial trade outpost here just before the first world war. And where there's a group of Englishmen, there's always a club."

"I see." She cast about for something else to say, starting to feel a little desperate. Her dilemma grew stronger with each passing minute—she had finished her meal and he had nearly emptied his plate. What then? Coffee and dessert—well, not for her. But how did she work this now? It had been too many years since she'd dated, and now she had no idea what to do. Besides, she was no longer certain she even *wanted* to take Peter to bed. Had she ever wanted to?

"Shall we dance?" Peter asked after a moment.

"Yes," she said thankfully. That would delay the moment of decision a bit longer, anyway.

A pocket-sized dance floor occupied the middle of the room, and a three man band on the bandstand, playing western lounge music. One other couple moved about the floor, a middle-aged pair that looked like they had been plucked off a dancehall floor out of the States—conservatively-dressed, overweight, polite, proper Americans.

Peter led her out onto the floor and took her in his arms for a slow two step. His hand on her back was sweaty. He seemed to be aware of it, for he barely touched her, as if contact with her bare skin would give him a shock. He concentrated very hard on the dance, not speaking at all.

Well, it had been a long time since she'd danced too. So Calli tried to relax and enjoy the moment.

Halfway around the floor, she ended up facing the other way and saw the rest of the room that had been hidden by a giant palm next to their table. A group of businessmen, had their heads together, over by the massive fireplace. Cigar smoke hung thick around their heads, and they laughed loudly over a joke, settling back in their chairs.

One of them was Nicolás Escobedo.

Calli tripped a little and clutched at Peter's shoulder to save herself. His hand clamped against her back, drawing her against him to hold her up.

"Whoa!" he said. "You all right?"

"Yes," she said a little shakily. Her heart hammered and she began to tremble.

"Do you want to sit down?"

"Yes...no, it's okay. I'm enjoying this," she said.

"You're sure?"

"Yes." She smiled at him.

He shrugged a little. "Okay, then."

They began dancing again. When Peter turned her next, she glanced back at the table of businessmen.

Nicolás Escobedo sat back in his chair, one arm draped over the arm. He watched her, while his three companions continued to talk. Calli covertly studied him before Peter swung her around again. A dark suit, but not quite black. Perhaps charcoal gray, or a gray green. The shirt was dark, too, and the tie matched it. He wouldn't look out of place on Wall Street.

With the next turn she looked again. He watched still and one long finger rested against his lips. He'd narrowed his eyes, as though her presence here disturbed him.

She felt a resurgence of the same anger that had gripped her last night when Nicolás had revealed his attraction to her and instantly pulled it out of her reach just because he wanted to. There had been no consideration for her in his decision, just some perverse desire to play with her, like dangling yarn in front of a kitten.

Why was he here? To play with her again?

Then her view vanished, for Peter had turned her again. The music stopped, and the musicians stood and nodded to them.

Break time.

Peter led her back to the table and they sat down. Their meals had been cleared, but as Calli no longer dithered about how the evening would finish, the acceleration of the end of the meal held little consequence. She would, somehow, let Peter know that if he pressed his luck, he'd find a willing mate. And she would cooperate with full enthusiasm. If she let herself sink into the experience, she could wipe out any lingering needs Nicolás Escobedo had stirred in her, and the slate would then be clean.

And after that, she would stay in bed with Peter and thank him the only appropriate way possible.

So all that remained now was to get to the end of the evening as quickly as possible.

Peter looked around for a waiter. "Would you like another drink?" he asked. "They have excellent tea here."

Tea. Calli shook her head. "I'd prefer coffee if I must, but—"

"Coffee. No problem." He waved his hand.

"No, really, I could live without it," she said quickly.

"It's no problem," he assured her.

She sighed, and sat back.

"It's Kaestner, isn't it?" said a new voice from behind her.

Calli didn't have to turn to look to know Nicolás stood behind her. The voice could belong to no one else. The American accent with the deliberate pronunciation, as if he concentrated on every word. Which he might well be. Even without the hint, no man she knew had that gravelly, low timbre that caressed her spine and made her gut turn with a slow roll that left every nerve in her body awake and tingling.

Peter stood up again, grasping the napkin in his lap and trying to shake hands at the same time. He did it awkwardly, caught by surprise. "Yes, Peter Kaestner, Señor Escobedo. I didn't realize you dined here—I wouldn't have ignored you."

"No, it's all right," Nicolás said, waving him down. "I am here on private family business—Ashcroft's is good for not being noticed, I've found. You too, I see."

"Yeah, you can really get away from people here," Peter agreed. "Please…sit down."

Nicolás sat in the chair to Calli's left and looked at her. "Miss Munro, yes? You were at the general's birthday party last night."

"That's right," Calli said. Her voice emerged husky.

Peter looked shocked. "You got an invite to *that*?"

"Callida has managed to make quite an impression on Vistarians in her short time here," Nicolás said.

"I guess," Peter said with a half laugh, half exhalation. He seemed genuinely bemused.

"We met at *Las Piedras Grandes*, didn't we?" Nicolás asked him. "At the opening ceremony for the mine?"

Peter nodded enthusiastically. Quickly Nicolás drew him out, opening up the conversation, getting Peter to talk about his work, his worries. Calli tuned the conversation out, watching the two men instead. While Peter spoke and Nicolás listened, Nicolás played with the stem of the empty water glass in front of him, absently sliding his fingers up and down the length of it. Calli watched the motion, almost hypnotized by it. His fingers slid up the stem, then up further still, around the bottom of the glass itself, to cup the curve there.

She released the breath she'd been holding. Was he doing it deliberately? But he never once even glanced at her.

Abruptly, she stood up. "Will you excuse me?" she murmured before either of them could react and hurried towards the door into the wide hallway that led to the front door. A waitress with a starched apron spoke to her, and Calli heard 'help' amidst the blur of Spanish.

"*Sí*," she said. "Washrooms? Um…" She frowned, recalling the phrases she had been studying, groping for an appropriate word. "*¿La conveniencia?*"

"*Sí*," the woman said, and pointed toward the wide carpeted stairs running up along the opposite wall of the hallway. The heavy paneling repeated there, and a thick railing of heavily carved wood glowed with age and good care.

"Up?" Calli questioned, also pointing.

"*Sí*, up." The waitress agreed with a wide smile.

The stairway broke into a square landing very close to the bottom of the case, and the wall along the side of the landing had a huge picture window, framed with lavish green velvet swags and curtains. At ninety degrees to the rest of the stairs, three more steps reached down to the hallway floor. Calli climbed the steps slowly and saw the reason why the window had been placed there: The lights of *la colina* spread out before her, undulating down the hillside and off to the north and south for miles.

She didn't pause to admire the view, for she wanted to reach a place where no one could find her easily. But she moved slowly. The longer she took to reach that place, the longer she stayed away from the table, the higher the probability that Nicolás would be gone when she returned to the table.

Why had he come over? There had been no reason that she could see. His talk with Peter had been virtually mindless, yet someone like Nicolás Escobedo did not engage in superficial conversation for no reason.

She found the washrooms, with the universal symbol for women, and stood at the basin, staring in the mirror but not seeing herself, tasting the roiling anger and frustration. Last night...and again tonight. He simply toyed with her.

But...no, that wasn't accurate. Her mind, trained for critical-thinking, nagged her into acknowledging the inconsistencies.

Calli spread her hands and leaned on the counter, letting her head hang as she pushed aside all the hurt feelings and her bruised ego, and separated out the facts. He had said...what?

I saw the light go out of your eyes when you heard my name, tonight. I saw you recall what you said at the police station. That is why I stand here now. I did not like watching that spirit in you die as you put it all together.

And the caress of his voice in her mind: *I dreamed of you, Calli.*

Abruptly, she shivered.

He hadn't been playing with her at all. He had revealed himself to make *her* feel better, then very carefully explained why he could not give in to the desire.

Calli rubbed her temple. God, and she had been at the point of dragging Peter to bed to get even with him. How stupid! How could she not have seen this before? "I'm out of practice," she whispered to the mirror.

That left one remaining question. Why had he come over to the table tonight?

If she hurried back to the table, would he still be there? Suddenly afraid, she raced from the room, intending to rush back to the table. He would have sensed her dismissal. He would not need it repeated. He would leave as quickly as politeness would allow. She had to get back.

Halfway down the stairs, she saw him. He stood next to the green swags, looking out at the view, but she knew instantly he waited for her. Her heart hammering and her body on high alert, she descended the rest of the stairs. All at once she was aware of the dress, her sheer black stockings—she was proud of her appearance. She was glad he had seen her like this.

She stepped down onto the landing and walked over to stand beside him, as if they shared the view. The skin on her shoulder prickled at the nearness of his arm, even though they did not touch.

"Why did you come over to our table?" she said.

"Did you think I could stay away? With you looking like that? I am a man, Calli, not a machine. Your appearance tonight...a man has only to look at you to know he should shower you with every sensual pleasure he can produce, that the rewards for such efforts would be ecstasy beyond his wildest dreams."

A shiver wracked her. Peter had not managed anything even remotely poetic. But Nicolás had responded. She remembered Minnie's advice and realized that Nicolás understood the difference.

"He's not worthy, Calli," he said quietly.

"He will do." She would not tell him that she had changed her mind about seducing Peter. There was no point.

"I'd assumed you had better taste," he said quietly. "He's a boy, and he cannot dance."

"And you can?"

"Better than he."

"But he took me out on the dance floor, while you will not dare. Who is more the man there?"

He reached out to grip the velvet curtain beside him and crushed it in his fist. "It is not lack of courage that prevents me."

"You made it clear last night that my life is none of your business."

In the reflection on the window, she saw his head drop, as if he didn't like the fact any more than she. "So I did," he agreed, his voice very low.

"Are you recanting?" she asked, her voice barely above a whisper, and her heart suddenly hurt as it pounded against her chest.

His grip on the velvet tightened. "I *can't*," he growled.

The exquisite tension in her subsided, like air from a tire. "I know," she agreed. All the pride, the excitement, fled. "I have to get back to Peter. He'll be wondering —"

But his arm wrapped around her waist as she turned to go. She inhaled sharply as he pulled her up against him, held there, his arm an iron band around her.

"Not yet," he said, his voice strained.

Heat. Solid, immoveable strength, the hard length of his body registering along hers. His hand cupped her hip.

Calli closed her eyes against the ferocious rush of undiluted desire. She began to tremble. "Don't," she whispered.

He drew breath. She could hear it and felt his chest expand against her shoulders. But he did not speak.

She opened her eyes. In the reflection on the window she saw his other hand come up to her bare shoulder, and hover there, as if he fought himself.

She held her breath, the skin over her shoulder tingling, all nerves stretched to their limits, anticipating his touch. Her thoughts paused, her whole body stilled…waiting.

But it was not a caress she received. His whole hand gently curled over her shoulder, and she realized that it trembled, too. The hand settled, firm and warm, as if by anchoring it so firmly he could resist moving it further. He let out his breath, stirring the curls by her ear, and grew still. His eyes closed.

Yes, he battled himself.

"There is a difference in you tonight," he said. "More than just the dress."

"I haven't changed."

"No, but you have...let go. What has happened, to make that difference?"

She thought of the stolen moment she had seen between Duardo and Minnie. "I have realized that some men will take what they want. You will not. I must find someone who will."

He remained quiet for a long moment. "If it is simply sex that you seek," he said at last. "Then you will not have far to look. But do you think Peter will appreciate what he has? Do you think he will be able to satisfy you beyond crude, coarse coupling?"

He spoke her own fears aloud. She sighed. "I don't know."

"I *do* know. Why must you do this? You did not, in Montana. I know that as surely as I know my own hand. The woman I see tonight...she does not normally show her face."

"I, too, am not a machine. You cannot stir these feelings in me, stoke them, and then expect me to remain untouched. I *dream* of you, Nick. And everywhere I see sensuality...lust...and know I will never have those moments with you that I dreamed of. I will take what I can, then."

"Not with him, Calli." His voice held a note of pleading…almost.

"You will not. He will."

She could feel him shake his head, even as his reflection made the same movement in the glass. "I could fill your mind to the point where you cannot think of another man. The idea of taking another would be as remote and alien to you as the surface of Mars."

"Arrogance," she breathed.

"*Knowledge*," he corrected. "I can feel you trembling against me, and I know how you have drugged my own mind these last two days, to the point where I cannot sleep. All I must do is stamp myself upon you a little more and I know you will not be able to think of another, for you are not like that."

"Nick…" She spoke his name half in warning, half in pleading. They walked upon treacherous ground now.

His hand on her shoulder slid, with a whisper of a caress, down to cup her breast. She gasped raggedly. The material of the dress was so fine and light it felt as if he held her naked breast. His hand was hot, large, against her flesh, delicious. She could feel the details on his fingers, the swell of flesh, the joints, the tips, searing her skin. His thumb rubbed against the nipple, little short strokes that tugged at the lace, and bumped over the tight nub of sensitive flesh. The chafing touch electrified her, sent a hard spike of pure pleasure straight to her clitoris, and her whole body clenched, tightened.

"God, Nick, please…" she moaned, her head falling back against his shoulder. Her shoulders pulled back involuntarily, thrusting her breast into his hand.

"You plead for me to stop…or for more?" he asked, his voice hoarse with pent-up emotion.

She clenched her jaw, determined not to speak aloud the rabid need she had for him. She cared not at all about their public place, that Peter might come looking for her at any moment, that anyone looking in the window would see them, would see his hand at her breast. She wanted more, much more, felt a ravening need to coax him by words and movements to take her right now.

He kissed her neck, right by the corner of her jaw. His lips were hot. "I see your jaw ripple. Ah, you are strong, Calli, I knew that. Do you know how much your strength is a goad, driving me to try to breach that strength, to have you whimper in my arms?" His voice by her ear sent another shiver through her. His heady, spicy and very masculine scent enveloped her.

His hand moved across to the other breast, but this time he slid it under the fabric. Calli sucked in a sharp breath as she realized what he would do. In her dreams she had ached to feel his hand on her bare breast, and had almost wept when the dream touch had not lived up to its promise. Now it would really happen and it wasn't just her breath she held — her pulse seemed to pause, her mind locked, and her awareness opened up, every nerve receptive to the tiniest stimulus.

The long fingers coaxed the lace aside, and slipped over the curve of her breast, grazing the puckered nipple. Then finally, *finally*, his hand settled around the globe of flesh and caressed the nipple directly. Heat, strength, control, sensuality…it all slammed into her mind at once.

She gave a little cry — it jerked out of her, and she tried to swallow it back, choke it to silence. But she could not prevent her head from rolling against his throat — the skin by her temple registered the heat of his flesh and the frantic beat of his pulse. But then his hand moved against her breast again, snagging the nipple. She gave a gasping groan.

"Tell me what is in your mind to make you utter that sound," he whispered.

"Your hand…I dreamed of your hand on my breast." Her voice was throaty, distorted by raw animal wanting. "But I couldn't feel it in the dream, and now you touch me just as you did in the dream, but it feels…so good."

She heard him swallow, the little ragged sound of his breath. "…God help me, Calli, but you are driving me out of my mind. The look on your face, your voice…do you know how easy it would be for me to tear this dress from you and lower you to the floor and take you right now? Here?"

"I would not stop you," she whispered.

His left hand, on her hip, moved restlessly, down to stroke her thigh beneath the dress, the little finger slipping between her legs. But it did not go higher. It fluttered against the sensitive skin of her inner thighs, stroking with delicate caresses. When his fingers discovered the lacy tops of her stockings, he made a noise that sounded half groan, half murmured growl.

"Tell me you can still think of taking another man to bed," he rasped in her ear.

The truth spilled from her. "Not in a million years."

His hands grew still. He withdrew his hand from her dress, and both arms came around her waist. "Then we are even."

She took a deep breath so that she could speak properly again. "So I am doomed to be tortured by what I cannot have, and you will go slake your need with whomever you please. You are being very unfair, Nick."

His lips came down upon the nape of her neck. "You misinterpret me. I have simply brought you to the point where I have been for two long nights."

She grew very still. "You mean...?"

"Yes, Calli. I have not been able to touch another woman since I met you." His tone became dry. "Although I have tried."

She closed her eyes. "Why me?" she asked. "Why, of all the women you have met? I know what I am. I'm a discarded economics tutor. I even have two cats at home."

His voice came right by her ear again, and she could feel it against her shoulders, too. "There was a moment, in the holding cell, when I first stepped inside. You had not seen me, but I saw you. You looked out the window, with your hands on the bars. I had just spent an hour sorting out the true story from the men in the hospital and the arresting officers and the liaison your uncle had called. So when I saw you I already knew that you had rushed out to Vistaria when your uncle phoned asking for your help for the summer, with little warning or preparation. Because he asked, you had come. Within an hour of landing in a country where you didn't speak the language, you had been put in a situation that would tax the nerves of most men, but I did not see a petrified, cowed woman standing at that window, and when you turned to face me, you did not plead or beg or whine. I saw your spirit, and knew it could not be crushed. That strength…is so very rare."

She absorbed his words with difficulty. "Oh, Nick, you're so wrong. I *have* been crushed. Ask Minnie. She will tell you I haven't yet dragged myself back to anything like normal."

"No." He shook his head. "You simply guard yourself now, that is all. The woman last night that looked me in the eye and planted that last barb, just to even the score…she was not crushed."

"And must I now guard myself against you?"

"I would never hurt you." Total conviction rang in his voice.

"Just standing here places me, both of us, in danger."

Again, she felt him draw a large breath. Bracing himself. And suddenly, as abruptly as she had been drawn to him, she was freed. She shivered as cool air touched the skin at her back, and turned to face him.

He stared out the window again. "You should go," he said, without looking at her.

"Calli?" Peter's voice.

She turned to see him emerging from the dining room. "Sorry, I got caught up," she said to him.

"Have you seen the view from here?" Nicolás added.

Peter climbed up to the landing and looked out. He gave a low whistle. "No, I've never been up here before," he confessed. "Quite a view, huh?"

"Yes, it is," Nicolás agreed. He pushed his sleeve back and looked at his watch, the gold band glittering in the light from the chandelier overhead. "You must excuse me, both of you."

"Of course," Peter agreed magnanimously. "It was good of you to stop and say hello."

"My pleasure," Nicolás murmured. He turned to Calli and gave a little nod. "Miss Munro."

"Goodbye," she said politely.

They watched him move to the front door, say something to the waitress that made her giggle with her tray covering her mouth, and shut the heavy door behind him. He didn't look back.

Exactly as it should be, Calli told herself firmly.

But she could still feel the imprint of his hand on her breast, the feel of his heart beating against her back, and knew her sleep would be as broken tonight as it had been for the last two nights.

"Could you please take me home, Peter?" she asked, abruptly.

* * * * *

Peter dropped her off outside the apartment, and she did not invite him in. Her silence on the way home clearly conveyed her mood, for he did not attempt to so much as kiss her. He simply braked and put the car in neutral, the engine running, his hand on the gear stick.

"Thank you for dinner," Calli said listlessly, feeling the enormous weariness wrap about her once more.

"No problem. Thanks for your company," he said. "Calli, did Escobedo say something to you? Something that upset you?"

"Why?" she asked.

"You've been silent ever since then...something must have happened."

"He was very polite," she said.

"Yes, he invariably is polite," he agreed. "But that doesn't mean what he's saying doesn't mean anything."

"He didn't say anything of significance. The view, the fiesta, Vistaria's wonderful future with the discovery of silver."

"All very politically correct." It sounded almost like Peter sneered but it was too dark to check.

One of the black taxis common around Vistaria pulled up in front of them, then, and the back door opened. Minnie almost fell out of the back seat, laughing. With her hand on the door she righted herself and stood up, pushing her clingy jersey dress down from around her hips to hang properly. It didn't seem to bother her that she stood perfectly spot-lit by Peter's headlights. A long trouser-encased leg pushed out of the taxi beside her, then Duardo uncurled himself from the back seat. He kept his head bent down, talking to the driver volubly, waving his hand for emphasis.

"That's Minnie, isn't it?" Peter said quietly.

"Yes."

Minnie turned to face Duardo, both of them standing in the angle between the open door and the side of the taxi. Duardo caught her face in his hands and kissed her hard and passionately as her arms curled around his neck. He grasped her thigh, drawing her leg up against his hip. The dress rode up her leg, revealing most of her thigh and the start of her bare buttock. At the same time his lips moved down her throat to the top of her breasts, revealed by the scoop neck of the dress. The hand on her leg slid around the curve of thigh to cup her buttock, his sunburned, olive fingers a sharp contrast to her pale white flesh.

Peter made a hissing sound between his teeth. "Jesus, Minnie," he murmured. "Who is that guy, anyway?" he demanded.

"He's okay," Calli said quickly. "He's a nice guy."

"I bet."

The pair kissed again, lingering, and Calli didn't want to climb from the car and alert them to witnesses. She cleared her throat, unsure what to do except wait out their passionate goodbye.

The taxi driver was not so patient. He tooted his horn, and Minnie pulled her mouth from Duardo's and appeared to chuckle. Duardo spoke, gave her another quick kiss, and let her go. She stepped back and let him get back into the taxi, and waved as it pulled away.

Calli got out of the car thankfully and shut the door, and Minnie turned to smile at her as Peter pulled away. Calli didn't wave.

"You look like you've been eating lemons," Minnie said.

"I'm very tired," Calli confessed.

"You're also damned early and you don't look like you have had a good time."

"I didn't," she confessed. "It was wretched."

"Ah. Then Peter's the jerk I always thought he would be." Minnie shrugged, and turned towards the apartment.

"You had a good time, though, I can tell."

"Mmmmm."

"Where did you go?"

Minnie laughed a little. "We planned to go to a night club with the others, but we never got there. We found a little bistro and then afterwards, well…" She gave a gusty sigh, and ran her hand through her hair.

"I assume the goodbye kiss we just watched was a mild rendition of the rest of the evening, then," Calli said.

"Fuckin' A," Minnie said, and laughed as she unlocked the front door and pushed it aside. "I gotta get some sleep. I'm exhausted."

"I'm not surprised," Calli murmured.

* * * * *

Calli's prediction about her own sleep proved correct. It was restless, shot through with dreams either erotic or downright disturbing — charged with a sense of impending doom. In the lucid moments of wakefulness between bouts of nightmares, she told herself that obviously even her subconscious understood the danger of entertaining even in her imagination any sort of relationship with Nicolás Escobedo.

Towards morning, exhausted, she dropped into a dreamless, heavy sleep. When she woke feeling only slightly refreshed, her exhaustion cemented her intention to avoid any more contact with him.

Then she saw the white lily lying on the untouched pillow beside hers, and her blood turned to ice water.

It hadn't been there when she had gone to bed.

Chapter Six

"Another party?" Calli said, wrinkling her nose.

"No, this one's a real party," Minnie explained, sliding onto the table top next to Calli's coffee and breakfast plate. "Not like that stuffy thing for the general. Duardo says proper Vistarian parties are not even like American parties—"

"How would he know what an American party is like?"

"They have TV here." Minnie rolled her eyes. "Half the shows they get here are American. Anyway, it's today. Sunday."

"Tonight?"

"No, today. Soon."

"Now?" Calli rubbed her temple. "Hell, they've just finished with Fiesta...isn't that enough?"

"Are you always this grumpy on Sundays?" Minnie asked, crossing her arms and tilting her head to one side.

"When I'm short on sleep I am," Calli muttered.

"You slept in late yesterday, and you came home disgustingly early on Friday night. And last night you went to bed early again. And it's now about nine. That's gotta be enough sleep for anyone."

"It would, if I actually *slept*." She thought again of the white lily in the vase on her bedside table. She hadn't been able to throw it away, even though its very presence made her deeply uneasy. That discomfort had robbed her of sleep last night and when she had managed to doze, lurid dreams of men stealing into the house had woken her.

"Well, if you're not sleeping anyway, don't bother trying. Come to the party."

Calli wrinkled her nose again. "I haven't got the energy," she confessed. "All that dressing up—"

"You can wear jeans," Minnie said instantly. "Come on, Calli. Please."

"Why do I have to go?"

"Because I won't go without you, and I want to see Duardo. He's going back home tonight."

"He doesn't live in the city?"

"God, no. He lives up in Pascuallita. That's where he's posted, at the base there."

All the way from Pascuallita... She recalled Nick's words when he had been shaking Duardo's hand.

"Okay," Calli said, understanding.

"Cool. They're picking us up at ten," Minnie said, sliding off the table and heading for her room. "I'm going to get dressed."

"No, wait—" Calli began, but the bedroom door had already closed.

With a sigh, she got up from the table and went to change.

* * * * *

A little less than an hour later, they heard a horn beep and went outside to find Duardo standing on the back of a beat-up, rusty and faded truck with an enormous engine cowling.

"Hell, it looks like Ford's first model," Calli muttered.

"Good morning, ladies!" Duardo waved them over. He wore jeans and a white shirt, which contrasted well with his tanned skin.

Minnie ran over to the back of the truck, and Calli followed more slowly. The high walls of timber planking provided back support for seven more people sitting on the floor of the truck. One of the women, Elvira, Calli recognized from the general's party. Elvira looked very much younger now in her pretty printed floral skirt and white cotton sweater with her hair down. Calli nodded to her. "*Hola*," she murmured. She realized she knew all but two of the soldiers, too.

Duardo bent over and held out his hand. "Put your foot there, and I will lift you up," he told Minnie, pointing to the edge of the platform.

Minnie looked down at her tight, mid-thigh length denim skirt. "I'm not hitching my leg up there," she said firmly, shaking her head. The others in the truck laughed. Her expression spoke clearly enough even if they didn't follow the English.

Duardo grinned. "No problem," he said. He twisted a little and said something quickly. Two other men got to their feet and moved to the edge of the truck bed, while Duardo jumped to the ground. He grasped Minnie's waist in both hands. "Lift your arms up," he instructed.

She lifted her arms, and the two men took an arm each. Then, with apparently no effort, Duardo lifted her straight up in the air, high enough for her to take a decorous step up onto the platform.

Duardo motioned Calli towards him.

"No, thank you," she said. "I can manage this." She stepped up to the truck bed and waved the two men away. They stepped back, grinning, and she could sense Duardo hovering behind her. But long legs and stretch jeans gave her an advantage. She tucked her knee to her chest and planted her sandaled foot on the wooden flooring. It wasn't even much of a stretch, especially after years of flexibility training for her karate. Pausing for a moment to balance herself with a hand on either side, she flexed her leg, pouring power into it. Straightening the leg, she raised herself up onto the floor. She ended up standing on the edge.

Duardo clapped and the men gave little whistles of appreciation, laughing and making comments. "Bravo!" she heard, and realized that these men, all soldiers, would understand the physical agility and strength she had just displayed. Smiling, she gave a little curtsey, and sat in the vacant space they made for her, between Minnie and a man in a black AC/DC tee shirt. He smiled at her, gave her a thumbs up. She smiled back.

Duardo settled down beside Minnie at the edge of the flat bed. They sat on the driver's side, so he leaned around the end and patted the side of the truck. "*¡Vayamos!*"

The truck jerked into gear, and with a belching roar, slowly moved off up the road.

Duardo leaned around Minnie and indicated the man on Calli's left. "This is Pietro," he said.

"*Sí,*" Pietro agreed with a grin.

"Hi Pietro."

Duardo indicated the others in the truck and they, in turn, all waved or said hello in English or Spanish, including Elvira, who attempted a shaky, thick 'how are you?' in English. In civilian clothes, without rank or title, they seemed very young, amiable people.

They made their way out of the city, climbing up and down foothills, moving onto a poorly maintained ribbon of tarmac with the thick vegetation that covered the island creeping close to the verge. Traffic kept the road clear of growth, but trees leaned in overhead, struggling for light at the edges of the canopy, and the road became a shadowed, narrow tunnel, lit here and there by patches of dazzling sunlight. Above the canopy, in glimpses, she saw pale blue, cloudless sky.

The people in the back paid no notice to their surroundings. They laughed and chatted amongst themselves, and Calli found herself relaxing. The roar of the engine and the vibrations had a soothing effect. She grew sleepy.

Pietro gave her arm a gentle nudge, and she opened her eyes. He offered an open bottle of Mezcal.

"It's watered down with lime juice and mineral water," Minnie said. "Very nice."

"It's too hot. You need water," Duardo explained. "Drink."

She took a sip and enjoyed the tang of the juice. It had been watered down a lot, and seemed very refreshing. The Mezcal merely added flavor. She took a longer drink and gave the bottle back.

The man with the incongruous name of Harry stood up and leaned over the boards at the side of the truck, calling down into the cab. Then he reached over and lifted up a guitar. He sat and settled it against his thigh and strummed some fast chords. This appeared to please everyone. The energy picked up around the truck. Harry laughed and began to play—intricate Latin-style music with a compulsive beat. The others picked up the beat, hands on thighs, feet tapping, clapping. There didn't appear to be any lyrics, but Calli heard Pietro next to her humming and slapping his thigh. After a while the music changed into a different melody, but the beat stayed the same. It seemed that Harry doodled, trying out different themes before moving onto something new.

When Harry tired of it, another man picked up the guitar, and a new lilt emerged.

Calli took sips from the Mezcal bottle when it was offered to her. Time passed pleasantly.

The truck began climbing up sheer mountainside, the road switching back on itself time and time again. The pavement here, and most especially the verges, was well maintained, consisting mostly of poured concrete and iron reinforcements. It seemed Vistaria had wisely chosen its priorities for road maintenance.

They travelled in full sunshine now. At this elevation, the sun beat down very direct and bright. Callie fished her sunglasses out of her shoulder bag and put them on. As they turned another hairpin bend she got a breath-catching view of the countryside. They'd climbed about a thousand feet, and the Pacific sparkled deep blue to the east. In between lay a carpet of green, rimmed by white beach. To the north, lay Lozano Colinas, *Las Colinas*, thick with buildings and roads, lapping up against the mountain chain that ran north and south along the spine of the main island. They climbed that same chain now, and the altitude made the engine of the elderly truck groan and work.

"This truck...this road...many. Many," Pietro said, with a big smile, lifting his voice above the music. He moved his hand in a flat sideways motion. "No worry."

Calli gave him a small answering smile. Had her concern been so apparent?

But Pietro's confidence seemed well placed, for despite some alarming noises, and the driver dropping down into such a low gear that Calli could have walked and made better time, the engine of the truck kept running. As the road flattened out and headed into a deep crevasse of the mountains, the truck slowly picked up speed.

The valley they were in tucked into a fold of the mountains, thick with trees. Surprisingly, a number of houses hugged the steep valley walls, dotted on either side of the road, some of them large, expensive-looking establishments, others barely more than two-room cottages with the traditional Vistarian gate and courtyard tacked onto the front.

"What is this place?" Calli asked Duardo.

"Dominio de Leo." He pointed back towards the Pacific, hidden by the sheer mountain beside them. "The army base is down there. Many senior officers up here. It is very...rich."

"Expensive," Calli said.

"Yes, so."

"But some houses here don't look that expensive."

"They were here before. Before the army base was built, and the officers found the valley."

"Dominio de Leo," Calli pronounced experimentally.

"*No*," Harry said from his corner. "*El dominio de Leo de príncipe* is right name. But not used."

"*El dominio de Leo de...*" Calli shook her head. "What does it mean?"

Duardo frowned. He seemed to be struggling to translate the name.

"It means the domain of Prince Leo," Minnie said unexpectedly. "Some Spanish prince probably took a fancy to the place. It's pretty nice."

"Yes," Duardo said, nodding. "Prince Leopold. He sailed here, long ago. Built a big house." He pointed further into the valley. "Gone now, but it was over there, they say."

The truck lurched to the left as it turned into a rutted, bumpy side road and came to a slow halt, with a squeal of brakes. The engine quit with what sounded like a heavy sigh of relief.

The silence that fell seemed almost profound.

Everyone got to their feet, stretching, wriggling, rubbing their legs and butts. The wooden floor was not the most forgiving surface in the world.

"*¡Hola!*" The shout came from the other side of the boards Calli leaned against.

She got to her feet, and saw over the sides of the truck that they had pulled up beside a modest house—more extensive than the two-room cottages she had seen, but not palatial by any stretch of the imagination. A bungalow like most houses here, with adobe walls, it had an elegant arch over the gate into the front courtyard. People emerged from the gate, shouting greetings at the new arrivals, including one very pregnant woman, who walked slowly but wore a very large smile. They waved, calling to each other as they spilled out of the truck and moved toward the house.

Calli looked around from her vantage point on the back of the truck. The trees crowded close here, and the ground dipped sharply from the nose of the truck forward. The truck stood at the end of a narrow, rutted path clearly used as a driveway. In another driveway on the far side of the house, three sedans had been parked behind the tail end of a fourth just visible behind the corner of the house.

"Come."

Calli turned around. Pietro stood at the end of the truck. With a smile he beckoned her towards him. "You come. We eat, no?"

"Sure," she agreed and moved to the edge of the truck. He stepped back and let her jump down by herself, then motioned that she should precede him toward the house.

Nearly everyone else had walked inside now, and the noise level already spiraled, even from out here. The party had begun.

The front courtyard was paved in terracotta tiles. The front door, a massive wooden thing decorated with metal studs and a wrought iron grill, stood open, revealing a passage that ran through the middle of the house. Calli looked up as they moved into the passage and saw a roof of exposed tiles resting on timber framing. On either side of her, rooms stood open to her sight, the fourth wall that would have lined the passage was simply not there. It made a charming and intriguing open style of house.

At the end of the passage, more daylight beckoned. A kitchen area on the right gave her a startling glimpse of an extremely modern-looking stainless steel stove top and range hood, a wide wall-oven and a double-doored fridge behind an island counter. On the counter sat a wooden chopping board, surrounded by tantalizing fresh produce. Out beyond the passage, she stopped to draw a second surprised breath.

Another courtyard, only knee-high walls surrounded this one. They had been clearly built so low to take full advantage of the view, which took in the trees carpeting the valley. The land dropped nearly the full thousand feet to sea level before climbing up again to the other side. The courtyard extended twenty feet from house to wall, and easily twice that from wall to wall—running the width of the house. Deep reddish-brown colored terracotta tiles paved the whole area. Colored and patterned tiles in deep blues, olive greens and yellows were embedded in odd places throughout the paving.

Trees that had had been trimmed and trained to provide shadow leaned over the walls. One of them stood at the far corner of the courtyard, its gnarled trunk made up of numerous thick cables. Most of the trunk easily measured fifteen feet across. The base of the tree flared even wider. The thick strands spread, burrowing into the earth. It looked like it had been there forever, and the wall had been built right up to the base, incorporating the tree into the walls. Calli had seen many trees like this in the city. Uncle Josh had called them banyan trees. They had been imported to the island from African territories by the Spanish. But none of them had been this big, this old.

While Calli paused to admire the view, three men helped the pregnant woman sink into an armchair sitting in the kitchen corner of the courtyard. Chairs and stools surrounded three low round tables, grouped across the courtyard, and everyone settled into them, chatting like long-lost friends. Clearly, everyone knew each other.

Movement to her right made her turn and check over her shoulder. Three men stood in the kitchen, one of them at the island, chopping a handful of herbs, while another one dug through the interior of the refrigerator. The third set out glasses.

The wall of the kitchen looking out onto the courtyard was actually three big glass panels. Two of them had been pushed along tracks to slide behind the third, leaving the kitchen open to the courtyard.

She checked over her left shoulder. The wall there was the same, pushed back to reveal an indoor lounge area, furnished with overstuffed sofas and spice-colored cushions.

People put plates and bowls of food out upon the tables. Colorful salsas, rolled tortillas, and many more dishes she could not name, made her mouth water just looking at them, with their sprinkling of fresh herbs, and garnishes of hibiscus and cucumbers.

Minnie came across to her, carrying two glasses. "It's some sort of punch. Alcoholic," she told Calli, offering her one.

Calli shrugged and sipped. The sweet-and-sour tang held a pleasant, rum-like flavor. "And strong."

"It's good," Minnie declared. "Come and sit down with us." She led Calli over to the table closest to the edge of the courtyard. Beyond the knee-high wall, the ground plunged.

Elvira sat at the table, and Pietro had just set down another steaming dish.

"Eat," Elvira said, handing Calli a large, bright napkin as she sat down.

Duardo brought the short man who had just been standing at the chopping block in the kitchen over to their table. "Calli, Minnie, this is Hernandez Mendosa, whose house this is. Hernandez is marshal at Lozano base."

Hernandez bowed to them, the hand gripping a tea towel held to his chest. "I welcome you to my home," he said formally. "I regret, my wife Menaka, she cannot stand with me. She is being comfortable." He waved to the armchair in the corner by the kitchen window, where Menaka sat rubbing her swollen stomach. "She is very tired."

"I'm sure," Minnie agreed. "It's very nice to meet you, Hernandez. You have a lovely home, and thank you for welcoming us into it. We appreciate your hospitality."

"Thank you," he said, and bowed again. "Will you excuse me, please? I must go back. These soldiers…they eat much."

Pietro chuckled, and Hernandez waved a hand at him, before heading back to his kitchen. Duardo dropped into a chair and reached for a plate.

"Is everyone here a soldier?" Calli asked, looking around.

"Yes, all," Pietro agreed. He ate busily. Elvira had risen from her chair and wandered over to the other table to select food from dishes there, talking and laughing with the people on that table.

A very fat man came to their table and selected one of the tortillas.

"And this is Pav," Duardo said.

The man laughed and nodded at them.

"'Pavarotti,'" Pietro explained, and patted the man's distended stomach.

"Right."

Pav moved away, and Calli leaned forward to examine the dishes. Duardo and Pietro immediately began explaining each one, the degree of spiciness, the ingredients. Elvira came back to the table, and added her own knowledge about the preparation of the dishes.

Pietro refilled their glasses of punch.

Calli ate and drank, laughed and relaxed in the security of being surrounded by people that enjoyed life and welcomed her. They were a lively group. As the pace of eating slowed, guitars were picked up. At first the music was slow, coaxing. But soon, one of the men stood up with a shout and stamped his feet, throwing his hands up in the air. It was a declaration. An entrance.

The guitar players picked up the pace. The dancer moved out onto the clear space at the end of the courtyard, tapping his way with expert steps, while the others cheered him on with claps and whistles.

Elvira got to her feet and ran over to him, then lifted her skirt a little to reveal her knees and tapped out intricate steps that sent up a cheer of encouragement.

"Elvira!" someone called, and two small brown objects flew through the air. She caught them deftly and paused to fiddle with them. Then she lifted her hand, with a graceful flick, and the castanets rattled out a tattoo. She stamped her feet in time.

A couple of people got to their feet, clapping along with the guitars, and another woman, who had not been on the truck, joined Elvira, her hands lifted in the same graceful motions as she began stepping out different steps.

"They seem to just do their own thing," Minnie murmured.

"Whatever the music tells them to do," Calli said. "They look great." She heard, with wry resignation, the touch of envy in her tone. That sort of seductive gracefulness had always been beyond her capabilities.

"You can do that," Pietro told Calli.

She laughed a little. "Not me."

"Yes, most certainly," Duardo added. He picked up Minnie's hand. "You, too. Come."

"Me?" Minnie asked.

He nodded.

Minnie let herself be led over to the other dancers, and Duardo placed her next to Elvira. Elvira picked up her skirt again and tapped out a very simple, half-speed set of steps, and Minnie followed. After a couple of repetitions, she got it down with a big smile and a laugh. Then Elvira repeated the step at the proper speed, rapping it out with a very Spanish-looking flourish, the castanets adding their compulsive rattle. Then she paused and waited for Minnie to repeat it.

Minnie repeated the pattern, with almost the same flourish, and Calli laughed aloud with sheer joy.

Elvira repeated the pattern again. Minnie immediately followed with her own repetition. Then they both danced out the pattern, keeping it going continuously, and Duardo began to clap out the rhythm, encouraging them. Elvira showed Minnie how to turn and move while keeping the beat, and Minnie followed, her hips swaying with the same elegant motion as Elvira. Slowly, she added arm movements.

Calli smiled, exuberance bubbling through her veins. Apart from the incongruous denim skirt and short hair, Minnie looked like any of the other women dancing there—flirtatious, seductive. Duardo moved around her with the strutty motion the men made as they preened beside the woman. They sent smoldering glances at the women over their shoulders, while their hips echoed the movements the women made. It was as sexy a dance as any tango Calli had ever seen, and she tapped her own feet, her hips twitching in time.

"Now you will know how," Pietro said, and picked up her hand. "You understand."

Calli willingly followed him to the group of dancers, and Elvira flashed her a wide smile when she saw her. She showed Calli the step, and Calli surprised herself when she executed it perfectly. It made sense to her, the beat and the motion falling into place along with the music. Except that the flat, rubber-soled sandals she wore wouldn't move easily on the tiles.

Elvira frowned and, over the music, called out something to Menaka, who sat in her armchair clapping as enthusiastically as anyone standing around the dancers.

Menaka nodded and called back. Elvira slipped between the bordering ring of spectators and disappeared inside the house. In a moment, she returned with a pair of black heeled shoes in her hand, each with a fine strap over the instep. Dancing shoes.

She thrust them at Calli. "Easier for—" and she stamped out a step or two, the heels of her own shoes rapping on the tiles.

Calli took them doubtfully, and slipped out of her sandals and put them on. They fit, which surprised her, for her feet were in proportion with her height, and Vistarian women seemed uniformly petite. She stood up and gave an experimental stamp, and immediately sensed the improvement. Her blood beating a tattoo in time with the guitars and the clapping, she moved to stand between Elvira and Minnie and picked up the pattern they followed. Excitement flooded her as the flow of the dance became clear. She relaxed her concentration, letting her instinct guide her instead, and the pattern came easily, naturally. Did she have a latent talent for this? Or had she simply been immersed in this culture for long enough to absorb the attitude, the...sexiness?

She really did feel a wholesome, exhilarating sexiness as she turned and tapped in time to the music. Her hands came up into the air of their own accord, weaving patterns that felt natural, inevitable. The clapping and shouting of the onlookers encouraged her to continue, to fling her head back and fall into the spell of seduction woven by the music and movement. She could feel her hair tickling the back of her hips where the skin showed between her jeans and tee shirt, and she laughed aloud for sheer joy once again. She hadn't felt this alive for years—with one recent exception.

She looked over and saw that Duardo had moved behind Minnie and shadowed her movements. It completed the pattern in her mind. Such a seductive dance must have an audience, an intended target, and it would be natural for the target to respond as Duardo responded—to be beckoned. As Calli watched, he reached out to rest his hands on Minnie's hips, then they moved in unison.

A hand came down on her own hip and Calli looked behind her. Pietro winked at her. "Don't worry," he told her. "Just friends."

She understood, let herself fall back into the beat, feeling Pietro follow her, his hands on her hips, lifting as he turned her, leading as they moved around the floor. Pietro was a good dancer, and Calli learned more as his hands guided her, as she followed his lead.

The music seemed to grow more frantic, the beat faster. She whirled, caught up in the rhythm. Abruptly it peaked, and with a final staccato beat of heels, they came to a halt, the music at an end.

For a tiny second silence held, while Calli drew an unsteady breath, her blood pounding in her ears. Then everyone clapped and laughed, applauding themselves. The dancers broke up, cups were refilled.

Acute disappointment circled through her. She didn't want the dancing to end.

"Later, okay?" Pietro said, plucking at his AC/DC tee shirt. "Time for rest."

"Sure," she said, forcing a smile.

Duardo, his hand still resting possessively on Minnie's hip, passed them and said, in a low voice clearly intended only for Pietro, "*Rojo*," and he nodded toward the house.

Calli's chest locked with a sudden, overwhelming mix of dread, hope and the return of the seductive excitement of the dancing, but this time it felt more primordial, more basic. It was pure wanting, bereft of any flirtation.

She turned toward the house, holding her breath. Was he…?

Nicolás Escobedo sat on one of the straight-backed chairs, a boot resting on the seat of another, his chair pushed back and balanced. Black jeans, a dark olive green shirt with the soft glow that spoke of silk. *Silk*, her mind whispered.

A couple of the men had approached him, and Nick looked up at them, spoke a few words. An exchange of greetings. Acknowledgments. But they made no fuss over him, no fanfare. She understood that Nick was not here as an Escobedo. Duardo had named him correctly. He was here as the quiet man who moved amongst them, directing, managing, putting things to right.

A few words for each of them, and they moved on, leaving him to his privacy. Alone, he settled back in his chair and turned back to look at her, his gaze direct, uncompromising. Had he been watching her dance?

Her heart gave a little thrill of a beat at the idea. But then she remembered the lily.

She walked over to stand in front of him and pushed her thumbs into her pockets, her hands curling into fists. "You were invited to this party too?" she asked.

"I'm invited everywhere."

"You don't go everywhere, though."

"I go where I'm needed."

"I don't think you're needed here."

"Are you sure?" he asked.

And Calli felt her spine, her whole body ripple. That response, and the aching, throbbing need pouring through her also tripped off her anger—she didn't like how her body longed for his touch when her mind had decided differently.

"Nick, stop playing with me. I don't need this."

He glanced around, a casual look. Calli knew he checked for eavesdroppers. Witnesses. Everyone appeared busy doing something else — talking and drinking, mostly. A little pocket of space separated Calli and Nick from them.

"Sit down," he told her.

"No."

"Sit *down*," he repeated. "This is one of the few places where you and I can talk in comparative security and by god, we will talk." He pushed a hand through his hair. "We *must* talk." His tone was insistent.

She sank onto the chair next to the one his boot pushed against, facing him. As she sat, Minnie came over and handed her a glass of punch, and moved away again. She seemed to be part of the unspoken conspiracy to provide them with total privacy right in the middle of a rowdy party.

"We already talked, I thought," Calli said, with a sigh. "You said nothing could ever come of this. I believed you."

He straightened up his chair, lifting his foot away from the other, and leaned toward her. "I meant what I said."

"Then why the lily, Nick? I know you put it there."

He studied her face, as if he absorbed the details, memorizing them. "Call it a supreme moment of self-torture," he said at last. "A moment of weakness."

"Do you know how insecure it makes me feel to know that despite locked doors you can invade my room while I sleep? I can't fight you off when I'm sleeping."

He nodded a little. "It won't happen again. Not unless you invite me."

"I will never invite you."

"It's better that way," he agreed. He reached out toward her face and very gently tucked a strand of her hair behind her ear. She could feel the warmth of him radiating against her cheek. Her heart jumped.

"Don't," she said sharply.

"I said that you had an uncrushable spirit, and I was right." He withdrew his hand and clasped it with the other, the double fists hanging between his knees. "I wanted to apologize. For the lily, for Friday night. You said I played with you, and I'm sure it feels that way, but it was simply…weakness. I have faced down rabid generals and armed guerillas in my time, but you are something I've never had to battle before. I faltered. It won't happen again."

In her gut, she knew he spoke the truth. After this day, he would go away, and leave her alone, and she would never feel the touch of his chest beneath silk, the feel of his hand cupping her bare hip.

She shivered. He sat inches away from her. She could reach out and touch him. But instinctively, she knew he would not allow it. The discipline, the iron will, had realigned themselves. He would resist his own weakness and fend off hers.

For the sake of Vistaria.

"Okay," she said with a sigh. "All right." And abruptly, she felt the return of the enormous, bone-deep tiredness that sapped her of energy. She managed to smile, and it came out crooked. "I believe you," she said.

Something must have shown in her face. He shook his head a little. "I don't know who Robert is, Calli, but right now I'd like to kill him. Because it is he who has planted the shadow of doubt in you that makes you think you're not whole and complete, that you aren't enough."

She jumped. "How do you know about Robert?"

"You mentioned him once. You said you hadn't felt anything since Robert, and then you stopped yourself from saying anything more." He leaned a little closer. "But I watched you dance just then, Calli. You felt whole, vibrant, alive. Didn't you?"

"Yes," she whispered.

"That is something Vistaria has done for you, I think," he said with a little smile.

"Not Vistaria," she said.

Just then, the world suddenly grew very bright and very hot. Something pushed at her from the left, and slammed into the side of her head, but she felt no pain. She felt nothing.

Then, even her sight faded.

Chapter Seven

"Calli! Calli, come on now, wake up."

Something tapped her face. She wished it would go away. She tried to turn away from it, but pain ripped through her at the small motion and she groaned.

"That's it. Wake up, Calli. I need you to wake up."

Nick's voice. His low caressing voice. He was here.

Then she remembered. "What happened?" she cried, and heard her voice as a croak.

"*No hay la línea de teléfono, señor,*" said another man.

"*¿Tiene cualquiera teléfonos de célula?*" Nick again. He spoke rapidly, precisely. Cool. In control.

"*Verificaré.*"

"*Sí, y Capitano Peña. ¡Rápidamente ahora!*" Nick said, his voice sharp. Then, "Calli, open your eyes. I need to see your eyes. Quickly, Calli. Look at me." The snap of command in his voice made her obey without hesitation. She opened her eyes and promptly shut them again as flickering light hurt them.

"No, Calli. Come on."

From close by she heard a woman scream. "Someone help me! Help! Please!"

Minnie. Calli opened her eyes and tried to sit up at the same time, and cried out as pain exploded in her head.

"Slowly," Nick said. She felt his hand on her shoulder, steadying her.

"Minnie!" she said, looking at him. He had a cut over his cheek, just under the eye, and blood ran down his face. His shirt was ripped; the edges, blackened. *Burned.* "Where's Minnie?" she cried, twisting around. She realized then that she had been lying on the ground. Nick crouched over her.

Details snapped into place, her senses pulling it all together. The house that should have been behind them stood no longer. In its place, a ball of flames reached high into the early evening sky, crackling loudly. Screams and moans came from all around her. Babbling Spanish.

"*Somebody help me!*" Minnie screamed her plea.

Calli tried to get to her feet, but Nick's hand on her shoulder kept her down. "Take it easy," he advised.

"Screw that. I need to help Minnie." Calli pushed at his arm and got to her feet, the dancing shoes crunching in rocks, dust, debris. She swayed for a second, the ground dipping around her, then steadied and looked around. "Oh my god," she breathed. There was little left of the courtyard but more rocks and lumps of concrete. The walls no longer stood.

Brushed away by a giant, she thought. "Minnie!" she screamed.

"Here! Over here!" Minnie yelled back. "Oh hurry! God, hurry!" Her voice came from the jagged, broken tiles at the end. Calli headed in that direction, crunching through the debris.

"*¡Señor! ¡Señor!*"

"Calli, wait!" Nick called.

She turned a little. One of the men from the party limped across to Nick, his face dirty and scraped.

124

"You go. I'll take care of this," she told him. She moved carefully to the edge of the tiles, feeling with each step if the tiles would take her weight. They sagged alarmingly under her step, and the broken ends sloped down sharply. An image of people moving on thin ice came to her, and she got down on her hands and knees, then stretched herself out across the tiles and wriggled towards the end.

The stately old tree that had provided most of the shade over the patio had taken a mortal blow. It had been pushed over the edge of the cliff by the blast. The tree's roots had been ripped from the ground, destabilizing the earth all around it. As it had tilted out into the valley, it had destroyed that corner of the courtyard and the weakened ground gave way beneath the tiles. But with such an extensive root system, the tree had not been pulled from the earth altogether. It leaned over the edge of the cliff like a monstrous great railway crossing boom, very nearly horizontal.

As Calli peered over the edge, little rocks and pebbles cascading down from her movements, the tree gave another deep groan and shuddered. The immense weight of the trunk and branches strained the injured root system. Soon, it would give away.

Another small gasping cry, directly below her, echoed the shudder of the tree. She looked down.

Minnie half-crouched on a tiny shelf, her arms outspread against the cliff for balance, her head turned into the cliff.

"Minnie!" Calli called.

She twisted her head to look up. "Calli! Quickly! You must help Duardo! Hurry!" Minnie nodded toward the tree.

Calli lifted her head and looked at the tree. It took a moment for her to see Duardo—he hung amongst the vines and leaves trailing from the end of the tree. In the dying daylight, she could see his eyes were closed and his head rested limply against his arm. But he could not be unconscious or his grip would have given way.

"Calli, you have to hurry. He was talking at first, but I think he's fading. If he passes out…oh God, hurry, Calli!"

For a tiny moment Calli lay there, flummoxed. *How do I do this?* Duardo would be no light weight. One thing seemed clear, though. She would have to go out onto the tree. It was the only way she could get close to him.

"Are you going to be all right for a while?" she said to Minnie.

"Yes, yes. Go!"

Calli wriggled her way over to the upended tiles and broken ground where the tree had stood for so long. The root system thrust high up into the air, the long tendrils, once buried in the earth, now stretched like threads. The bottom half of the tree still held the earth, but the center of the trunk had split like kindling. Calli jumped and snagged the base of one of the roots and hung there for a second. The root, a foot in diameter, ran like a tent rope down to the earth, disappearing under the edges of the tiling. She drew herself up and kicked with her feet to find footholds on the base of the tree. The heels of the shoes caught at projections and snags, giving her a foothold.

Calli pushed herself up above the root, supporting herself on the broad beam like a gymnast, then worked her way over the very sharp slope down to the trunk of the tree itself. It wasn't as straightforward as walking across a log, but the multiple stems created ruts and runnels that gave her footing, until she reached the first of the major branches. She got down on her stomach, and studied the way ahead.

She lay well out over open air now—the ground sloped sharply away, a good thirty-five feet down. Duardo hung just ahead, perhaps two feet, but nearly six feet below her. She would have to climb down into the branches to reach him.

"How you doing, Minnie?" she called.

"Just shut up and get him!" Minnie yelled back.

"Working on it. Is there a branch right below me?"

"Yes."

"Big?"

"As big as your butt."

"That'll do," Calli murmured. She would have to slide over the side of the trunk and find the branch and grab it before gravity took her the rest of the way down.

She was scared spitless.

"Duardo! Can you hear me?" she called out.

No movement. No sound.

"Just don't let go, Duardo. I'm coming to get you." She couldn't think of any Spanish at all. She took a deep breath. "Here I go." She slid over the sharp ridge of the trunk, her knee and hand trailing to give her some sort of hold, and reached out under her for the branch Minnie told her was there. Further than she'd thought. For one breathless, faint moment of panic, she actually hung in mid-air, unsupported anywhere. Then her left hand curled around the big branch, and she slithered onto it, her legs clutching around it for dear life.

Her heart hammered, but she forced herself to keep moving. Wriggling again, she moved up the branch, closer and closer. She could see Duardo's hands, now, gripping a handful of vines and whip-thin branches. Finally she lay right over him. She reached down but couldn't reach his head. Instead she patted his arm. "Duardo!" she called. "Duardo!"

The glossy black hair, covered in wood chips and twigs, moved. He stirred and looked up at her. Calli caught her breath at his unfocused gaze. Even as she watched, his eyes rolled up.

"No!" she yelled, and shot out her hand for his wrist as his fingers loosened and the vines began to slip through his grip. She had no idea what she intended to do beyond holding him here. She felt the flesh of his wrist under her fingers and brought her other hand around the branch to grip beneath her fingers.

Minnie screamed.

Abruptly Duardo's full weight pulled on her arms, and the branch she lay upon drove into her chest. She gasped, pain ripping through her shoulders, as Duardo dangled from her hands, a complete deadweight. He had passed out.

She drew a few slow breaths. The branch pushed against her chest hampered her breathing, but she could breathe, and that was enough for now. She turned her head towards the hill, where she could see Minnie hugging the earth, the broken tiles a few feet above her head. Calli lay lower than the tiles and couldn't see the remains of the house or anyone on the courtyard, but she could hear shouting, strident voices, and the crackle of flames. The fire still climbed and she could see the tips of the flames licking the trees.

Duardo's feet still dangled twenty-five feet above the ground.

She drew another slow breath, filling her lungs, and shouted as clearly as she could. "Nick! Nicolás! Over here!"

For a minute or two she kept up the shouting. She knew it could take a while for her to be heard because she competed against the drama playing out up above. So she conserved her strength, breathing deeply, and kept shouting, while her shoulders burned and her fingers cramped cruelly.

"Nicolás!"

"I'm here." His voice, from behind her. Steady and quiet. She felt movement on the tree, heard it creak.

"Be careful!" she warned. "But hurry. I don't know how long I can hold on."

"You can hold on for as long as you need to." He sounded totally confident, and much nearer. The tree definitely bounced and stirred.

"My fingers are going numb."

"Doesn't matter. Your muscles are far stronger than you think. It's your mind that makes them weak. It's your mind that decides to let go. You should know this, Calli. Karate, right?"

"Yeah. A century ago, seems like."

She felt movements through the branch against her chest. His voice sounded close by, now. He chuckled. "But you know I'm right. As long as you decide you're going to hang on, you can outride any pain, any desire to let go and get rid of the pain. You just make a decision, and that knowledge, that certainty, will let you hold on."

She tried to nod, but her cheek scraped on the branch. "Okay," she said.

"Minnie, we'll get you in a minute. You must hold on, too."

"I ain't goin' nowhere," Minnie muttered.

Small movements. A pause. "I'm going to shout," Nick warned. And he did shout, a stream of Spanish.

Voices lifted in response, and she heard steps on the tiles. "*¿Señor?*"

The crunching on the tiles reminded her of her perilous crossing. "Tell them to be careful, there's no support for the tiles," she said.

"I have," Nick assured her. He spoke some more, and from the cadence, the clipped sentences, she guess he gave orders. She heard a scurry, people hurrying, murmured conversations. More movement on the tree.

"It won't hold up many more," she said.

"It will last long enough," Nick said from right behind or above her. She felt a touch on her back. "That's me," he told her. "I'm right above. I'm going to have to—"

From the corner of her eye, she saw his boot land on a smaller branch just to her left, but behind and little lower than her. At the same time, she felt weight and warmth on either side of her hips. He straddled her.

"Okay?" he asked.

She felt a giggle rise and tried to squash it. "You only had to ask," she said. "You didn't have to arrange all this to get me in this position."

"And chance you turning me down?" He tapped her belt. "Is this leather?"

"Yes."

"I'm going to take it off you. Can you lift one hip so I can get at the buckle? I'll keep you balanced."

She lifted her hip, and felt his hand slide beneath. "Higher," he said. She pushed with her knee and lifted higher. The end of the belt slipped out of the buckle, the buckle loosened, the belt slid around her hips and pulled away. Thankfully, she lowered herself back to the branch, her hip flexors and thigh trembling with the effort to maintain balance in that awkward position.

She could feel Nick moving above her.

"What happened up there?" she asked.

"Explosion. From the kitchen. We'll find out later."

"Is everyone all right?"

"Later, Calli," he said.

Everyone was *not* all right.

He leaned out and reached for a branch below her. It was thinner than the branch she lay on, but still sturdy. He lowered himself slowly, with perfect control. The athletic move spoke of muscle power totally beyond her own capabilities. Hanging by both hands meant his legs brushed against the unconscious Duardo. Nick rolled himself up and hooked his legs over the branch he hung from, reminding her of a similar movement made by trapeze artists at the circus. He had to pull himself up with his arms to bring his legs high enough to do it. Then he let go of the branch and rolled back down again. Now he hung upside down, right next to Duardo.

The movements on the tree grew closer. Quiet murmurs. Then hands on her calves, holding her steady.

Nick reached into the ragged remains of his shirt and pulled out two belts, one of them Calli's. Putting the other between his teeth, he looped Calli's belt around Duardo's abused wrist, just below her fingers. He slid the buckle tight like an emergency tourniquet. He put the other end of her belt against the free end of his own, and threaded them both through the buckle of his belt. He pushed the tongue of the buckle through the holes of both belts. This created a secure loop in his belt. Nick pushed the loop over his arm, high up over the elbow, and took a grip on the leather down by Duardo's wrist and tested it.

He looked up at Calli. "Do you know what I'm doing?"

"You're going to take his weight."

"Yes. Then I need you to climb down his body and hang onto his legs, because we're going to swing you."

"*What?*"

"Yes, like a pendulum. That will bring you over to the high ground there, right in front of Minnie."

"Wait!" she called, and frowned, thinking it through. "I get to the ground, hang on to Duardo, then what?"

"You'll see. Just take care of that for now. Climb down, hang on."

"Okay…" She took another breath.

He lifted his free hand to touch her shoulder. "As soon as the weight goes, your arms are going to feel numb and completely useless, but you have to use them to climb down. It has to be you, you're lighter."

"If you're trying to scare me, Nick, it's too late."

He smiled a little. "You'll be fine. I'm going to take the weight, now, okay? Let go when you're ready."

She looked at her hands around Duardo's wrists. "My fingers won't let go."

"Think of what it would be like to put them into nice warm, soapy water right now, the warmth seeping through to the bones."

She thought of her kitchen back home in Montana, the morning sun shining in the window over the sink, water in the sink. She would plunge her hands into the water, and spread her fingers, enjoying the sensation…

And her fingers uncurled as if she had flexed them just like in her mind.

Duardo dropped another few inches, but Nick's grip on the leather stayed firm. He checked the strain on the leather then looked up at her.

Her shoulders were white ice, cold and locked solid. She gave a little choked groan and rested her head against the branch, fighting back tears. It really felt as bad as Nick had forecast. She was glad of the hands holding her steady on the branch because she could not have held on for herself.

"Calli." Nick's voice.

She turned her head to look at him. He had curled up a little to watch her.

"Ready?"

"Okay." But she lied. She wouldn't be able to do what he wanted her to do.

He pointed to his eyes. "Look at me. Watch me. Okay?"

She nodded.

"Reach out for my hand." He held out his left hand, across his body, for his right arm stretched below, holding up Duardo.

She reached, and her arm obeyed her. But it felt lifeless, light and insubstantial. No strength there. She forced her finger to curl around his hand.

"Now lower yourself down."

It took all her courage to lower herself off the branch and let go. For a moment she hung purely by Nick's grip. But that brought her swinging into Duardo's body.

"Oh, sorry," she said, reflexively.

"I don't think he noticed. Can you grip the leather?"

She knew what to do now and reached out to grip the leather above the buckle around Duardo's wrist. Trying to imitate Nick's controlled movements, she transferred her weight from her left hand in Nick's to the leather belt. Nick let her hand go. She let herself down, hooked her arm over Duardo's shoulder, then let go of the leather. With mental apologies to Duardo, she hooked her right hand into the band of his jeans, then let herself down. She wrapped her left arm around one thigh, and let herself slither down until she had her arms about Duardo's calf.

She looked up, and saw Nick's face, the fierce concentration, as he watched her. On the branch where she had been clinging like a burr, Pietro sat straddled. Another man...José, she thought, sat right behind him. A third sat on the main branch, and a fourth behind him.

"Okay!" she called. "Quickly!"

Nick had both hands around the leather now. Straining, he pushed with his arms. The tiny movement traveled down to her and translated into a miniscule sideways motion. But Nick kept the effort up, pushing and releasing, pushing and releasing, until gradually the arc of her swing grew wider and wider. Gravity added its effect.

"Watch the ground," Nick said.

She twisted her head around. With each inward swing of the arc she moved closer and closer to the ground. A few more inches and she would be able to put her foot on the ground.

"Find something you can grab!" Nick called.

She looked, and saw one of the emerging tree roots had formed a big loop. There was nothing else but raw earth and rocks. "I see it!" she called back.

"When you're ready, grab it, and keep hold of Duardo!"

She swung outward, swooping across the valley. She didn't let herself look down. Instead, she watched the loop of tree root come rushing towards her, imagined reaching out and grabbing it with one hand.

Now. She reached out, snagged the root with her hands and found it cool and grubby. But it held.

She thrust out her foot and dug for a foothold as the pendulum motion tried to take her backwards. The strain transferred to her shoulder, but it was minimal compared to the pull from holding Duardo's full weight. She still hugged Duardo's leg to her, but now she stood anchored to the ground, a bare six feet from the top of the cliff, but those six feet consisted of almost vertical, unstable earth.

Distantly she realized that the men on the trunk clapped and cheered. She hooked her leg through the root and turned to look at Nick, hanging patiently, his arms outstretched.

"Ready?" he asked.

"Yes."

"As Duardo is lowered, get a better grip on him, so he doesn't roll down the valley."

"Okay."

Nick rolled his head up to look at Pietro. "*¿Listo?*"

"*¡Sí!*"

"*¡Ahora!*" Nick shouted. He let go of the leather with his left hand and flexed, rolling up, and thrust his hand towards Pietro, who clamped both hands around Nick's wrist.

The tug on Duardo's leg came but Calli, forewarned, hung on.

"*¡Obtuvolo!*" Pietro declared triumphantly.

Got you, Calli guessed.

Nick and Pietro adjusted their grip, so that each had their fingers gripped around the other's wrist. Pietro reached over to grip the man next to him in the same way. In turn, the man reached to the one next to him, and so on along the tree.

Nick looked down at her. "I'm going to drop, and Duardo will too." He unhooked one leg and pushed with his boot against the branch to release the other. But he didn't drop like a stone. He rolled slowly, and Duardo's body sank towards the ground. Calli hauled on him, bringing him to the ground close by her, again gripping the band of his jeans and hanging on grimly.

Pietro did the same as Nick, letting himself fall off the branch in a controlled motion, and now the two of them hung in the air, a human chain. The third man, José, slipped off the tree, and Nick dangled closer to her. Duardo had reached the ground fully now, so she pulled him up and thrust her leg in front of him so he would not roll. That left her hands free. She reached up and caught Nick's leg and hauled him sideways, toward the high ground. A fourth man slipped off the tree, and suddenly Nick stood beside her.

He gave a shout, and the chain of men on the tree trunk who anchored them slowly began to move back to the base of the tree, towards the cliff and the broken tiles. As they moved, Nick reeled Pietro in so that he could stand. Then José.

Finally, a chain of men stood strung along the cliff, up onto the tree base. The men on the tree climbed off and lay down on their stomachs on the edges. They reached down with their hands.

Nick hooked his own leg around the same root Calli used as an anchor. He bent down and with another flex of muscles, picked Duardo up in a fireman's lift. He looked up above him. "*¿Listo?*"

"*Sí.*"

With both hands beneath his torso, Nick lifted Duardo straight up into the air. Many hands reached for him then lifted him up and over the edge. A little cheer sounded above them.

Nick looked behind Calli. "Minnie, your turn. Calli, you'll have to lift her over here."

Calli looked at Minnie's tear-streaked face. "No problem," she said cheerfully. "She's always been a squirt."

Minnie gave a big sniff.

"Minnie, you don't have any room to do anything but push off with your hands and fall into Calli's arms. She'll catch you."

Minnie looked at Calli. "Drop me, and I'll never talk to you again."

"Deal," Calli said.

Minnie took a deep breath and launched, arms outspread, straight at Calli. Minnie's weight slammed into Callie, and she felt herself toppling over. But Nick's arm was there, against her back, holding her up.

Minnie gave a shudder and a hysterical little laugh, but Nick patted her cheek. "Not yet, Miss Minerva. Hold on for a few more minutes."

Minnie took another deep breath and nodded.

Nick threaded his fingers together, to form a step. "Kick your shoes off. Step on my hands, then my shoulder, and then the men will lift you up. Okay?"

She nodded and sniffed again, wiping her forearm across her cheek, which simply smeared the dirt and tears even more. Calli propped her up while she pulled off her shoes. Then she stepped onto Nick's hands and he boosted her up so that she could use his shoulder. She stepped up and the men lifted up and over the edge as if she weighed nothing. Another small cheer sounded.

"Your turn," Nick said in Calli's ear.

"What about you?"

"I'll be right behind you."

She kicked off her shoes, regretfully casting them aside. She had enjoyed the few minutes she had been wearing them before the explosion. It was unlikely she'd experience anything quite like that ever again.

She stepped onto Nick's hands. He boosted her as if she weighed the same miniscule amount as Minnie, which she knew for a fact she did not. She barely put any weight on his shoulder. Many hands caught at her arms and drew her swiftly up. The motion shot pain through her shoulders, but it was over before she could protest. She found herself laying once more on the debris and sand scattered across the tiles.

She wanted to stay there, to rest and recover, but the same many hands hauled her up, made her sit and move out of the way. They raised her to her feet, and led her to a battered, but still whole, chair, where she sat, grateful to be still for a moment.

She watched as Nick was hauled up over the edge, and then Pietro, José and the last of the human chain clambered up. Pietro's AC/DC tee shirt hung torn and dirty now. His face was smeared with ash, but he smiled brightly.

Many more people moved about the remains of the courtyard now, including men in uniform. She remembered the valley was a popular residence for army officers. The explosion would have brought them running.

A very senior-looking officer, a man with graying hair and a buffet table's worth of medals across his chest, walked up to Nick. As Nick brushed himself off, the officer saluted.

Nick spoke. It sounded like a question.

The officer pursed his lips then shook his head.

Nick looked down at the ground and sighed. After a moment he straightened again. "Okay," he said, and spoke more Spanish. Short sentences. Emphatic.

Orders.

The officer saluted again then turned on his heel and strode away. He called out to others, who came running to his side as he walked, some wearing uniforms, some not.

He issued orders, too, and they scurried off to do his bidding.

Nick stopped in front of her, picking up her hand, pulling her from her comfortable seat, while all around them the courtyard seemed to suddenly burst with activity. Lights came on everywhere, and she heard the distant *thwock-thwock* of helicopters.

"Come here," he said.

She allowed herself to be led to the dark far corner of the yard, the left side where, just beyond the jagged remains of the courtyard wall, the truck in which they had traveled here was parked. The triangular-shaped side pocket lay in quiet shadows.

He turned her to face him, letting her rest up against an intact section of the wall. The cut below his eye had stopped bleeding, but his face was still dirty and scratched. "You look like hell," she said.

"You should look in a mirror," he said, with a grin. Then his grin faded. "Calli..." Then he shook his head. "You're a hero, Calli. You saved Duardo's life, and every man here knows it. But there will never be any acknowledgment of what you did here tonight. There can't be."

"I don't want it."

"You deserve it. And there are a handful of Vistarian men who will, for the rest of their lives, consider themselves in your debt because of what you did for their captain. But they cannot speak of it, and neither can I."

"No problems."

"Yes it *is* a goddamn problem!" he said sharply, and his fist slapped the wall by her head. "We should not be in such dire straits that we dare not breathe about the efforts of an American amongst us, but we are and it is only going to get worse."

"Worse?"

"Much worse. This is the beginning, I think. I will know more later, but if I'm right, then this is the first faint sounds of disaster for Vistaria."

"You mean...this explosion was deliberate?" Calli shook her head. "Someone blew up the house on purpose? My god..." She caught at his arm. "Nick, I know someone was hurt. Is Duardo...did he...?"

"Duardo will be fine," he said quickly. "But Menaka died. She sat right next to the kitchen...she had no chance. Nor did Hernandez."

"Oh, Nick...and the baby?"

"Lives, poor orphaned soul. They delivered it a few minutes ago."

"Elvira?"

"She is badly hurt."

Deep sadness welled in her, and she hung her head. Nick drew her to him, and she rested her cheek against his chest. She could hear his heart beating, but nothing stirred in her. The waste, the pointless loss, pained her too much.

And then a more terrible possibility occurred to her. "Nick, this didn't happen because of Minnie and me, did it? They didn't do it because we came here?"

"No," he said quickly. "This valley is full of army personnel, and a party at any house here with a concentration of officers...it's a natural target, if you're looking for targets. It's just that no one thought they were looking for targets." He sighed.

She closed her eyes, and let her hand rest against his shoulder, feeling the silk and the firm, warm flesh beneath.

His arms came around her, tightening. Then with a low groan, he pulled her away from him. "I only have a moment, Calli. You must listen, for this is important. You and Minnie will be flown back to *Las Colinas*. I've arranged medical care for you both—you'll be checked and treated as needed. And you'll get fresh clothes, a chance to clean up, then you'll be dropped at your apartment tonight just as if you had been to the party. You may feel the need to tell your uncle what happened and I can't prevent that, but you must not tell anyone else. Things are going to start happening now, and you must be kept out of them. Do you understand?"

"Yes."

He paused and drew back a little, as if he had been expecting a protest from her.

"I'm not stupid, Nick. I can see what is happening here as well as you. If this was not an accident, then the rebels have made their first move. You have to find out how they knew about this party, how they managed to penetrate it without detection. The only way that could have happened is that you have rebel sympathizers inside the army. That means everyone is suspect, no one can be trusted."

He smiled a little and cupped her cheek. "You continue to astonish me," he said.

His praise, his admiration, warmed her. It made the touch of his hand more than a simple comfort. She could feel her senses wakening, stirring. But she pushed aside the distraction because another horrible possibility occurred to her. "It also means you're a possible target, doesn't it?"

His hand dropped away. "Yes," he said flatly. Truthfully.

From the valley came a roar of an engine. A rhythmic percussive sound that beat at her ears, inside her head. It was a helicopter, very close.

A man stepped around the corner. He carried a rifle and wore a bandolier of rifle shells over one shoulder. "*El helicóptero espera, señor.*"

"*Gracias. Deme un momento,*" Nick murmured.

"*Sí, señor.*" The man stepped back around the house.

Nick turned back to her. "This is a race, Calli. If we can find them, root them out, then we may still win the day. We have to pull their teeth. Weaken them before we can dig them up out of their mountain strongholds. And we must do it quickly, before this gets out of hand. So for now everything must appear to go along as usual. The mine must still operate, people will work, live, and we must give no indication that we are hunting them. And you must stay out of it."

She gave in to her need to touch him and rested her hands on his chest. "I'm afraid for you, Nick."

"Don't be. I have the nine lives of a cat, don't you know?"

"*¿Señor?*" The soldier had returned.

Nick barely glanced at him. "The helicopter is here for you," he told her.

"I know." She looked at the soldier. "*Uno momento más, por favor.*"

"*Sí,*" he agreed and moved away again.

Nick smiled. "You've been studying."

"I'm a fast learner," she said, and gave a little laugh. "Economics seems very remote right now."

"You have one moment more," he reminded her.

She gripped his shirt. "It's not enough," she confessed. "I'm confused, Nick. I thought I had it sorted out before all this happened, but now…I don't know. You're right to send me away. All I know right now is that I don't want to leave you."

His hand settled around her neck, curled around it, as if he would draw her face to him, and she held her breath, her heart suddenly leaping and her pulse fluttering. He gazed into her eyes.

"Nick," she whispered. "Nicolás Escobedo. *El leopardo rojo.* I have seen you all ways. I want them all."

He closed his eyes. She knew he battled temptation and his own better judgment. Right now, though, she didn't care about prudence and good sense. She only cared about the truth in her heart—and damn the price of speaking it aloud.

"*¡Señor!*" came the imperative call.

Nick growled under his breath, and opened his eyes. He pushed her gently towards the waiting soldier. "Go," he told her.

And she was being hurried away, towards the military helicopter, with no answer, not even hope to cling to.

Chapter Eight

For the first time since she had landed in Vistaria, Calli slept the sleep of the dead. They had been dropped at the apartment a little past midnight after being checked over and given a shower and a change of clothes, although Calli was barefoot. They could find no shoes that fit her. She dropped into bed as soon as she had seen Minnie tucked into hers, and slept dreamlessly for ten hours.

Minnie had woken her a little after eleven a.m. Her cousin bubbled over with happiness, for Duardo had phoned and assured her he was okay. And now Minnie straddled Calli's back and did her best to work the stiffness out of her shoulders. Calli had found herself nearly unable to move for the soreness.

"Calli, the way the men deferred to Nicolás Escobedo yesterday...he's the one they call the Red Leopard, isn't he?"

"Why do you think that?"

"Red hair, red leopard. And Duardo said '*rojo*' yesterday just before you went over to talk to him. He's the one that helped you in the jail. That's how you know him."

"Yes."

"You know who he is, don't you?"

Calli sighed into her pillow. "Yes."

Minnie kneaded and worked at one of the knots by her right shoulder blade. "He would be a very dangerous man to get involved with."

Calli jumped a little at her unexpected statement. "I rather doubt he'd trouble with the likes of you and I, Minnie. He's virtually royalty here, or so your dad keeps telling me."

"Maybe. But he wants you anyway."

This time the leap of her heart made her whole body twitch. Calli rolled over, dislodging Minnie, and drew the gown back around her shoulders. "How do you know that?" she asked her cousin.

"I know men. Much better than you, Miss Academic. I saw him watching you, and later when you talked, just before the explosion. He wants you. Most people wouldn't see it, but it came off him in waves. He barely held himself in."

Calli chewed at her lip. "No one else would know?" she repeated.

Minnie wrinkled her nose. "Unless they could tune into that sort of thing, like me."

"God, I hope not," Calli muttered.

"You can't get involved, Calli. Not with him."

"I know."

"You told him no, didn't you?"

"Well, more or less, but…"

"*But?*" Minnie pounced on the prevarication.

"But afterwards…" She shook her head. "After the explosion, Minnie, it felt like nothing really mattered, like I should just cut through all the bullshit and tell it like it is. And I did. I told him how I feel."

Minnie drew her knees to her chest and hugged them, resting her chin on them. "What did you tell him? That you're in love with him?"

"It's more...in lust. I know I go a little crazy when he's near. I can't breathe properly. The ache to have him...it's overwhelming, and I can't think of anything else. It's the first time I've felt that since..."

"Since Robert," Minnie finished.

Calli shook her head. "I've never felt this, not even with Robert. Not this way."

"You don't think that could be love?"

"I don't even know him," Calli protested.

"You don't have to know him," Minnie whispered, and Callie was alarmed to see two big tears roll down her cheeks. She brushed them away impatiently.

"What is it?" Calli asked. "Duardo?"

Minnie half laughed, even as she began crying in earnest. "I'm such an idiot," she said. "But watching him hanging there yesterday, God, Calli, I would have died if he'd let go, if you hadn't been able to hold on for as long as you did, if Nick hadn't come along."

Calli felt her own eyes welling with tears, in reaction to Minnie's genuine distress. She rubbed her cousin's shoulder, trying to find something appropriate to say. "It could just be the stress of the occasion," she offered.

Minnie gave a gigantic sniff, like a little girl. "Yeah, and tell me that the way you want Nicolás Escobedo is just the stress of the moment," she said.

Calli stayed silent.

"There you go, then," Minnie said.

* * * * *

Uncle Josh listened in total to silence to all Calli had to say, and even Minnie repressed her natural tendency to slide in shocking side commentary. He remained silent for long moments after she had finished, absorbing it all.

Finally he blew out his breath, making his cheeks pop. "I'm glad you were there, Calli. For Minnie's sake. Thank you for that. But what concerns me more is Escobedo's airy assurance that Americans are safe. Why would we be safe?"

"There's no advantage to hurting Americans," Calli explained. "Or anyone but the Vistarian Army, who are the power-holders."

"And how long will it take the rebels to figure out that the army needs us here to get to silver production going? And how long after that will they start taking potshots at us?"

Calli had no answer for that, but she knew Nick would have and wished he were here to supply it.

"Can you give me any reason why I shouldn't phone Dan Mellon right now and recommend we shut down the mine and ship everyone back home?" Josh asked.

"If you do, then the president will have no chance of sorting this out at all. None. The rebels will have won."

"We didn't come here to get mixed up in their politics," he replied.

"Dad, you threw your lot in with the government just by coming here," Minnie said. "You can't leave them to the wolves now."

"Maybe, maybe not. I don't like this at all. Knowing this—in a way I wish you hadn't told me. It's a responsibility."

"It is," Calli agreed. "What if you spoke to Nicolás Escobedo yourself, Uncle Josh? Would that reassure you?"

He thought about it, and shook his head. "It's not just me I have to think about, or even you two. It's the whole damned company. It's everyone out here."

Minnie sat forward on the sofa. "What if Dan Mellon spoke to Nicolás Escobedo? Or even the president?"

"That," he declared, "would make a difference." Then he looked at them both. "Don't tell me you can pull that off?" He looked sharply at Calli. "You can?"

"Not without Minnie's help," Calli said. "Minnie has to make a phone call."

Joshua turned his head to look at his daughter. Minnie shrugged. "What can I say? It's this *femme fatale* quality I have."

He shook his head. "I get the impression you're not joking, and I don't know that I want to know the details. Okay, make the call."

* * * * *

It took one phone call and a great deal of waiting but eventually the phone rang, and Uncle Josh went off to a meeting with a worried look. He returned several hours later, very quiet.

"We're staying. For now," he added. "Nicolás Escobedo can be very persuasive."

"What did he say that convinced you?" Calli asked.

"It's more what he didn't say. The President was very clear about economic impacts and even the impact on the company should we pull up stakes—they have a surprisingly sophisticated understanding of our own financial situation. He insisted it hadn't been proved yet the explosion at Dominio de Leo was rebel action. And rebel action or not, it had been aimed at the army. No one else. Dan Mellon didn't accept any of it. That's when Nicolás leaned forward and said in a quiet way he would personally guarantee no harm would ever come to any American in Vistaria. Not one. Because the moment that happened, his country would be lost, and he had no intention of losing it to rebels who would run it into the ground inside a generation. And Dan Mellon looked at him and nodded. And that ended it."

Minnie smiled.

Her father lifted a finger. "But you stay away from the army from now on, Minerva. It's too dangerous. I can't lock you up behind palisades because you're a grown woman, but I wish to God I could. I want you to promise me."

Her smile faded. "I can't promise that, Dad."

He stared at her, surprised. "Why not?"

She put her hands together in her lap. "There's a man. A captain in the army."

"With you, there's *always* a man, Minnie. D'you think just because I'm your father I'm deaf, dumb and blind?"

"This is different," she said firmly. Simply.

"Calli, help me," he pleaded.

"I can't," Calli said softly. "I believe her. This is different."

He scrubbed his hand backwards and forwards through his hair. "Oh hell's bells," he muttered. "Minnie, don't you understand that hanging around with army personnel is liable to get you into trouble?"

"It already has."

"I could ship you back to America," he said. "In fact, I'm thinking of sending your mother back home anyway. The climate here isn't helping her."

"I'd just leave home," Minnie said quietly, without undue emphasis.

He growled a little under his breath, and Calli knew Minnie's passive, truthful answers drove him into an unaccustomed corner. She put a hand on her uncle's forearm. "I'll watch out for her, Uncle Josh. And we will be very careful. We know, better than you, the dangers here."

"Do you? Are you so sure?" he shot back. "I was in Vietnam when the communists rolled their way through town. Revolutions are the ugliest events in the world. Terrible things can happen. No one is spared."

Calli tried to keep her gaze steady. "I will watch out for her."

"You already have, I know," he said, relenting. Then he straightened and put his hand over her own. "Stay away from Nicolás Escobedo, Calli. I know there's a connection there, but he is a far different sort of trouble than an army captain. When revolutions happen, the heads of government tend to end up very dead, and so do their kith and kin. Stay away from him."

"That's an easy promise to make," Calli assured him.

Josh considered this for a moment, then looked at Minnie. "An army captain, huh? And Vistarian. Here's me hoping you'd settle for a Wall Street guru, when you finally took the plunge, and look after me in my old age."

* * * * *

In the cooler evenings, Minnie's mother sat with them at the dining table, and tonight Beryl even cooked a little. She talked of her return to the States, and it seemed the impending departure energized her. It saddened Calli that Beryl's health prevented her from enjoying the beauty of Vistaria, but knew the return would do her good.

They were still eating when a child came to the door bearing a huge bouquet of vivid colored flowers. She curtsied when Minnie answered the door, and held out the flowers with a lovely smile.

Minnie took them, and read the card tucked in amongst them. "Ah!" she said, and held them out to Calli. "They're for you." She smiled.

Calli opened the little card.

Thank you, Miss Calli. D.

She looked at Minnie. "You knew."

"He said he might. I encouraged him like mad." She giggled. "They don't have a delivery service here, so he had to pay a local kid."

Calli looked at the flowers. Many of them she could not name, but they were gorgeous. Beryl exclaimed over them while Calli got water and a vase. "Whatever is this D person thanking you for?" Beryl asked.

"Calli saved his life," Minnie said.

"No, really," Beryl insisted.

"Really," Minnie insisted right back.

"Oh," Beryl said in a small voice.

Josh looked over his glasses at them. "D?" he asked.

"Duardo," Minnie said.

"Army?" he asked, suspicion tingeing his tone.

"Captain," Minnie said happily.

Josh's gaze swiveled to Calli. "I see," he said. He went back to his meal.

After dinner, when Calli stood out on the balcony grabbing some fresh air, Josh found her there, and shut the sliding door soundlessly. He came and leaned against the balcony. "Tell me about this Duardo," he said. "Is he a good man?"

"Yes," Calli said, without hesitation.

"Does he care for her?"

"Yes."

"Enough?"

She sighed. "I don't know, Uncle Josh. I think so...but I don't know. All I can say is that I'll watch out for her."

He thought about that one for a while. "It's hard. I know she must take these bumps, make her own way, but it's hard to watch your only daughter risk...everything. I remember your father saying the same thing about Robert and now I know how he felt."

Calli sighed. "I'm glad he died without knowing what Robert did."

"He knew, Calli. He knew in his gut."

She looked at him. "He never said anything."

"You'd made your choice. What could he say? He just hung around, hoping you'd figure it out, or else to be there to help you to pick up the pieces when it all fell apart, as he knew it would."

"It must have killed him to stay out of it," Calli murmured, feeling a sting of tears. "Maybe it did. They said the cancer was stress-related..."

"No, Calli, don't go wearing that one too. You carry too much already." Josh's hand touched her shoulder briefly.

She blinked the tears away. "He knew in his gut, about Robert?"

"Yes."

"You believed him?"

"Without doubt."

"That's how I feel about Duardo, Uncle Josh. In my gut, I know he's good. Minnie will be okay."

Again he stayed silent, absorbing it. Then he straightened. "Thank you," he said softly and went back inside, leaving her with her thoughts. But she had been alone barely a minute when the door slid aside again and Minnie stepped out. She held a cardboard box.

"Another delivery for you."

"Who is it this time?"

"I don't know. Open it."

Calli pulled the string off the box — it was the size of a cake box, but brown like wrapping paper. She flipped the lid open. Inside sat a pair of Spanish tap shoes and resting on top of them a small, flat, thick blue velvet-covered presentation box. She smiled when she saw the shoes and held them up to Minnie. "Guess," she said.

"Don't have to," Minnie said quietly. She took the big cardboard carton from Calli, and held it while Calli opened the smaller velvet one.

Inside lay an intricately worked silver belt buckle, made up of delicate filigree threads, and adorned with green stones. Emeralds? A card sat tucked behind it. Calli plucked the card out and handed the box to Minnie silently.

Minnie gasped. "Holy Toledo!" she breathed. She pulled the buckle out and turned it over. "Yes, it is! This is Vistarian silver — see the stamp? And these must be emeralds. I know they dig them up in the northern ranges."

Calli opened the envelope. Inside was a small card.

In my soul, you will always be dancing. Keep it so in yours.

No signature, but she didn't need one. The strong, character-filled flourish on the down strokes was all she needed to know who signed it.

She handed the card to Minnie and leaned against the balcony rail again.

Minnie leaned beside her and swayed against her, a little companionable jostle. "I think you're in trouble," she said softly.

"Me too." She dropped her head into her hands.

"My warning this morning came too late, didn't it? You're already involved with him."

"Yes. No...I don't know. I think so...But, oh God, the risk, Minnie!"

"Isn't just getting out of bed a risk?"

"Yes, but the odds now..."

"So what?"

Calli looked at her, a little surprised by the fierce tone in her voice.

"A long time ago, Calli, when you first met Robert, you said something to me I've always remembered. I asked you how did you *know* Robert was the right one, that he was worth giving up college for, to support him while he went through medical school, and you said—do you remember?"

"No."

"You said that lots of people fear risk, of the price it will ask of them at the end, yet you'd read about people who lay on their death bed and they don't bewail the price of risks they've taken. They regret the risks they didn't take, the things they didn't do because they were afraid. And you didn't want to get to the end of your life and regret what you didn't do."

Calli remembered the conversation now. "Instead, I've spent five years bewailing the price I paid for that risk."

"I think you've paid enough," Minnie murmured.

Chapter Nine

"There he is!" Minnie said, her voice lifting.

Duardo, again wearing jeans and a black sweater, lifted his hand when he saw them. He waited across the street, but Minnie rushed across with barely a pause to assess traffic — she dived between cars, causing at least one set of brakes to squeal sharply, and made the other pavement with a jump. Still running, she pushed through the people strolling the avenue, taking in the evening air, and threw herself at Duardo, literally wrapping herself around him, her legs around his waist, her arms around his neck. He held onto her, grinning, and ran his hand through her hair, then kissed her, passionately and long.

When Callie crossed the street and made her way through the flow of pedestrians to the place where they stood, Minnie had regained her feet and Duardo caressed her face. The gentleness of his touch made Calli's heart ache. Oh, how she hoped for Minnie's sake that he loved her!

Duardo turned to face her, came to a loose attention and bowed. Vistarian men did it often, she realized, and it did not seem silly or archaic. It seemed like a very genuine expression of honor. Then he took her hand and kissed the back of it. "Miss Calli."

"Thank you for the flowers, Duardo."

"They were not enough," he declared. He lifted her hand to his head, pushing her fingers under the hair. She felt beneath her fingers a long, hard welt of skin about an inch across.

"Ugh," she said.

Minnie lifted her hand to feel, too, and pulled it away with a grimace.

Duardo just grinned. He pointed to his temple. "I still see double a little. So I am off duty until I see just one." He tucked Minnie under his arm, and squeezed her. "We walk, okay?"

"Yes."

Calli noticed bruises and scrapes around his wrist, peeping beneath the sleeve of the sweater, but he used that hand without hesitation, gripping Minnie's. "Hey, you guys should go on without me," she said. "I can go get dinner somewhere."

"No," Duardo said firmly, even as Minnie protested. "You come with us."

"I don't want to be in the way," she said.

"No," Duardo said again. He pulled her around and made her walk beside him, keeping a grip on her elbow.

Realizing she wouldn't be able to leave them alone without creating a scene, she tried to relax and enjoy the stroll. A lot of people seemed to be doing the same thing, in twos, threes, even more. It seemed fashionable to stroll the Avenue of Nations in the evening. The cars on the four-lane paved road also moved leisurely, and passengers in the cars would call out to pedestrians. Along the pavement many pushcarts sold flowers, food, cheap jewelry, clothing and trinkets, but it didn't appear to be a hard commercial push—they seemed content to watch the crowd go by and make social contact with people they knew.

"This street, they see many parades," Duardo explained.

"It's wide enough."

"That's the palace up there, isn't it?" Minnie asked.

Calli looked up. The road sloped upwards from here, a gentle incline that ended at a semi-circular building in white stone, bathed in spotlights.

"That is *el Edificio Legislativo*," Duardo said. "The President's residence is behind it, and there is lots of park in between."

At the top of the hill, the road widened out into a very large circle, matching the curve of the legislative building. In the middle of the circle was a fountain, which seemed to be the center of social activity on the Avenue of Nations. Many people sat around the fountain, and many more lingered in the area, talking and walking about.

A wrought-iron fence separated the public circus from the legislative building, and in the middle, two gates stood open, with armed soldiers at attention. Duardo headed toward the gates.

"We're allowed in there?" Calli asked.

"The public, no. But me, they let me in. I am part of the government." He lifted his hand in a salute to the guards, who brought their feet together at parade attention as they passed by. Duardo walked over to the gatehouse, where a man in normal army uniform sat behind the glass. He chatted to him for a minute and pulled out his wallet from his back pocket, to show ID.

Finally, the man behind the glass pushed a clipboard through the slot, and Duardo signed it. The man gave a salute, which Duardo returned, and then tucked Minnie back under his arm. "No sweat," he told Calli.

"I'm sure they don't let just any soldier in here, though," Calli said.

"Ah, no, but I am walking wounded. They feel sorry for me." He grinned.

"You're lying, but okay," Calli said.

"It is perfectly true!" Duardo protested.

A great archway lay ahead. It actually burrowed through the middle of the building, in the manner of some of the European buildings where the road ran through the middle for coachmen and horses to drop their privileged passengers right at the door. Duardo led them under the arch, and their footsteps echoed flatly across the old cobblestones.

At the other end of the archway, the road became a covered walkway, well lit, with slim columns lining each side. It was a modern addition, designed to provide shade and protection from daily rain for those walking to the legislature. Along the walkway, guards stood between the pillars at regular intervals, facing each other. The walkway ran straight toward another three-story building, but this one unlit by spotlights. Lights illuminated rooms here and there, but many of them remained dark. The Presidential residence.

Duardo did not walk down the pathway. Instead, he slipped out between the pillars, across well-tended lawn, and around huge beds of flowers surrounding shady trees, in a big arc that would eventually bring them towards the north wing of the palace.

"You're heading somewhere," Calli guessed. "This isn't just a stroll in a pretty garden."

"We are just walking," Duardo said. He halted them suddenly, a hand on Calli's arm, and called out something in a low voice. An equally low response came from their right, and Duardo answered. Then Calli heard the sound of metal clinking. Duardo let her arm go. "Come," he declared.

"We just got challenged by someone with a gun!" Calli said. "Hidden away where no one could see them."

"You do not think those guards standing so stiff would be able to see everything, did you?"

"They didn't just let you in here on a whim, did they?" Calli said.

"Not quite," Duardo admitted. He brought them to a halt, next to a tall bed of flowers and grasses. She could smell the dry, herbal smell, and a strong, almost intoxicating scent of some sort of lily nearby. They faced the covered walkway, about thirty feet away from it, and they would be quite invisible in the darkness beyond reach of the lights.

"See?" Duardo said, nodding towards the walkway.

Calli drew a sharp breath, her heart jumping. Nick walked down the walkway, obviously in a hurry.

"He has been alerted by the gatehouse," Duardo said. "No one comes in here without *el leopardo* knowing about it. And because it is me, he hurries to find out what is wrong, for he knows that I would not come here without just cause. In a moment, when he finds me gone, he will go back to the palace, puzzled and concerned."

"Why, Duardo?"

He looked at her and in the darkness she saw him smile. "It is time for you to surprise him instead of always being surprised by the leopard. Take the choice away from him this time."

There remained so much unspoken in his words, a wealth of knowledge and understanding that made her a little uneasy.

Minnie held out her hand. "I told Duardo, Calli. All of it. Even Robert."

She was suddenly glad of the dark that hid her burning cheeks. "Jesus Christ, Minnie!"

"This is right," Minnie said firmly. "Take the risk. Take the leap."

"Yes, the leap," Duardo said. "Minnie knows. You listen to her. And you, the strong one, here is what you must do." He took her arm and led her around the far side of the flowerbed beside them. They came right up to the palace itself, on the far corner. The stone walls were still warm from soaking in the day's sunlight. Duardo pointed up at the second balcony, and then at the concrete screen that blocked off the end of the lower floor veranda. "A good ladder, yes?" he asked.

"Up there?" Calli asked.

"His rooms are there, where he stays when he is in the city."

"How do you know so much, Duardo?"

"In the last few days I have learned very, very much, because I met you and Minnie. I have become...a channel."

"Conduit."

"*Sí.*" He glanced over her shoulder. "He comes." He patted her shoulder, and abruptly, silently, left. The trained soldier moving in stealth.

Calli moved around to face the concrete blocks. Their intricate patterns provided toe and finger holds everywhere. Duardo proved right—it was virtually a ladder. She began to climb, wishing she had worn jeans again, but at least her short skirt didn't get in the way. It just didn't protect her knees very well. A cotton skirt and spaghetti strap top would not have been her apparel of choice for climbing walls.

The blocks went all the way to the roof of the building, which meant when she'd climbed high enough, she had to move sideways to reach the actual balcony rail, a concrete balustrade a good two feet thick. She jumped down to the floor and looked about. A huge old banyan tree spread its branches out a few feet further along the veranda, giving her a place to hide from observers down below.

She sat on the balcony rail behind the tree and rested against the pillar there, completely hidden except for anyone who might be standing at the end of the second floor balcony. If Nick's rooms were at the end, as Duardo said, then he would have to walk past her to reach either one of the three French doors there.

She hugged her knees to her chest and it reminded her of Minnie's confession the other day. What would Nick say? The speedy approach of the moment of confrontation made her heart beat so hard it hurt.

She heard a door close and footsteps coming closer. Then she held her breath as he passed her. He had his head down, his hand in his pocket. Deep in thought, again.

Calli slipped off the balcony and ran up behind him, intending to catch at his shoulder and turn him around. But her sandals must have made some noise — perhaps her clothing rustled. Before she even laid a finger on him, he had spun and caught her wrist in a vise-like grip. He thrust her up against the wall; the impact pushed the wind out of her. He'd pinned her arm above her head, his arm across her throat, his body slammed up against hers, holding her there — all before her own instincts were even triggered. Her gasp of surprise remained locked in her chest. She stared at his eyes, barely four inches from hers.

They stayed locked in that position for what seemed like eternity, while her heart stopped beating altogether. He had thought her the enemy, had defended himself with a speed and agility that told her he was practiced at this, that he was prepared. It gave her an insight into his life that she had not considered before.

All the words she had prepared, the explanations and justifications, had fled her mind. She simply stared at him. The cut beneath his right eye had almost healed. He seemed otherwise completely untouched.

She was absurdly glad to see him.

With a groan, he let her wrist go, and the arm against her throat slipped over her head to pull her to him. Then his lips crushed against hers—he kissed her with a thoroughness that left her breathless. He kissed her face, her eyes, her nose, her chin; he rained kisses upon her in a soft barrage that left her trembling for more.

His hand held her head steady while he plundered her mouth. She felt his heart under her hands, under silk, and she groaned a little, her eyes closing.

His arms tightened around her and he picked her up, bringing her with him as he turned and pushed open the French door. He pulled her inside and shut the door with one hand. She heard a solid, small thud. He pushed her up against the wall again. His mouth came back against hers. He kissed her with a thoroughness that left her breathless.

His hands seemed to be everywhere at once, building an erotic storm of sensations that she could not track individually and could not prevent. Caresses covered her body, through her clothing, under it, she didn't know.

If he wanted her now, this moment, she would comply willingly. She wrapped her leg around his hip, and threaded her fingers through the soft, heavy silk of his hair, and opened her body and soul to him, drunk with the joy of it. Eons passed within a heartbeat.

Eventually Nick lifted his head from tasting the skin at the base of her throat. He kissed her throat, her chin and finally her mouth. Then he grew still, his head resting against hers. They breathed heavily. His body, a solid mass, held her against the wall—a support she needed. She could feel his cock, thick and hard, against her hip, and delighted in the tangible evidence of his arousal.

Finally, he shifted his weight away from her, a little at a time, then stepped away from her altogether.

She marveled that she was still completely dressed.

Nick backed away to the center of the room, his gaze not leaving her. "Why did you come here?"

"For you."

He shook his head a little. "Heads will roll for this," he said, his voice low. "How you got in here—"

"Your security is intact."

He considered that. "Duardo," he said at last and gave a short laugh. He walked back towards her and reached out to the low cabinet by her hip. An automatic pistol lay there—she had not noticed it until now. Nick picked it up, and with an absent-minded motion, flicked something on the gun that clicked audibly. He pushed it inside his jacket.

She remembered the quiet knock she'd heard when he'd first pulled her in here. He had been putting the gun down.

Nick gave a grimace. "I had the gun in my hand before I even turned to confront you," he said. "Such is my life."

She felt a touch of fright, but knew that now was the time to say what she had come to say. She spoke the words. "Is there room in that life for me, Nick? Even a temporary, hidden corner of it?"

"Temporary?" He looked at her sideways. "You would settle for that?"

"Temporary can last a long time," she said as airily as she could manage. "Besides, there are no guarantees, are there? That's one thing Dominio de Leo taught me. You may have all the best intentions, the greatest plans in the world…and it doesn't matter a damn. It can all go —" She snapped her fingers. "Just like that."

He sighed and pushed a hand through his hair. "Calli, the risks —"

"And I could get run over by a bus tomorrow."

"The odds will be even shorter if you become involved in my life," he said.

"I don't care."

"I do. I don't want to see you hurt."

She straightened up from the wall, and walked towards him. "Then keep me at your side. I know I'll feel safe there."

"That could be a dangerous illusion for both of us."

She'd drawn very close now, but he gave no sign of relenting. She indulged in her private pleasure: she slid her hands under his jacket and rested them against his chest, feeling the warm, delicate silk, and the heat of his firm flesh beneath. She looked up at him, pleased that she had to lift her chin to look him in the eye.

"I'm willing to accept the risks, Nick, if I can have you — even for a short time."

She saw him swallow. "Why me?" he asked, his voice low.

"The bastard son who cannot use his mother's name?" she whispered.

"Yes," he ground out.

So many answers occurred to her. She picked and discarded a dozen, but it came down to the fact that he had seen something in her...a potential she had begun to discover for herself. "You know me," she said at last. "Better than I know myself. And you accept it."

Her fingers resting against his chest were not enough. She followed a blind instinct, leaned forward to kiss his neck, to follow the beating pulse with her lips, tasting him, the salty heat of him, up to his ear, where his hair tickled her cheek. She lifted her hands and pushed the jacket off his shoulders. The jacket hit the floor with a heavy thud. Of course, the gun.

His pulse raced beneath her lips and she heard his breath, a little unsteady, next to her ear, but he did not move. She thrust her tongue in his ear, and he rewarded her with a deep groan. The sound fluttered through her with little tendrils of pleasure. His hands came down around her waist, almost defensively. But he did not push her back.

Encouraged, she brought his head down to hers and kissed him firmly. Her hands dropped to his waist, to the belt there.

His hands came to life and snagged her wrists. He held her still. "Not here," he said. "Not where Vistaria can intrude at any moment." He looked her in the eye. "I want you for myself, with the world shut firmly outside the door."

She shivered at the implied promise. "Where, then?"

"My place."

She gave a little laugh. "Where is your place? I thought it was here."

"Here?" He looked around the room. "This is just a tool." He took her face in his hands and gave her a firm kiss on the mouth, then smiled. "You are relentless, Miss Callida. You drug my sleep, invade my thoughts, and breach every defense I've built. I must concede because I am helpless to do anything else, but at the same time there is a voice inside me telling me this is right."

"Hooray for small voices," Calli murmured, unable to prevent her own smile of pure happiness.

He pushed her away from him a little, and bent down to pick up his jacket, and slide it back on. "Forgive me, but for now, we must be careful," he said.

She nodded. "But soon, Nick. Please make it soon."

"Is tomorrow soon enough?"

"No," she said quickly.

He raised his brow. "I see. Then tonight it must be."

"You're serious?"

He laughed a little and kissed her mouth, his fingers sliding into her hair. Her breath deserted her again, and she held onto his jacket. When he released her she shook him a little. "Tonight?" she repeated.

He frowned a little. "Can we be together tonight? I think the laws of physics are against us there. But I can start the arrangements right now, and we can start out tonight. I'm afraid that is the best I can do. Can you live with that, Calli?"

"If we start at once, yes. But Nick, can you walk away from here, just like that?"

"There's an advantage to being a bastard son without a formal position," he said. "I can come and go as I please."

"Stop teasing."

"I'm not teasing," he said flatly. "I exaggerate just a little, though. I will have to make certain arrangements, but they can be put into place tonight."

"You would do that for me?"

"Certainly." He raised his brow again. "What is it?"

She shook her head. "It's just that…after fighting so hard to reach this point, I suddenly feel like I'm freefalling."

He pushed his hand into his pocket. Studied her. "That's because the brakes are off, Calli. I've wanted you since the moment I saw you, and I've fought harder and longer than I've ever fought to resist you, but no more. I want you so badly that if I took you now it would not be soon enough to suit me…so you will find me more than willing to speed up arrangements in any way I can."

She swallowed, her throat suddenly dry and raspy. "And heaven help anyone who gets in the way?"

"Yes, indeed," he agreed, his voice very low. His eyes, his gaze burrowed into her soul again. Then he cleared his throat and looked away, and Calli shook off the spell.

He walked over to a desk in the corner, and lifted the phone. "One moment," he told he, and spoke into the phone. He had a quick exchange in Spanish, then covered the phone with his other hand. "Calli," he murmured.

When she looked over, he waved his hand in an unmistakable 'come here' motion. She walked over, and he sat her on the desk, facing him, her thighs on either side of his legs. As he spoke into the phone he watched her, his eyes never leaving her face. His other hand pushed her hair back over her shoulder, then lingered, the thumb caressing the flesh at the base of her neck. It sent little ripples of pleasure through to her breast. Her head fell back a little. She arched her back, forcing the taut nipple through the clinging jersey.

It seemed that his eyes darkened, reflecting stormy emotions, but he had a calculating look on his face. He enjoyed his power over her.

Well, it could be a two-way street. She reached for his belt buckle. She laid her hands on the end of the belt, and looked up at him, lifting her brow inquiringly.

His hand came down to cup her breast, the thumb sliding over the nipple, and she jumped and gasped. The touch speared straight down to her already throbbing clitoris.

Staring him straight in the eye, she pulled the end of the belt out of the carrier and slipped the tongue from the hole. Only the pressure she applied to the belt kept it closed. Gradually she let the tension ease, allowing the buckle to slide along the leather.

Nicolás finished the call and hung up. He caught her hands in his. "You play a wicked game," he said, delighting her with the throaty growl in his voice. He fastened the belt, then picked up her hand and kissed the back of it. "All has been arranged."

"Really?"

"You doubt me?"

"No…it just seems a little simple."

"Simple enough. I always keep my options open. But you must play your part now, Calli."

"What do I do?"

"You and Minnie must go to Pascuallita with Duardo."

"That's it?"

"Tonight."

"Oh, yes, that might create some problems."

"Can you handle them?"

"I think so."

"Good. Duardo can pay penance for interfering with my personal affairs by playing nursemaid to two American women who want to sightsee around the top of the island. He will be bored and charming in turns, and you two will pretend a total fascination with the country."

"That's the easy part. Vistaria *is* a fascinating country."

He smiled a little. "Vistaria can also be a deadly country. Don't underestimate my fellow countrymen, Calli. You have only seen a glimpse of the passion and determination that runs in their blood. Vistaria has been self-determining since we threw off the Spanish yoke, and men will give up their lives to ensure it stays that way."

She thought of the gun in his jacket. How could she underestimate Vistarians when the gun proved that

Nicolás would not take any chances? "I won't," she said softly.

"Good. Now, you should scale whatever wall you scaled to reach me and go give Duardo his orders."

"And then what?"

"Enjoy your trip to Pascuallita." He lifted her off the desk and walked her towards the door, his hand on her waist.

It was moving too fast. "Wait," she said quickly, turning. "What happens then?"

"I will find you."

She shook her head. "It doesn't feel that way. Nick, I'm afraid that if I step out of this room, I'll never see you again."

He didn't dismiss her fears as foolish. "Do you trust me?"

She answered honestly. "With my life."

"But you still believe I will not come to you. Hmm." He thought about it for a moment, then reached into his pocket as she had seen him do a hundred times since she had known him. His hand emerged, snarled with a gold chain. He lifted it up, so that the pendant attached to it swung clear. "St. Christopher," he explained. "Patron saint of —"

"Travelers," Calli finished. "My grandmother was Irish."

"My mother was Irish, too. This pendant traveled with her father through Europe during the war. She wore it until the day she died, and swore it saved her life a hundred times in Northern Ireland. She gave it to me, and I have carried it with me ever since." He held it out to her.

"No, Nick, I can't."

He shook his head, as if to refute her protest. He turned her around. "Your hair. Pull it aside," he told her.

She pulled her hair aside and watched as the pendant descended in front of her. It settled on her chest. Then he turned her back to face him. "Believe that I will come for you," he said, and kissed her gently.

Chapter Ten

They traveled by train, a slow, picturesque journey through the mountains. The train stopped at every station along the way and at every stop it seemed that dozens of people got off and three dozen more got on.

The windows remained wide open throughout the trip and fresh air bathed their faces as they sat on the wooden seats facing each other, their luggage piled up on the seat next to Calli. Duardo, she noticed, did not give Minnie any of the overt signs of affection she had seen in the city. As he approached home base and his family, did he grow more wary of his reputation? She didn't speak of it, but worried that perhaps while he had been in the city Minnie had provided a nice distraction and now he had been forced to bring her back home, he carefully put distance between them.

Minnie did not seem to notice the difference in his behavior, but then, she had accepted with serene calm everything that had happened since Calli had shinnied back down the bricks of the Presidential residence last evening.

Calli had found them sitting on the lawn at the base of the flowerbed, Duardo's arm around her, and their heads close together. When her vision had adjusted to the dark of the night, she had seen that only a few dozen paces away, a soldier stood with his rifle resting across his hips, not overtly watching them, but hovering, just the same.

Calli had dropped to the grass in front of them, and told Duardo what Nicolás had said. Duardo had listened with his head cocked. It seemed he read more into Nick's instructions than she did, for he accepted the news with a sober expression, the twinkle of merriment in his eyes fading.

"I'd like to see Pascuallita," Minnie said simply.

They had traveled back to the apartment, catching the last streetcar of the night. There, they had packed hurriedly. Calli finished before Minnie because she had less to pack. They'd discussed the pros and cons of telling Joshua exactly what they planned, then decided a note would delay the delivery of the news until they had left the city. They'd written a jointly authored letter, assuring him they were snatching a last-minute chance to tour the north of the island. They promised to phone him from Pascuallita.

Then on to the house where Duardo had been staying in the city, this time by taxi, which they had managed to hail from the main street that ran below the apartment. Duardo quartered in a small, older house with a distinct lean, tucked away off the main square. Four or five army people shared the house. Duardo packed quickly while Minnie and Calli sat on the front stoop to wait for him — he had explained a little awkwardly that it would not be appropriate for women to go inside a male-only household. He slipped out through the door barely fifteen minutes later, an army issue suit bag over his shoulder and a Nike sports bag in his other hand.

They had walked to the train station, at the bottom of *las colinas*, passing through silent streets where it seemed everyone slumbered. At the train station they had curled up on benches and dozed with their heads on their luggage until the ticket office opened an hour before the train departed.

After the tickets had been bought, Duardo had disappeared into the men's room with his luggage and returned, shaved and clean. He also wore a light windbreaker, protection against the pre-dawn chill.

Now they were on the train, despite the heat of the day and the collective humidity of a dozen bodies squashed in around them, Duardo had not removed his jacket, although he had pushed the sleeves up. He left it zipped a third of the way up, too, which prevented the jacket from falling open.

Calli waited until they approached the next station, then sat on the edge of her seat and twisted around, as if she inspected the view out of the window beyond their luggage. When the train came to halt with the shudder and jerk she had been anticipating, she let herself fall sideways, her shoulder landing against Duardo's chest.

She apologized, pushed herself back upright and ignored Duardo's thoughtful expression. Minnie already showed signs that the restless night had caught up with her, so Calli waited. Soon, Minnie's eyes slid closed, and her head bumped against Duardo's shoulder. He lifted his arm and settled her head on his legs, and she curled up like a kitten and slept.

Duardo looked at Calli expectantly.

"How many people around us understand English, do you think?"

He didn't look around, which told her that he had already assessed everyone near them. "None. They have made no reaction to comments we have made."

"You have a pistol under your jacket."

"Yes."

"Why? Are we in that much danger?"

"Pascuallita is only five miles away from the area of a known rebel camp. I must act as if I am in enemy territory."

"It is your home town, isn't it?"

He grimaced. "Many call Tel-Aviv their home town, too. And Belfast."

"There has been trouble there?"

"Once." And unconsciously, he rubbed his thigh.

"You were part of that trouble, weren't you? You were caught up in it."

"Yes."

"That is what you did that earned you honor, that got you invited to General Blanco's birthday. You said you protected your country."

"And I did," he agreed.

"Would you be carrying the gun if you didn't have us with you?"

"Maybe not. I do not know. But you *are* with me, and—" He glanced around quickly, and said, "Nick asked me to get you to Pascuallita, and so I shall."

"What did you tell the guard last night? The one that tried to stop us when we headed for the palace?"

"Pardon?"

"The one that put his rifle back on safety and melted back into the dark. I've been thinking about it, Duardo, and it seems very odd to me that a security detail surrounding a presidential residence would allow an American woman to climb up into the building even if she *was* with one of their own. You said something— enough to allow me to wander freely into Nick's rooms. What did you say?"

He considered her for a moment. "I told him that—"
Again the quick look around, an awareness of his audience
disciplining his tongue. "That the long blonde heroine of
Prince Leopold's domain wished to speak to Nick."

"And just like that, he let you through?"

"Your reputation has spread throughout the army,
Callida. You are the strong one. They will allow you
almost any liberty, if you say you want it."

She ran a hand through her hair, suddenly uneasy.
"Don't tell me they have some cute little Spanish name for
me, like Nick's?"

Duardo grinned. "I translated it literally. 'Long,
strong, blonde'."

"Ouch."

He laughed properly then. "Vistarians are all poets,
even the soldiers. You cannot stop them weaving tales
around everything."

"I'm not a hero, Duardo. You know why I did what I
did, and it wasn't for the sake of Vistaria."

His laughter fled. "It does not matter why you did it.
You were scared, and you didn't know if you could do it,
but you did it anyway. *That* is a hero. Me, I will always be
grateful you did what you did." And he looked down at
Minnie and caressed her cheek.

That gentle sweep of his fingers reassured Calli more
than anything he could have said.

"So, what do we do when we get to Pascuallita?" she
asked.

"Act like tourists, did he not say?"

"Are there lots of tourists in Pascuallita?"

"A few, but it is an uncomfortable journey, so not as many as there should be. Pascuallita is very handsome."

"Pretty."

"*Sí*. The mountains, the old houses. To me it is simply home, but people tell me that it is charming."

"So charming, the rebels are within spitting distance," Calli muttered. "What was he thinking of, bringing us there?"

"He lives there," Duardo said unexpectedly.

"He does?"

"Not in the town, but nearby. That is why I met him once before I met Minnie and you. When…" He touched his thigh. "He came to speak to all of us who fought that day."

A shiver climbed up her spine suddenly. *Nick's home.*

"How long till we get there?" she asked.

"An hour, maybe. We will be there in time for a late lunch."

* * * * *

Duardo took them to a public house across the road from the railway station. It appeared to be a custom of his when he arrived back in Pascuallita because the man behind the bar greeted him cheerily by name.

They slid into a booth with high benches and wooden walls that virtually blocked the table from the view of all but someone standing right next to it. Duardo ordered quickly, chatting with the waiter. When the waiter nodded and walked away, he shrugged a little. "You must trust me. They don't have a menu here, and I know what is good."

"That's fine, Duardo," Calli assured him.

Minnie, looking fresh and rested, rolled her eyes. "Just don't let her gobble it down, Duardo. She turned purple in the face last time because she bit into something too hot for her. You let her do that again and she'll sue you for damages to her tongue."

But Duardo seemed incapable of accepting teasing in his new role as their appointed guardian. He shook his head. "You will like this," he said.

While they waited for the food, Calli employed Duardo as an interpreter and arranged to use the hotel's telephone. She placed a call to Josh's office at the silver mine on *Las Piedras Grandes*, repressing her frustration at having to deal with an operator to place a simple long distance call. Using good English, the operator told her it would take a while, so Calli sat back at the table, a few feet away.

"What does *piedras* mean?" she asked Duardo.

"Rock. Boulder."

She laughed. "*Las Piedras Grandes*…the big rock."

"It is, too," Duardo said. "Right at the end of the main island is *las piedras*. There is nothing on it."

"Nothing but silver in vast quantities," Minnie said.

"Yes, but for many years, nothing."

"How big is it?" Calli asked.

"You can drive across the island in twenty minutes," Minnie said.

Duardo nodded. "I believe that is true. I have not been there."

"No? Northern boy, huh?"

"Most certainly," he agreed easily.

The food arrived then, steaming hot bowlfuls of what Calli took to be stew, and plates of crisp tortilla-like wafers. There was also a bowl of something cream-colored and of the same consistency as a dip.

In Lozano Colinas, most of the dishes consisted of lots of fresh produce—salsa and piquant salads, along with just-browned meats and freshly-made tortillas. But in Pascuallita, the emphasis appeared to be different.

"No spoon, no fork," Minnie muttered.

"No. Like this," Duardo explained. He picked up the crisp wafer, dipped it in the creamy stuff, and took a small bite, and indicated that they should, too.

It tasted bland.

"Now try this," he instructed, and dipped the wafer into the bowl before him. The wafer emerged thickly coated with sauce, and carrying a spoonful's worth of what looked like carrots and perhaps meat.

Calli dipped into her bowl and ate. The stew was a savory delight, the vegetables crisp, the meat tender and the spices hit the back of her tongue and surprised her with their subtleness.

"Like?" Duardo asked.

Minnie frowned. "It's not curry, I know that, but it reminds me of curry. It's great," she assured him. "But what is it?"

"Whatever it is, it's never been in a can," Calli declared. "That sort of flavor you only get from blending and cooking well."

"Three days," Duardo said.

"And the meat?"

"Wild mountain goat. There are many around here. Try it with the tapinade."

Calli ate with a relish, for she was ravenously hungry. They had only had chocolate and some crushed cookies on the train.

"This is what you eat all the time?" Minnie asked.

"Often. People cook here more than they do in the city. It is traditional. And it is cooler. Nearly two thousand feet. We have bigger mountains in the north." He did not hide his pride.

The call to Uncle Josh went through just as she finished her bowl. Calli sat at the bar and swiveled so that the customers sitting a few stools along from her would not be able to easily eavesdrop—even if they did know English.

"Calli? I got your note. You're in Pascuallita?"

"Yes, we just got off the train a while ago, and we're eating right now."

He was silent for a moment. "I suppose there's a good reason you're up there?"

"Yes."

"Should I be concerned, Calli? You left with no notice, in the dead of the night. And Pascuallita…I've heard rumors that Pascuallita would be where the rebels would strike first."

"Have you heard that something might happen?"

"No…but, just be careful. Duardo is with you?"

"Yes."

This time his silence was even longer. "Is he armed?" Uncle Josh asked, his tone awkward.

"Not that you'd notice to look at him, but yes, he's carrying a gun," Calli said softly.

He sighed, and she could see him in her mind, rubbing his hand through his hair. "Okay. Is Minnie there? Let me talk to her."

* * * * *

After lunch, they stepped out of the tavern and looked around. The train station was directly in front of them, but because of the mountainous terrain, the platform lifted twenty feet or so higher than the road. Bright red, yellow and blue safety rails edged the platform, and tubs of flowers sat beneath them, nodding in the little breeze that passed up the street. It was mid-afternoon, but lots of people still moved about the street.

"No siesta?" Calli asked.

Duardo shook his head. "No heat," he explained. "Why sleep away the day?"

Even though it was certainly cooler at this elevation, there was still a mugginess in the air that reminded her they were in the tropics.

"Well, we'd better be tourists," Minnie said, dropping her sunglasses over her eyes, hitching her heavy overnight bag over her shoulder and looking around with interest. "Where are the shops, Duardo?"

"Ah, shopping, of course," he said with laugh. "How silly of me to forget a matter of such importance." He arranged his bags in his left hand, tucked Minnie's hand under that elbow and turned her to face downhill. "This way," he instructed. He waved for Calli to walk along beside him, but he did not gently guide her with a touch to her arm or back as he had done in *Las Colinas*. The reason, when she figured it out, took some of the pleasantness out of the afternoon: he kept his gun hand free.

The narrow, winding streets in Pascuallita discouraged any vehicles with more than two wheels. The streets had been constructed around the original buildings, which had been built on the flattest piece of land to be had. The streets had been laid on the land that remained — the steepest land. Sets of steps and terraces broke up many of the streets, which further reduced traffic.

Bicycles could be seen everywhere, and many of the younger people used skateboards and in-line skates, but most people walked. There was a lot of foot traffic, more of it the deeper they wound into the heart of the town.

At one intersection of three different streets, Calli heard her name being called from the street on her left. She looked that way, startled. At the far end of the street an open topped jeep sat. Nicolás Escobedo leaned against the front grille, his arms crossed, a black hat shading his face, sunglasses obscuring the dark blue eyes.

Calli controlled the first impulsive sound of delight that came to her, but couldn't stop herself from brushing past Minnie and Duardo and hurrying up the narrow little alley. She stopped in front of him, her backpack slapping against her shoulder. "You came," she said simply.

"And you thought I wouldn't."

"I couldn't see how...never mind. You're here. Although *how* you got here..."

"Later," he said, and lifted his chin. "Duardo..."

Duardo and Minnie had followed her up the alley. Nicolás held out his hand, and the younger man dropped his bags and shook it, but didn't smile.

"Anyone?" Nicolás asked.

"No."

"You have my thanks."

"For you, *señor*, anything."

"I will take it from here," Nick said, straightening up. "You will come to my house, yes?"

Duardo looked a little awkward. "No, *señor*, as much as I regret missing such an honor, I have something I must do."

Nicolás dropped his chin to look over his sunglasses at him.

Duardo moved his feet, and shrugged, and Calli realized that he had turned slightly red. "I will visit my mother. I want her to meet Minnie."

Pleasure touched her, but she suppressed her smile. Minnie looked up at him with a small smile of her own.

Nick nodded. "Of course." He glanced at Calli. "Excuse me for just a moment," he said, and pulled Duardo aside. They dropped into low, quiet Spanish.

Minnie grabbed Calli's arm. "Oh hell, now I'm terrified," she whispered. "You don't meet their mothers here unless it means something."

"Which is just what you wanted, so why the terror?"

"What if she hates me? I'm American, I'm...I'm...I'll never measure up."

"You'll be fine," Calli assured her.

The two men finished their conversation and returned to the front of the jeep. Duardo picked up his bags again, and picked up Minnie's hand in his right. He nodded at Calli. "*Adios, la dama fuerte*. I will take good care of your cousin."

Calli heard Nicolás chuckle, as she touched Duardo's arm. "Thank you, Duardo."

She watched them walk back down the alley, suddenly shy—she battled her own terror. Deliberately, she looked at Nick, but couldn't tell through the sunglasses whether he watched her or just happened to be looking in her direction.

"*Strong lady?*" he said.

She grimaced. "It's not as picturesque as red leopard," she returned.

He pulled a key ring out of his pocket. "I think it fits you perfectly." He opened the passenger door of the jeep for her and moved around to the driver's side and settled in the seat.

"What did you mean when you said 'anyone' to Duardo?" she asked.

He paused with his hand on the keys, already inserted in the ignition. Then, he started the engine. "I asked him if anyone had followed you from *Las Colinas*."

She shivered. "How did he know to watch out for that?"

"He's one of the best captains in the Vistarian army. When I asked him to bring you here, he knew what I expected of him." Abruptly, he switched off the engine, and turned to face her in the seat. He took the sunglasses off, and reached out to pull the edges of her shirt aside. She realized he checked to see if she still wore the medallion, and he smiled a little when he saw it there. Then he drew her forward and kissed her, and his lips were warm, firm and demanding. His tongue swept into her mouth, and she could feel her shyness, her awkwardness, the sense of unreality slipping away.

This was Nicolás. Nick. He was real, and hot beneath her fingers.

He drew back a little, but his hand rested loosely around her waist. "No more worrying," he declared. "You made a decision back in the city to accept the risks, yes?"

"Yes."

"And so did I. So, we do not worry about the future now. Just this moment."

"Well...okay."

He shook his head a little. "No, Calli. I mean this. Here, I am me. Just me. Nicolás, that you call Nick."

She gave a little smile and tapped his jacket, down low on the left hand side, and her fingernail rapped against metal as she had known it would. "No, you're not *just* Nick," she said softly. "You will never be just Nick, but that's okay."

He studied her, that same cool assessing look he had given her in the prison cell. Then he swiveled back to face the steering wheel and put on his sunglasses. "I think, perhaps, you are even more of a realist than I," he said, and put the jeep into gear, and took off with spinning wheels.

She tried to calm her jumping heart. "You don't like that?" she said, lifting her voice above the engine noise.

"Right now, no," he said. He smiled a little. "But that's just because you've made me feel foolish. You are right, *la dama fuerte*. We accepted risks, which means we can't afford to ignore them or pretend they're not there. So...home, by the most direct route, and without scenic stops. There, at least, we shall be as secure as we can be."

He drove through a maze of streets and it seemed that he backtracked sometimes. She realized he worked to avoid the terraced roads a car could not use. Then they were beyond the town, out onto a narrow mountain road, with a sharp drop down to Calli's right. They headed northwest, further into the mountains.

"How far?" she asked.

"Twenty minutes, more or less. Depends on the weather."

"Rain?"

"Fog," he said. "Makes turning the hairpin bends an exercise in caution."

"You live very much out of the way?"

"Just enough." He paused while he negotiated a sharp curve. "About five years after I got back from the States, I bought up half-a-dozen slice farms and built a house at the top of them."

She took a moment to absorb the wealth of information in that simple statement. Nick liked living out of the way. He'd acquired at least six properties to build a house upon. His out-of-the-way property was not a little cabin in the woods, then. "Slice farms?" she said at last.

"I'll show you one, later," he promised. "My neighbors still work their farms."

"And you lived in the States while you studied, right? Philosophy and economics."

"Mmmm." His attention had drawn to the road ahead, and he slowed the jeep, creeping around a bend. Hidden on the other side of the blind corner, a dozen or so mountain goats meandered across the road. He beeped the horn to encourage them to move out of the way. They wandered to the side, barely pausing to look at the jeep.

"You knew they were there?" Calli asked.

"They were on the side just there when I came down the hill earlier."

"They look just like the ones we get back home."

"They probably are. The British traders introduced a lot of western ideas and animals into Vistaria in their efforts to make the world England."

"You don't like that, do you?"

He took a while to answer. "I grew up listening to my mother's stories of Belfast and the mighty English fist. No, I don't like it. Not for Northern Ireland, nor for Vistaria."

She didn't know how to respond, for she had caught a glimpse of the passion he had for his country, the dedication he brought to his work. She represented a country that most of his fellow Vistarians viewed as a threat. Yet she sat here beside him on her way to...

"Tell me about your dreams, Calli," he said, making her jump a little.

"Dreams?"

"You said you dreamed of us. Together."

"I did."

The quick montage of images, faded by constant review, flipped through her mind. But still they had the power to stir her, to catch her breath with their power, their raw sensuality.

"Tell me about them," Nick coaxed, his voice low.

She licked her lips, suddenly shy again. Even when she had lived with Robert, she had not discussed such intimate details as dreams and fantasies. She couldn't recall if she'd even had them.

He glanced at her and smiled a little. "Ah, Calli, it's clear you've never been with a man who cares about such matters. But I do. I want to know what's in your heart, your mind, your soul, and every inch of flesh and blood in between."

She deliberately changed the direction. "You said you dreamed of me, too."

"I can tell you my dreams, Calli, but I'd rather show you, and for that I need both hands free."

"Show me?"

"Oh yes," he said, his voice lower still and suddenly a little hoarse. "I have the details memorized."

She shivered, despite the sun.

"Give me the one image that has stayed with you," he said. "I know there must be at least one. A moment from your dreams. Just as you did that night at Ashcroft's, when I touched your breast. You said you had dreamed it, only—"

"The reality was better than the dream," she finished. Despite her awkwardness at discussing such intimate details aloud, she grew warm, moist, and her nipples began to tingle. She shifted her legs, the thighs rubbing each other, and the heated folds of her cleft moved against each other. Delicious friction. "Your hand on my hip," she said, and her voice was husky, too.

"Tell me what it looks like in your mind."

She cleared her throat a little. "We're lying together. Naked. Your hand is around my back, and I can feel your...you, against me. And your other hand slides under the back of my knee, and pulls my leg up against your hip. Then it moves up my leg, and curves around my hip. The heel of your hand and your thumb sweep across the skin just next to the hip..."

She risked a glance at him and saw him swallow, his Adam's apple dipping sharply. The corner of his jaw flexed a little, as if he clenched it. She dropped her gaze down to his crotch, to the folds of denim. Was he aroused? She couldn't quite tell, but it seemed so.

"Yes, I'm hard, Calli. I've been that way since I saw you at the end of the alley."

Her heart gave a giant leap. She looked at his face, but he watched the road again, and the sunglasses and the shadow thrown by the brim of his hat hid even more. "How did you know…?"

"I know you, remember?" he said, with a little smile. "Am I wrong?"

"No," she confessed. What was the point in denying it?

"Ah…you're such a delight. A realist and a romantic in one long, delicious package. You've just let the realist stay in charge for too long. Since the long-departed Robert, I'm guessing." He did spare a swift look at her then. "Did he prey on the romantic in you?"

"I suppose that's what he did do," she said slowly, thinking it through. "He convinced me he loved me, and that we'd be together forever…only he had to get through medical school, first."

"So you moved in with him, left college, supported him and loved him," he finished. "Until he got his internship."

"Yes," she said, very softly.

His hand came down on her thigh and squeezed gently. Empathy. He knew. He had seen it all without explanation.

His hand stayed on her thigh, moving a little. Restless.

She swallowed back her sudden excitement. She wanted him to move his hand higher, and her clit gave out a throb, almost in pleading. She resisted the urge to spread her thighs a little, to give him better access, for that would be too telling...too... *Too what, Calli?* she asked herself. *He knows I want him.*

But before she could give the explicit signal his hand lifted away.

"Why don't you take off your panties?" he asked, his tone conversational.

Her heart gave another almighty leap. Thready, silvery excitement slithered through her. The pounding anticipation made her voice thick and unsteady as she said: "How safe is it here? Can you put the gun aside?"

He seemed to consider that. "Aside, but not too far aside," he said.

"Do it. And take off your jacket too," she told him.

He shot a look at her, an indecipherable glance with the sunglasses obscuring his eyes. "So..." he said slowly. He reached inside the jacket and pulled out the same automatic pistol she had seen in the palace last night, and after checking the safety, slid it onto the shelf below the windscreen. Then he pulled off the hat and threw it into the back of the jeep. His dark red hair, which looked almost black in dim light, ruffled in the wind, the deep red highlights gleaming.

"Sunglasses, too," she insisted.

"Of course," he said, with a little smile. He took them off, folded them up with one hand, and tucked them into his jacket pocket. "Better?" he asked, looking at her. The indigo eyes narrowed a little against the sun.

"Much better," she assured him. "The jacket."

"You'll have to help me."

"With pleasure."

He grinned a little and held out his right arm so she could tug the jacket down over his hand and let him slide his arm out. Then the left arm. He leaned forward, and she pulled the jacket away from him and dropped it into the back of the jeep, over his hat.

His shirt, what looked like a normal short-sleeved business shirt, billowed around his shoulders and chest, moving in the small breeze created by the passage of the jeep. She studied his thick, tanned forearms, the wide wrists, as he held the steering wheel.

"The shirt, now," she said, her heart beat picking up speed.

"You first," he countered.

Fair's fair. She pushed her sandals off with her toes and reached up under the cotton wrap skirt, the same one she had been wearing since the previous evening. She had not had time to do more than throw on a shirt and a light jacket over her clothes when they had packed. With trembling hands she drew her panties down her legs, and dropped them into the back of the jeep. She felt wickedly bare, accessible. Her thighs relaxed, falling open. She breathed heavily now.

"The shirt," she said.

"You do it."

Oh my…

She got up on her knees, anchoring herself with her hand over the back of her seat, and reached over to slip the first button undone. Nick stayed silent, his eyes on the road ahead, as she undid the second, the third, the fourth, fifth. She had reached the waistband of his jeans, now, and she pulled out the shirt, and undid the final button. The shirt flew open like a parachute blossoming in the wind stream, revealing the broad expanse of his chest: tanned skin over well defined muscles, and below the two dark, erect nipples his abdomen rippled, the 'six-pack' clear and hard.

"Oh..." she breathed, and rested her hand on his shoulder, feeling the heat and soft yield of his flesh.

"What?" he asked quietly.

"I knew you were strong, but not this strong."

"You like what you see?"

"Oh, yes." She pulled at the sleeves of his shirt, quickly removing it altogether, leaving him topless. His shoulders had powerful round caps of muscles; his biceps and triceps flexed under the skin with each movement of his hands on the wheel. A scar, pale and faded from age, marked his right shoulder. She touched it.

"Bullet," he said softly.

"A long time ago," she guessed.

"I was fifteen. Later, I will tell you the story. But for now, it's your turn. The shirt."

That was easy. She turned to sit down again.

"No. Stay on your knees. I want to see it all."

She kept her position and fumbled with the buttons one by one, then tugged at the knot of the tails at her waist. Awkwardly, she shrugged her arm out of the sleeve, then changed her grip on the seat so she could remove the other. Abruptly the wind caught it and tugged it out of her hand. The shirt went sailing high up into the air.

Nick laughed a little. "I'll give you another," he promised. "I know how limited your wardrobe must be."

"Fine. You next."

"What do you want me to remove?" he asked, his voice dropping.

She swallowed, the excitement pounding through her making her throat dry.

"Your jeans. Undo them."

He considered that for a moment. "I'll give you three buttons for your top."

Buttons... She didn't think her excitement could lift to a higher level without actual physical contact, but the mental image of him slowly undoing the buttons on his jeans caused her pulse to leap.

"Yes," she breathed.

His hand fell to the top button on his jeans, and flicked it undone. Then it dropped down to the next hidden button on the fly and slipped under the denim to ease the button undone.

She held her breath.

The third button slipped open, and the parted sides of the jeans sagged open, revealing more tanned skin, the ripple of muscles. She couldn't see anything else.

"Your top," he said, very low.

Wickedness, wantonness, threaded through her. She sat down on her heels, still sitting sideways, and slipped the straps of the top from her shoulders, letting the jersey settle down her breasts a little. Nick watched from the corner of his eye, snatching quick glances.

She pulled the top from her skirt and crossed her arms, gathered the top up in her hands. After pausing for a teasing moment, she pulled the top over her head and dropped it into the back with the rest of their clothes. Her nipples, brushed by the currents of cool air, crinkled immediately and she gasped a little.

"Beautiful," Nick said, his voice so distorted with excitement it was almost unrecognizable.

She raised up on her knees once more, deliberately letting her breast rub against his arm, and thrilled when she heard his breath catch. With a daring that seemed a little shocking, but terribly exciting, she leaned against him properly, and ran her hand over his chest, his stomach, lower, to slide inside his jeans, where she felt the silky hardness of his cock, beating against his stomach. Her touch made him groan.

She fumbled with the last of the buttons on his jeans and pushed the denim aside with trembling, impatient hands, and he lifted his hips a little, accommodating her. His cock sprang free. She grasped it, marveling at the thick length, the rounded head, so dark with blood and visibly throbbing. She swept her hand the length of him.

"Ahhh, Calli, I can't..." Nick said desperately. "No, I can't wait." He pulled her hand away from him and braked. With one hand he steered the jeep off to the side of the road as much as he could. As soon as the jeep came to a halt he killed the engine, reached over and picked her up by the waist and brought her across his lap, straddling his hips. Her back was against the steering wheel, pushing her towards him.

His hands on her hips trembled, but he guided her and she felt the blunt tip of his cock against her vagina. She was slippery with moisture, as ready as he.

"So hot..." he muttered, and pulled her down as he thrust upwards into her.

She cried aloud at the penetration, at the thickness of him, the nearly forgotten but impossible to forget sensation of a hard cock inside her and her fierce satisfaction. Nick's eyes closed and she saw the tendons in his neck straining as he pushed into her.

He opened his eyes and licked his lips. "Christ, Calli, I thought I would have more finesse than this, but you are too much."

"I like it that you can't wait, that you can't control yourself enough."

His hands left her hips for a moment to fumble at the button on her skirt, pulling it away, leaving her naked. "I wanted it the other way. I wanted you screaming my name, as you writhed beneath me." He ran his hands over her body, up to her breasts, which he cupped. He stroked the nipples with his thumbs, making her gasp and buck. Her whole body clenched in response.

"I'll have my way yet," he said, "but not this time. This time I've waited too long..." He gripped her hips again, and she felt him lifting her, his cock sliding out of her.

"No!" she said quickly.

He pushed back inside her again. Hard. It made her groan with satisfaction.

His lips moved to her chin, searing a moist path over her chin and down her throat, to the well-defined dip between her breasts, just above the St. Christopher medallion. He licked the skin with a murmur of appreciation.

His hands found her breasts, stroked them. He avoided the nipples, but ran his fingertips around the swell at the bottom of each breast, over the tops. His hands fluttered, driving her mad with the need for him to touch the nipples themselves.

But instead, his tongue flicked out to stroke one nipple, sending a lighting bolt of pleasure through to her clitoris, making her clench around his cock. He gave a little murmur of appreciation and continued his assault on her breast with both hands and his mouth.

He stroked the nipple with his tongue, then took it into his mouth. He teased it with his teeth—little nips and swirls of the tip of his tongue as he sucked the nipple in. Then he transferred his attention to the other nipple, while a hand played with the deserted one, rolling it, stroking it, running his fingers across the tip one after another.

For endless minutes he showered attention upon her breasts. Calli relished the attention, for Robert, the only lover in her life until this moment, had rarely spent so long a time on her enjoyment. The pleasure coursed through her with a strength she'd never experienced before. Her heart raced, her breath came shallow and unsteady. She twitched, writhed, her whole body focused upon what Nick did to her breasts, her nipples. The endless stroking, the swirling caress of his tongue…each touch of her astonishingly sensitive nipples brought her closer to orgasm. She gave a little moan, the sound slipping from her involuntarily. She gasped now, little hitches of breath as the pleasure built and built. Her head fell back against the windscreen, and her eyes closed. She was close, so close…

She felt Nick's hips move under her. His cock throbbed. The muscles of her vagina had been convulsively clenching and relaxing around him. She was slick, hot, and having him inside her while he ravished her breasts pushed her closer to her climax.

"Oh…Nick…!" she breathed. She wriggled against the wheel, the pulsing surge of pleasure building swiftly. "Don't stop…please don't," she gasped.

He kept stroking and sucking on her breasts, while one of his hands brushed down her stomach, between her legs. She caught her breath in anticipation, knowing he intended to stroke her clitoris. The stroke, when it came, was subtle, delicate. Just one—but enough to make her buck hard. Her climax exploded through her, stealing her vision, straining every tendon in her body, but it did not end there. Nick's tongue still stroked her breasts, and his hand again brushed her clitoris, a butterfly touch, and she convulsed again, a fresh wave of electrifying pleasure pulsing through her. And a third time. This time she heard herself cry out, her throat aching from the primordial sound.

"Make it quick," she begged. "Hard."

"It can be nothing else." He gripped her chin and turned her lips to his. He kissed her quickly, then gripped her hips and lifted her again. She felt him throbbing inside her, and knew his orgasm was seconds away. She saw it in his eyes, in every straining muscle in his body…and then he pushed into her again and his body seemed to lock, his hips thrust upwards, and his mouth opened in a soundless cry.

She held still, marveling at the power of his climax, at the raw pleasure of it, as she felt his hot seed spill into her. The sensation was as heady as the climax itself.

His hips lowered back to the seat and he fell back against it, his chest heaving, his hands loose on her hips.

She collapsed against him, utterly spent.

In the silence she heard a bird coo, somewhere in the trees above them.

Chapter Eleven

After a moment or two, she became aware that his hands still stroked her, this time along her back, following her spine and over the curve of her buttocks. His touch didn't stimulate, but the very pleasant sensation kept her nerves tingling.

Where their flesh touched, she felt heat between them and a hint of sweat. Her cheek rested against the back of the seat, right next to his head. Her arm felt like a deadweight, but she lifted it enough to cup his cheek and moved her head a little to kiss the other one.

"Thank you," she murmured.

"I believe I should be saying that," he returned. His voice sounded raw. He moved so he could turn his head to look at her. This close, his indigo eyes mesmerized her. "We should get off the open road," he said.

"We should," she agreed. "But I think all my bones just melted."

He gave her a wicked smile. "I thought mine had, but it's just temporary." He moved his hips a little, and Calli felt his cock move inside her. She caught her breath at the exquisite sensation. He was thick, hard. "See?" he added.

"You would prefer to drive even in this condition?" she asked.

"I would not have stopped in the first place except that you pushed all good sense from my mind." He grasped her hips and helped her rise from his lap. When he slid out of her, she couldn't help the little noise of disappointment she made. He swiveled and placed her in the passenger seat, showing some of the strength promised by his physique. Then he carefully eased his jeans back over his hips and did up a few of the buttons on the fly. Not all of them, for even the few he tackled strained to cover his erection. The tip of his cock showed just above the fastened button.

"Besides," he added, as he started the engine and backed up the jeep a little so he could regain the thin strip of tarmac, "The longer I am in this state, the longer I can pleasure you."

She could feel herself blushing, even though she knew it was ridiculous to react that way. She was also acutely aware of her nakedness. "This is a busy road?" she asked, lifting her voice over the wind a little.

"Pretty busy."

"How do you pass anyone here?"

"Carefully."

"Slowly, then?"

"Very slowly."

She shivered, suddenly nervous. "I should get dressed then."

"We'll be turning off in a minute and then the only people we'll see are farmers. Stay that way. I like the view."

She studied him. With his bare chest, and the jeans barely covering his cock, he was virtually as naked as she. "Undo the rest of the buttons, though," she said.

His smile was slow and seemed filled with delight at her command. "As my lady pleases," he said, and reached down to release the buttons once more. His cock sprang up straight.

"That's better," she said.

"Hang on," he warned, and turned the jeep into a rough gravel track that seemed to head straight up the side of the mountain. But after the initial sharp descent the gradient decreased, although they continued to climb, rounding a dozen hairpin bends along the way.

"How long?" she asked.

"Impatient?"

"Yes."

"Minutes, that is all."

The jeep climbed a little more, then the road evened out and arrowed straight into the trees, which grew as a shady tunnel over the top of them. Two hundred yards further on, the trees thinned out, and Calli saw the jagged peak of a mountain directly ahead. Nick turned the car to the right, towards the mountainside, and then she saw the house.

It was a low thing of glass and thick black timbers, bereft of any adobe, and nestled into the trees. Behind the flat roof of the house, she saw a waterfall cascading down the side of the mountain.

Nick pulled the jeep up sharply at the front of the house, where inlaid cement flagstones led right to the front door. He climbed out and strode around to Calli's side of the car and opened the door. She caught only a glimpse of the unfastened jeans barely hanging onto his hips before he scooped her up and carried her towards the house.

"Now who's impatient?" she asked, looping her arms around his neck.

"Damned right," he growled. He pushed the door open with his shoulder—apparently he saw no need to lock his house up—and then they were inside. A green oasis with raw terracotta tiles, and large walls of glass. She saw nothing else before Nick pushed through another door and lay her on a wooden surface. A table.

He moved around the side of the table, and bent over and kissed her, while his hand ran across her body, smoothing its way across her ribs, her stomach, to the small patch of hair over her mound.

"You are so beautiful." His lips brushed against hers as he spoke. "I could explore for a decade and not tire of it."

She groaned into his mouth as his fingers slipped inside her and stroked up and down the length of her vagina. The irregular shape of his fingers moving against her felt far different than his cock. His thumb caressed her clitoris, again the delicate touch that electrified her, yet at the same time made her desperate for more.

"Nick...you...I want you inside me."

"So do I," he muttered, and moved around to the end of the table. She heard the whisper of denim and knew he'd stripped off the jeans. He lifted her legs over his arms.

"Hurry," she said.

"Shhh...Such a moment should always be savored." He paused with the head of his cock right against her vagina, pushing a little, but not quite entering her.

Calli's heart trip-hammered with anticipation. "Nick...!"

He slid into her slowly, so slowly that she thought she might die of frustration and need. But finally he rested, buried to the hilt. The heat and size of him made her groan. "Good," she said thickly.

"Very good," he agreed.

He pulled out of her at the same unhurried speed.

"You're killing me!" she cried.

"You have to feel it, with every inch of your body. Focus on every little sensation, every quiver, every spasm...delight in it." Despite his words, he sounded strained, under pressure. And his eyes were half-closed, watching her. A bead of sweat formed at his temple.

He pulled all the way out of her, then just as slowly pushed back in again. This time Calli tried to extend her senses, to focus on the sensations. She could feel the ridged head sliding into her, opening her up, the touch of his pelvis against her clit when he was fully inside her. She could hear his breathing, rough, ragged.

And despite the slow, slow thrusting her heart was thundering, her body pulsing, every nerve end a sensitive livewire triggered by the slightest touch. Her head rolled to one side and her eyes closed as Nick pushed into her once again. He paused, and she could feel him quivering against her, the little thrusts and spasms that said he neared the limits of his control, too. That pushed her excitement up a notch, and she swallowed on a throat gone dry.

"I can't...stand it," she pleaded, her own hips moving restlessly, her legs quivering against his arms.

The rate of his thrusting picked up speed. A little. But after a moment he swore, his voice hoarse. "Again, too much," he gasped, and suddenly he thrust hard, quick, his fingers digging into her thighs, the tendons in his neck showing the strain.

The pressure against her swollen and sensitive clit, the quick little pushes, sent tremors of pleasure bursting through her already quivering, desperate body. Her climax slipped over her like a hot wave of electrical light. While her heart and mind hung suspended, every nerve flared in response.

Nick slammed into her one last time with a choked cry. She felt him pulsing inside her and the hot spill of semen, even as her own body clenched around him in orgasmic pleasure. For a moment he sagged over her. He lowered her legs, then propped himself up with one trembling arm and gave a deep, gusty sigh.

Then he slid his arms under her shoulders and lifted her up off the table. Calli twined her legs around his hips instinctively, as he turned around. He surprised her by sitting on the table, and settling her legs around him, so that she sat in his lap. His cock was still buried inside her.

Nick stared into her eyes, and brushed tendrils of hair from her face. "Welcome to my home," he said gravely.

She gave a tiny laugh. "That was quite a welcome."

He smiled. "It is a better welcome than most Vistarians extend, and we are known for our warmth and generosity."

She wrapped her arms around his neck. "Thank you," she said.

He still stared, still studied her. The humor faded from his face. "If I considered myself a superstitious man, I would say you have bewitched me, Calli Munro."

"You are not superstitious?"

"I thought I was a realist, but you are teaching me otherwise," he said. Before she could respond, or even begin to untangle his meaning, he hugged her, very tightly, holding still for a breathless moment. She closed her eyes and enjoyed his scent and the heat of his flesh against her cheek and chest. It was a moment she knew would stay with her forever.

Then he let her go, and lifted her up and onto her feet. She sighed a little at the loss.

He stood and picked up her hands. "Realism says we must eat soon. And I'm sure you would sell your soul for a shower, yes?"

"Yes!"

He tugged on her hand. "Come."

She followed him from the dining room, more than happy to watch his tight tanned buttocks work as he walked. His wide shoulders were complemented by a lean, muscled back and tight waist and hips, and she marveled again that his clothes had hidden such delightful details so well. He did not have the distorted size and shape of a dedicated body builder, but clearly he worked his body hard.

The house seemed to be made almost entirely of glass between the black pillars and beams. Natural light flooded the house, warming the tiles underfoot, and feeding the tubs of plants everywhere.

Nick led her into a spacious bedroom. A thick Persian carpet covered the tiles, and a low bed with a dark green quilt nestled right up against the glass wall. The floor of the room lay at the same level as the ground outside, making the room effectively part of the glade.

On the other side of the room another door was set in the only solid part of the wall. Nick crossed over to open it. A bathroom, she realized, when she stepped inside. But a bathroom with a difference. The wall with the door held the essential plumbing and equipment—sink, toilet, cabinetry. Opaque glass blocks that had a showerhead and taps inset, made up the far half of the wall to the left. The rest of the room, all of it, had clear glass walls. And thundering down the mountainside, directly outside the wall, was the waterfall she had seen earlier. It was close enough that a little spray landed against the wall from the impact of the water at the bottom of the stream.

Nick turned on the shower, then tested the water.

"It's…stunning," Calli finally managed.

He glanced over his shoulder at her. "I never get tired of it," he admitted. "I built the house with this one room in mind, and the rest just formed around it." He flicked water at her. "Nice and warm," he promised.

She undid the leather thong that held her braid and shook out her hair.

Nick watched with narrowed eyes. She had seen that expression before, when she had done something that jolted him into a new perspective, that gave him pause for thought.

"God, you look…wild, with your hair loose," he said. "Why do you tie it up all the time?"

"At home, it's to keep a professional image. Here…it's because of the color." She stepped into the spray of water and gasped at the heavenly warmth.

Nick frowned.

"Too much realism for you, Nick?" she asked.

His frown deepened. "For this moment, yes," he said. He stepped into the water and wrapped his arms around her, and she felt his head rest against hers. He sighed a little.

"I'm sorry," she said softly. "I shouldn't have been so…practical."

"No, don't apologize. I'm being a fool, trying to leave the world at the door."

"You can do that," she assured him. "We can be what we want, no limits, just for this short while, and the rest of the world can go hang. Then after, you can get on with your life, and I'll be safely back in the States."

"Okay," he said heavily.

* * * * *

Nick left the bathroom before her, explaining that he wanted to start dinner. When she emerged later, wrapped in a big bath sheet, she found her backpack sitting on the end of the bed. Next to it lay a white glossy box.

She walked over to the bed and rummaged through her backpack, but couldn't help glancing at the box curiously.

"I saw it in my dreams," Nick said from behind her.

She whirled. He wore blue jeans and a black sweater. Unlike the business suits and shirts she had seen him until now, the sweater emphasized his shoulders. "What was in your dreams?"

"The…garment in that box. I saw you wearing it in my dream, and the next day — the very next day, I saw it in a window. It would please me if you wore it."

She opened the box and saw layers of powder blue chiffon, silk. "I thought you weren't superstitious?"

"Ah, but I *am* a liar." And he turned and left the room as silently as he had arrived.

Calli dropped her towel and pulled the garment out of the box. It seemed to be a cross between a nightdress and evening gown—she couldn't decide which. The chiffon lay over the top of the silk. Carefully, she worked her hips into the dress, for it fit tightly and the dress had neither zipper nor fasteners. It was cut on the cross, which gave her the room she needed to get it over her hips. The bias cut also meant it clung. Everywhere. The top was a little looser, and when she slid the straps over her shoulders, the fabric between her breasts hung very low, enough so that it revealed the swell of her breasts. The back of the dress resembled the black lace one she had worn, skimming down in a deep vee to finish just above her buttocks. The straps of the dress crossed her back and attached just above the end of the vee.

The hem of the dress brushed her toes, which Calli found remarkable, for any floor length gown she bought always had to have the hem dropped. Had he seen to that already? She picked up the hem and saw the faint signs of previous stitching.

Yes, someone had extended the hem.

She walked over to the mirror, and discovered the silk was so fine and delicate that every rub and swish of the chiffon against it transferred to her skin. As she was naked beneath the dress, her nipples and mons were delicately brushed. The subtle touch was undeniably arousing.

She looked in the mirror. The dress outlined her hips, her abdomen, and seemed to reveal more of her breasts than it covered. She felt more naked in the dress than she did wearing no clothes at all.

* * * * *

Calli made her way back to the dining room, figuring the kitchen had to be somewhere nearby.

As she had been dressing, evening had fallen, and it was already quite dark outside the glass walls. The dining room was empty. The door on the other side of the room led to the kitchen, also empty. But good cooking smells came from the stove, and a chopping board, a knife and vegetable scraps lay on the counter.

She went back through the dining area and down some steps, where she found Nick looking out through the glass towards the trees. Far to the left, she could see the luminous spray of the waterfall.

"Stop there," he said, his voice low.

She stopped, realizing he had seen her reflection in the glass. "Why?" she asked.

"Straight ahead, next to the tree in front of me. See it?"

She tried to look through the glass. "No."

"Next to your right hand, the light switch. Turn off the lights."

She touched the switch, and the lights all shut off. She blinked, trying to adjust to the darkness. It wasn't that dark after all. The sky was inky blue, but not yet full dark, and the moon was still quite full even though it waned now.

She looked at the tree Nick had singled out.

"See the eyes?" he asked.

She looked again. Something moved a little. Eyes reflected the moonlight back at her. She caught her breath.

"What is it?" she asked.

"Jaguar," Nick murmured. "I think she lives around here."

"She's beautiful."

The cat, reassured by the absence of light, prowled out from under the tree into the full moonlight. Her black coat shone with indigo highlights that reminded Calli, eerily, of Nick's eyes. The cat turned her head, sniffing, scouting her way ahead. She gave a low growl, almost a clearing of the throat. Even through the glass, Calli could hear the deep rumble.

Then, as if she had reached a decision, the jaguar leapt over the root by her feet and padded away towards the stream.

Nick turned to face Calli. His gaze slowly traveled up and down her body, and he drew in a deep breath, let it out.

"It will do?" Calli asked. She nervously brushed at the chiffon.

"You have an aura, standing there in the moonlight. You are glowing." He moved across the room to come up behind her where she stood on the edge of the carpet. "Did you plan this?" he whispered, his hands sliding around her waist.

"Plan what?"

"To stand before the glass so I could come up behind you. Do you know how I have replayed that moment at Ashcroft's over and over in my mind? How I have wished it might have ended another way?"

His hands slid up the dress to cup her breasts, and she drew in her breath sharply. "It was one hand," she whispered.

"Ah, yes." He slipped his hand beneath the silk and cupped her breast. She swallowed hard as low-key pleasure spurted through her, and her tender clitoris awakened. In response, her shoulders straightened and she thrust the breast he held more firmly into his hand. The movement made her ass cheeks press back into him. His thumb rubbed the nipple. In the glass she saw his black shadow by her shoulder, the dark arm across her chest. He spread his other hand out across her abdomen, splayed flat, possessive.

"More…" Her voice came out weak.

"Mmmm…" He kissed the nape of her neck, making her shiver. "Much more. But later. For now, I must eat real food."

Her stomach grumbled a little and he laughed. "And so must you."

* * * * *

They were eating—a spicy casserole with a salad and lots of crusty rolls and pale pats of butter—when a quiet tap-tap-tap sounded.

Calli frowned, unsure what she'd heard, but Nick lifted his head and cocked it, his whole body straightened in the chair, alert.

"What is it?" she asked.

"Shhh…"

The tap-tap-tap sounded again.

Nick stood and picked up the jacket slung over the back of the chair next to him, and put it on. "Stay there," he instructed, as he might a child. He left the room, using the archway that lead directly to the front door—the one he had carried her through only a few hours earlier.

Her body tingled at the memory.

She continued to eat, her hunger still not fully satisfied. It felt like she had not eaten for a month. But she also listened, trying to hear what Nick did. As she scooped up another spoonful of the casserole, she heard what she assumed must be the front door open and close. Then nothing.

Several minutes later, the door opened and closed again, and a few seconds after that, Nick returned. He lowered himself into the chair, and picked up his fork again. "I apologize for the interruption," he said.

A small chill touched her spine. "What's wrong? What has happened?" she asked.

"Nothing. Why?"

"You haven't taken off your jacket."

He paused, looking at her as though he weighed his answer, then continued to tear into a bun. "It is somewhat cool outside. I want to be warm again before I remove it."

He had the same look as when she had seen him in the cell. The cool, assessing look that missed nothing, and gave nothing away. His voice was the same rough burr she remembered from the first time they had met. The low, controlled voice of one used to command.

"Bullshit," she said. "You're not Nick. You're... *el leopardo*. Whoever it is at the door has made you start thinking of Vistaria, your affairs."

He put the bun down and slid his hand into his pocket. She had seen him make that habitual motion dozens of times and realized he was reaching for the St. Christopher medallion. It was an instinctive and secret reach for comfort, for reassurance. *El rojo leopardo* could not afford to reveal weakness or hesitancy, after all.

But he had placed the medallion around her neck. He had given it to reassure her.

Yes, Nick was thinking of his country now. The reach for the medal told her that.

Nick withdrew his hand. "You're very perceptive."

"Tell me."

"I would not burden you with my petty concerns."

"When they trouble you so much, they're my concern too. "

He reached out and laid his hand over hers. It felt cool. "I'm sorry," he said. "I thought that here we would be insulated from such things."

"We are, mostly. I don't pretend to know what your day-to-day life must be like, Nick, but I know it must be a good deal busier and carry far more interruptions than the six hours I've experienced so far."

"That is true."

"If this is a petty concern then share it with me, and let me help it go away for a while."

He shook his head. "I would not sully your thoughts with even a petty Vistarian concern. I would prefer you remain aloof from it all. Untouched."

"That's impossible, Nick. I got involved when some asshole decided to blow up a party full of young army officers."

He smiled a little. "Is that your oblique way of reminding me what Vistaria owes you?"

"Hell, no. I just want to help."

He sighed and ran his fingers through his hair. "A local farmer came here a little while ago. He said there are signs of soldiers in the area. Footprints in muddy fields, flocks of birds disturbed. Small signs."

"Isn't the rebel camp somewhere around here?"

"No one really knows where it is. Besides, they keep on the move. The area where we think they are is many miles south of us. On the other side of Pascuallita."

"So who are the soldiers?"

"It may not be soldiers. Or rebels. It could simply be someone wearing army-issue boots. There's a healthy trade in used and surplus army equipment in Vistaria."

"But someone is hanging around here, right?"

"The signs stopped appearing two days ago."

"But you're still worried."

"The worry is passing," he assured her.

"And you're also a liar," she said softly.

Chapter Twelve

They did not make love that night. The farmer's visit had popped the bubble of isolation. Calli sensed the demands of Nick's world reaching for him, calling for his attention. She did not intrude on his thoughts. She took care not to give any hint of her need for him, although she badly wanted him to take her in his arms. She needed him to assure her it would all go away, that he could be hers for just a little longer.

When the moon hung high and small, he picked up her hand and helped her to her feet. "I'm sorry, Calli. This is not what I intended."

"It's all right," she assured him. "I'd be a stupid fool to think it could all stay away for as long as I wanted."

"I shared that wish," he said. "So, let's see what we can do to preserve what we can, hmm? A night of sleep, that might be free of dreams now I have tasted the reality, could be enough to push the ghouls away. And I will make it up to you tomorrow, I promise."

So they had gone to bed.

Nick held her beneath the green quilt, and kissed her cheek, but she knew his mind was elsewhere. He was preoccupied.

Sometime later Callie woke to a soft growling by her head. She jerked fully awake, trying to orient herself. She lay on one side, her back up against Nick. He hand his arm over her waist, his hand cupped her breast.

The low growl came again, very close. She stiffened.

"It's all right," Nick said by her ear. "She's just nosing around outside. It's a restless night for everyone."

"You can't sleep still?"

"I've slept, but sleeping seems such a waste of time while I have you in my arms. I feel I must make the most of the time I have."

"You've been watching me?" She turned so that she could see his face.

"And thinking, yes."

She turned all the way over to face him. The moonlight illuminated his face a little, but his eyes hid in shadows.

"Black thoughts," she whispered.

He was silent for a long moment. "Yes," he said at last, his voice soft.

"Tell me," she coaxed.

He sighed. "My deepest fear is that Vistaria will be lost. The balance here is so precarious, and there are so many wrong turns that even one of us could make. And that one turn might be all that is needed to destroy the balance."

"Is that why you worry so much?"

"It's not worry that distracts me." He touched her cheek. "If it was simply worry, then I would not have been such a poor host this evening."

"What is it, then?"

"The weighing of decisions, of actions. Each and every one of them must be considered. I must constantly guess, estimate and measure the possible consequences."

"I was one of those decisions, wasn't I?"

Again, he sighed deeply. "Bringing you here was purely selfish, Calli. I gave it no more thought beyond what *I* wanted, with no thought of the risks."

"And tonight, you've started to wonder what the price will be for that indulgence," she finished.

"A little, yes." His hand came down to rest on her waist, heavy and warm. "But only a little. I will not regret this, and neither should you."

She could hear a tightness in his voice. Fear? "You don't sound very convincing, Nick," she said softly.

His silence seemed to throb between them, speaking of the tension within him.

Calli brushed her fingers across his cheek and kissed him very gently. She meant it simply as a sign of empathy, affection, but it gave her an idea. She sat up and turned to face him on her knees. She pushed at his shoulder, coaxing him to lie on his back. It was like pushing on a rock-face, but he lay down anyway. "What...?" he began.

"Shhh..." She leaned over him and kissed him, tasting his tongue and lips. She let her lips travel where they wanted over his face, his neck. She trailed them up to his ears, and down again to his collarbones. His skin tasted salty, soft to her tongue and lips. His hand rested on her thigh and she paused. "You don't have to do anything," she said softly. "This is for you."

"Calli—"

"It's all right. I know you're troubled. Let me help ease your mind. Relax. Let it happen, Nick."

"But..."

She put her finger on his lips, silencing him. "If you're about to tell me it's your role to give pleasure then you can remain silent. You have given me so much pleasure this day, Nick. It's my turn. Let me do this. Let me give pleasure."

His lips moved against her finger. A kiss. "As you wish," he murmured.

She smiled a little and bent down to kiss him, letting her breast rest against his chest. "Yes, this is my wish," she said, and kissed her way back down to his collarbones again.

She did not speak the rest of her thought aloud: that it was only a part of her wish. The wish she hid from him had been growing all evening, shaping itself in her mind.

She spent long minutes tasting and stroking the flesh over his shoulders and chest, teasing the taut flat discs of his nipples with her fingernails, listening to his breathing and the small little sounds of reaction to what she did. She slid her tongue down the shallow indentation of his abdomen, swirled around his navel, and smiled at the catch of his breath.

"You're enjoying this, after all," she teased.

"It is...very intense, to simply accept it," he murmured, his voice thick.

Calli nudged his thighs apart and settled herself between them. His engorged cock lay on his stomach. When she leaned over and blew on it gently, she heard his breath hitch yet again. What a delicious sound.

Carefully avoiding the throbbing shaft, she nibbled and tasted his skin all around. She felt the taut plane of muscles beneath bunch and quiver in reaction. For a long moment she paused, her mouth hovering over his cock, then moved on to taste along the length of his thigh to the inside of his knee. Then over to the other knee, and a slow crawl back up to his hip, along the inner thigh...

Bringing her back to his cock, which strained and jerked. She slid her fingertip along its length, to linger for a moment on the very tip, and it reared. Quickly, she gripped him in her hand, and Nick gasped. "Hot," he muttered.

"Hotter still," Calli responded, and bent to take him into her mouth, her lips sliding over the thick head.

His hips lifted beneath her and he gave a groan that seemed to be pulled from deep, deep within him.

She swirled her tongue around the ridge of skin edging the head of his cock, and drew him into her mouth, deeper, then let him slide out. From the corner of her eye she saw Nick's hand claw at the sheet beside her knee. Encouraged, she kept up the motion, exploring the shape and size of him with her tongue, teeth and lips, her hand cupping his testicles, gently caressing them.

He panted now, clenching and releasing his butt, his muscles spasming. Almost...almost...

At the last minute she pulled away, licking her lips for the taste of him.

Nick gave a growl of frustration and she lifted her head to watch him fall back onto the mattress, the tension released a little when he realized she would not allow him to climax.

It was a small little power she had, yet one that would bring immense pleasure if she wielded it properly.

To be able to provide such pleasure gave her joy. It touched again the secret wish building inside her. To always provide such pleasure to Nick...what a joy that would be.

She bent to take his throbbing cock back into her mouth again, and Nick gave a small hiss of what sounded like pain.

"Ah, Calli, to tease so isn't ladylike," he said, his voice husky.

She sucked at him, letting her tongue answer him.

He arched against her, his hips bucking hard. She could feel the tension building in him again, his thighs tightening. As soon as she suspected his climax approached, she halted for the necessary few moments for it to subside, before taking him back into her mouth.

She repeated the rise and fall cycle over and over again, until Nick writhed beneath her, panting and quivering at her slightest touch. His hands clenched at the sheets, mauling them. The tendons of his neck and arms corded under the skin, and his whole body quivered, drum tight. Sweat glistened at his temples, reflecting the last of the moonlight.

She slithered up the length of his body, letting her breasts brush against him, and kissed his dry lips. "Shall I let you come?" she whispered.

"Ah, please…!" he croaked.

She settled her knees on either side of his hips and lowered herself until she felt his cock pushing against her slit.

She heard Nick's breathing pause at the touch.

She sank down, taking him into her, feeling the hot thickness of his shaft spread her apart. He gasped unsteadily.

She paused, savoring the feel of him deep inside her. She stored the impression in her memory. She would need such memories later, when she returned home.

Slowly she drew up, up, to a point close to where he would slip out of her, then slid down, down, back slowly down again.

Nick gave a low animal growl, deep in his throat. His hands gripped her thighs. Squeezed. The hard pressure of his fingers on her thighs and the flex of muscles in his strong wrists and forearms drove her.

Slowly, she rose and fell upon him again, lingeringly. And his fingers tightened, dug a little deeper.

She read from his quivering, bow-taut body and the erratic breathing that she had brought him to the outer limits of his control. Only a little more pressure would break that control. She watched, alert for the smallest sign, as she maintained the long, slow stroking of his cock, clenching her muscles around him to intensify the sensation for him.

Then the moment arrived.

"Calli…!" he said in a desperate cry.

She gathered herself, increasing the speed of her movements, bringing on the climax that could no longer be held back, and Nick thrust against her, once, twice, a third time, and then a fourth, the longest, and his cock jerked inside her.

He fell back on the mattress once more, completely spent, his body as limp as a stringless puppet.

She settled onto the bed beside him, and when she judged by his breathing that he was calm once more, she eased him over on to his side and pulled the cover up over both of them.

"Sleep," she whispered, and kissed his temple.

She snuggled up behind him, threading her arm under his and over his torso, to rest her hand against his heart. With sleep-slowed movements, he picked up her hand, kissed her fingers. She sensed he intended to return her hand to where it had been resting, but the motion was not completed. His hand grew heavy, and dropped away from hers.

He slept.

* * * * *

A little later, she roused from a light slumber. Nick still lay beside her, but now he rested on his back. She couldn't tell if he slept or not. At her movement, his hand sought hers and brought it to his lips. This time he completed the act properly, and she felt his lips touch the back of her hand squarely.

"That's very Vistarian," she said. "I like it."

"I am Vistarian…despite my coloring. Sometimes I think I am more Vistarian than my brother who has a fondness for all things American." All the tension and worry had left his voice. He simply observed a fact now.

"You mean José? Does he know about me, Nick? Does anyone?"

"Duardo and Minerva know."

"My uncle suspects, I think."

"A great many people have suspicions. Suspicion comes easily to Vistarians these days. Truth…is in short supply."

"You say you love Vistaria, but you speak of the people so…callously sometimes."

"Love always includes acceptance of weaknesses, haven't you noticed? I know Vistaria and her people too well, love them too much, to ignore their weaknesses.

Besides, in a country this small where everyone knows just a little of everyone else's affairs, suspicion sprouts far too easily."

"Cynic."

"Realist," he corrected.

"I'm the realist. You're the…" She cast about for the right word, but the only one that came to her was *savior*, and she fell silent, confused. Sadness touched her. His talk of love had released her awareness, opened her perceptions. She couldn't speak, couldn't find the strength to pretend nothing had changed in the last second or two.

"I'm the what?" he asked. "The doomed romantic?"

She found her voice. "Now you're being cynical again," she teased, pleased with the casual tone that emerged. It hid her momentary confusion, and the welling sorrow. "Try to sleep."

"*Para usted, mi dama fuerte, yo trataré,*" he murmured.

She turned away from him and lay her head back on her pillow, letting the sadness that had washed over her dominate her mind.

For only now she recognized *she* was the doomed romantic. Yes, Nick had coaxed that side of her to re-bud and bloom, but now she faced an awful truth: she loved him. And within the next day, or perhaps two if she was very lucky, he would say goodbye and they would never again lie like this together.

La dama fuerte, she mentally whispered. *Hold it together, Calli. Walk away with your chin up. That's the bargain you struck, and now you must live with it.*

Chapter Thirteen

The next day she found out what a slice farm was.

"There's not enough flat ground in Vistaria for bulk crops," Nick told her as they walked around the property. "And there's not enough people to make the farming of a single product viable. Vistarian farmers figured out for themselves how to farm vertically, centuries before the scientists started talking about micro-climates."

He pointed to the top of the mountain. "Up that high, you get frosts. So they plant cherries, apple trees. A little further down, apricots, plums and some of the hardy vegetables." He pointed to the steep slopes a little lower than where they stood. "There, you will get coffee and lots of herbs. Down further still, pineapples, many more vegetables and spices."

Each time he pointed, Calli picked out a terraced piece of land laid out in orderly gardens.

Nick brought his two index fingers together up in the air and traced an elongated triangle against the mountain in front of him. "There is not as much land at the top to share around, and more is given at the bottom for the crops that need room. So you end up with a piece of the mountain that looks like a slice of pie."

"A slice farm," Calli murmured admiringly. Simple concept, but very practical. Practicality seemed to be the flipside characteristic of Vistarians, offsetting a love of drama and passion in their leisure pursuits and entertainments—like the Luna festival.

Nick's house sat on one of the middle terraces of the old farms he had acquired. They climbed to the upper levels to investigate the source of the waterfall — or at least, Calli wanted to investigate despite Nick's assurance there was nothing to see.

By the time they climbed up the winding path for two terraces, she was breathing raggedly, and her thigh and calf muscles screamed for mercy. "My god, the farmers must be just bouncing with good health climbing these things every day!"

"They're very tough," Nick said, grinning. He breathed easily.

"Hell, and I thought I was fit!"

"You're not at sea level, here."

"Montana isn't at sea level, either. And you're not even breaking sweat. I hate you."

Nick laughed. "Army training here is very rigorous, very thorough."

"You're not in the army."

"No, but I've taken every training camp, every course, every discipline they have." He headed for the rocks that hid the top of the waterfall from sight.

"Why would you do that?" Calli asked, scrambling to catch up with him despite the burn in her quadriceps.

"So that every soldier knows the training they receive is a valuable thing, that civilians, even their leaders, desire it."

She watched him climbing from rock to rock. "I bet you were good at it, too," she called out.

He paused and waited for her to catch up with him. "I had to be. The brother of the president of the nation could not fail. It would not inspire confidence in the Escobedos."

No wonder soldiers like Duardo admired him and officers obeyed his orders without question. He had proven himself to them over and over again.

She reached the rock he stood on, and he turned her towards the north. "See, the stream comes from much further up the mountainside. You can trace it back to its source but from here the only way to do that would be to actually walk alongside the water."

"That's bad?"

"Water takes the steepest course down a mountain side." He grinned. "Basic mountain climbing training. Don't follow water courses. Up or down."

"Well, my knees are ready to give in, so I'll actually listen to you this time. Can I see the waterfall itself?"

"I can do a little better than that," Nick promised her. "Let's go back down." He helped her back down the rocks, and they headed towards the house. This time Calli *knew* her legs would give out on her. She'd never thought going *down* a mountain would need more muscles and control than going up. It seemed like she was leaning backwards, every muscle clenched so gravity wouldn't pull her down the slope.

By the time they reached the level of the house, she was sweating freely, and her breath came just as raggedly as when she had made the ascent. Nick, of course, still strolled as if it were a Sunday in the park.

The idea of falling, cool water seemed delightful, but when they arrived at the foot of the falls, Nick picked up her hand and tugged it. "This way," he said.

"But...!"

"Trust me," he said. He led her around the bend of the creek, where it hugged the stone outcropping and bent north. The path sloped down to follow the course of the water.

"*More* down hill? And following water?" she complained.

Nick looked over his shoulder. "It's worth it," he assured her.

There were rough stairs cut into the bank, which took some of the strain from her legs. She cautiously followed Nick down the steps. A dozen of the broad steps curved around the base of the waterfall, down to a flat, round apron of close-cut turf edged by rocks and unkempt grasses and bushes on the right. On the left, the rushing stream tumbled over a ten-foot drop of rounded rocks into a deep, large pool. The water was crystal clear.

The pool had no edge.

Calli looked at it sparkling in the sunlight. There was no bank. She realized she was looking at the edge of another small waterfall. The water slid over the edge without ripple or spray, creating the illusion that the water simply held itself there.

"Can I go wading?" Calli asked, swallowing with her dry throat, her toes tingling as she imagined the touch of the cool water.

"It's much deeper than you think."

"You swim in it?"

"Often." He smiled a little. "Though it's not good for laps."

"Don't care," Calli said, pushing off her sandals. She reached for her top, and paused, for Nick still watched her. "You're coming in, aren't you?"

"In a minute," he promised.

She hesitated, wondering why he waited. "Why in a minute?" she asked.

He seemed almost awkward as he answered. "I like watching how you move. Especially when you're not hidden behind cloth."

There were a dozen things he might have said that would have been more intimate—that he liked her naked body, that he liked watching a woman taking off her clothes—and none of them would have made her blush as deeply as his simple, unexpected answer did. She couldn't think of a response that wouldn't sound totally dumb, so she took off her top instead. With another small hesitation, she undid her skirt and slipped out of it. She was naked beneath, and wondered if he would realize she was bare beneath her clothes to give him easier access.

Her cheeks burning even more, she stepped into the pool. Her foot didn't meet the bottom when she thought she would, and she plunged in up to her neck. She gave a little gasping shriek and struggled to find her footing.

"Oh god, it's ice water!" she cried.

"Of course. It comes from a glacier."

She glared at him. "*That's* what you were waiting for," she accused him.

"Yes. But the rest of it was true, I swear," he said, laughing.

She splashed at him. "Come and join me," she said softly.

His laughter was replaced by a smoldering, knowing expression. He understood.

He stripped quickly, and walked to the edge. His cock hardened, and Calli felt excitement spill through her. She let herself float in the water, studying him as he paused on the brink. He was tanned all over, proof that he had not lied about swimming here often. His well-muscled body gleamed with a slight sweat from his exertion climbing the slopes. The sweat emphasized each dip and swell. His eyes were a mesmerizing dark blue in the direct light.

She shivered, from more than the chill of the water.

Nick stepped off the edge, judging his footfall, so that he stood merely thigh deep, then pushed off into a glide through the water towards her. The water lapped about his shoulders as he stopped in front of her. He pulled her into his arms, and she came willingly. Though he was warm, in contrast to the water, his erection had not withstood the temperature—as she discovered when her hips bumped against his. One of his hands slid around her ass and held her against him.

"*Gracias*, Calli," he said.

"For what?"

"For forcing the issue. For insisting on this…little pocket of time. For knowing I didn't have the courage to take it for myself."

Tears gathered in her eyes, the pressure of them almost painful. She was glad they stood in water, and her face was wet, hiding them.

She had to swallow hard to clear her throat enough to talk. The need to speak her heart and mind pushed at her. Her time with Nick was nearly over. Even Nick sensed the end drew near, and now wanted to tie up loose ends, finish things off properly.

"I was just being selfish," she said at last, and her voice was thick with the dammed tears. She hoped he'd assume it was the touch of his hands and body that was the cause of her thick voice. And before she gave away more than she intended or her voice or face betrayed her, she lifted herself up and kissed him. His arms tightened, holding her in place, as his mouth opened beneath her lips. She thrust her tongue inside, tasting him, exploring the even edges of his teeth, the sweetness of his mouth. She licked his damp cheek, then slid up to his ear and flicked her tongue around the curves and ridges before probing inside.

He groaned, and his hand on her buttock pressed her harder against him.

The little movement sent water that hadn't been warmed by their bodies eddying around them, and she shivered suddenly, almost violently.

Nick chuckled, and the sound reverberated against her.

"We need to get you warm," he said.

"I'm all for that," she agreed. "But it's so nice here."

"I'm not taking you far," he said. He stepped back, bringing her with him through the water. He was heading for the little cascade on the far edge of the pool. Now she was closer she could see why the spill seemed so clear and soundless.

The edge was made almost entirely of a flat, wide rock, roughly four feet across. The water slithered noiselessly across the flat top, and rippled down the sloping side to the streambed two feet below.

The floor of the pool gradually sloped up to that rock. When they reached it, the water was only hip deep. Calli was more than grateful for the touch of the sun and the ambient warmth.

Nick helped her sit on the rock, which had been worn smooth from eons of water eroding the surface. He knelt and spread her legs on either side of his hips. She sat with her back to the lawn, her legs damming the flow of the stream. Water gently pushed at her left hip and thigh, a cool caress that passed around her buttocks. She shivered again.

"Let me do something about that shiver," Nick murmured, kissing her. His lips moved down to her throat, then quickly to her breasts. He took a nipple into his mouth and the heat, the stroking of his tongue and the touch of his teeth ripped a groan from her. She propped herself up on her hands, her head falling back, as he lapped at each nipple in turn. Her thighs fell apart even further, in offering.

In response, his mouth drifted down to her stomach, and the muscles there quivered and clenched in response to the nibbling and the licking and stroking of his velvet-hot tongue and lips, and the caress of damp locks of hair across her skin.

She shivered again.

Nick lifted his head and smiled a little. "I'd have thought, coming from Montana, you would be used to cold."

"Cold, perhaps, but not the touch of wet hair on my skin."

His smile broadened. "Ah…a shiver of delight. Then I must do it again."

He tugged at her wrists, lifting them up, then pushed at her shoulders. She lay down on the rock, her heart jumping, for she knew what he intended. She had never had a man's mouth on her pussy before, but before she could even begin to worry he kissed the taut plane of flesh along her hipbone, the hugely sensitive areas that had her breath catching in her throat and all thought scattering.

His tongue slid in between her folds and stroked her clitoris, and she cried out with shock and pleasure. The soft, subtle stroking sent warm waves of ecstasy through her. Her body clenched in desperate little spasms as he flicked her clit and thrust his tongue inside her vagina, before sliding his tongue the length of her slit, to swirl around her clitoris once more. Her chest hitched in small panting breaths, thrusting her breasts up.

His hand fluttered between her thighs as he began to stroke her clitoris with his tongue — steady, firm strokes.

"Aaaahhhh!" The exclamation emerged as a groan. "Nick…!"

The softness of the caresses, the delicate, hot touch, was like nothing she had ever felt before. Her concentration narrowed down to what Nick was doing to her with his tongue. All other sensations were shut out while she reveled in the pool of pleasure swirling through and around her. She could feel her orgasm building up, the quick final rush starting to sweep through her.

Then Nick pushed his fingers inside her, sliding along the walls of her vagina, caressing. The good hard pressure of his hand combined with the relentless silvery delight of his tongue was too much. She climaxed with a cry that strained her throat, and tightened every sinew in her body. Powerful waves of excitement surged through her as he kept up the assault on her clitoris, and she shuddered and quivered with each pulse.

Before her body could relax and her nerves flatten, before she could ease back onto the rock beneath her, Nick's hands were on her thighs, lifting her hips. She felt his cock pushing at her vagina as it throbbed still from the climax. He slid into her, his hands on her hips anchoring her for the deep thrust, and groaned. "Ah, god, the heat!"

Her muscles clenched around him and he gasped.

"The touch of raw silk," he murmured, and thrust again.

Her exquisitely sensitive clitoris sent a little quiver through her at the touch of his pelvis as he pushed deep into her.

"Yes…" Nick murmured, his thrusts speeding up. He wrapped her legs around his waist.

The little kisses and caresses of his pelvis against her clitoris were like the touch of his lips and tongue. She clenched around him even tighter. The feel of his thick, hot cock sliding inside her was delicious.

She felt many delicate touches at her breast and looked down. Nick's hand hovered just above. He had dipped it in the pool and let the water drip onto her breast. The heavy water drops rolling off her superheated skin were like small caresses. Her nipples tightened almost painfully at the sensation. When the last drop fell, he grasped her breast and rubbed the tip of her nipple with his thumb.

She let her head fall back again, her eyes closing, as the multiple sensations built up. Unbelievably, she could feel another climax begin. Her body locked up tight, as the heart-stopping moment stretched out — a high musical note held endlessly, the single note ebbing and pulsing with a life of its own.

"Yes...!" Nick said, his voice thick. In a little uncontrolled jerk he came with a deep groan, as her climax shattered and passed. His hot, thick semen filled her as he pulsed and quivered deep within her. When the climax passed he kept still, locked against her, until at last he gave a shuddering sigh and relaxed. His cock slipped out of her.

"Ohh..." she protested at the withdrawal.

"Wanton one," he teased, and climbed onto the rock. He lay beside her, his thigh resting over her hip and between her thighs in an agreeably possessive way. He propped his head up on one arm and smiled down at her.

"I will never look at this pool the same way again," he told her, and kissed her forehead.

She gave a little laugh. "You flatter me. I am not the first woman you have brought here," she said with certainty.

He frowned a little. "There has never been a woman I wanted to see this, to bring here, to my...place. Until now."

She stared at him. "You're not joking, are you?"

His hand, the one that did not prop up his head, had dropped to her waist and now idly stroked her skin, making the quiescent nerves twitch a little. "No joke," he assured her. "You are the only one who has ever found her way this far into my life."

This time she had no disguise and no time to hide her reaction. The tears sprang without warning and rolled down the sides of her face. She did not dare say a word, for she knew she could not speak without sobbing. She did not wipe at her tears for she didn't want to draw attention to them, either.

Nick wiped them for her. "Such courage," he said. "You've dared much, haven't you? Yet you're overwhelmed by the mention of your own achievements. You think so little of yourself, Calli. I wish I could teach you to see better, to see how I see you."

"I'm sorry," she said at last when she thought she could speak and not betray herself further. "I didn't mean to spoil the mood."

"Nothing you could do could spoil the mood right now." His hand came down to rest on her again, this time over her breast. "This is the time I like best, when the physical needs have been filled and raise their demands no more. Then, in the moments after it's just emotion. Feelings."

"Happy ones, they should be," Calli said, and gave a little sniff.

"Happy, sad, regretful, it doesn't matter what they are, for they are nearly always *truthful* ones, and that is when you learn the most, if you watch for them."

She put her arms around his neck and drew him down to kiss him, but did not answer. Above all else, she could not afford to let him see the truth.

* * * * *

They lingered by the pool until the sun was high.

Hunger drove them indoors in search of food. By the time the meal was prepared they were so ravenous, they did not bother with the dining room. They ate standing up in the kitchen.

After her last mouthful, Calli burped.

Nick laughed. "For such an uncivilized meal, only a very civilized espresso will finish it off properly."

"God yes, coffee!" Calli agreed.

Right by her elbow, a phone rang. It was so unexpected she jumped sideways and turned to look at the counter, her heart hammering. Only Nick's jacket lay there.

He reached past her to pick up the jacket and pull out a cell phone from the inside pocket. His eyes had narrowed, as if he thought hard, his mind miles away. In Lozano Colinas, she realized. That's where his mind was.

"*¿Sí?*" he answered. His frown deepened. Then he took a deep breath, the kind a person takes when they've received bad news. His eyes closed briefly.

Calli's heart began to beat so hard it hurt. It wasn't just the knowledge that this call marked the end of her time here. It was also the news that Nick now heard, that made him look suddenly much older than his thirty-eight years.

"*Gracias,*" he murmured, and ended the call. He dropped the phone onto the jacket and leaned against the counter, his head low.

Calli rested her hand on his shoulder, unsure of whether he wanted comfort or not, but unable to stand by and watch him suffer alone. But she didn't prompt him to tell her about the call. He would, or he would not. She had no right to insist on anything, anymore. So she simply shared her empathy in silence, knowing it was one of the last things she could do for Nicolás Escobedo before he went back to his life and the country he loved.

Finally, he straightened and picked up her hand and held it in both of his. His sigh gusted out. "Fighting has broken out at the mine on Las Piedras. Two Vistarians were killed."

"Fighting? Who is fighting who?"

"Vistarians," he said simply. His expression was bleak. "It's the rebels, Calli. They've come down from the mountains, much sooner than we thought they would, and not where we guessed they would strike first." He pushed his hands through his still damp hair. "I have to go."

"Of course you do."

"You must return to the city, you and Minnie. And you must wait for your uncle to return from the mine. The army has standing orders to evacuate any foreign nationals, especially any Americans, as a first priority if violence breaks out. They will get him and his people out and back to the city. You must stay with him until we know if this is the beginning of a sustained attack or if it's simply a skirmish."

"Do you think it's just a skirmish?"

"I don't know," he said. "The timing, the location, go against all good strategic thinking, so there's hope this is a single moment we are dealing with. But until we know for certain I want you in the city, and safe."

"Is the city safe?"

"Safer than Pascuallita." He picked up the cell phone again, and paused to think, then punched in a number. The conversation, all in Spanish, seemed to be with two people for after a short time he paused, then his manner became more abrupt, brusque. He closed the phone with a snap, and thrust it into the jacket. He put the jacket on.

"Pack your things, Calli. Quickly. We must leave at once."

Chapter Fourteen

Calli had heard that Pascuallita was four hours away from the city by road. Duardo managed the trip in three hours and fifteen minutes—a jolting, panic-inducing race that wiped any lingering emotions from Calli's mind.

Nick had driven her to Pascuallita, and on the northern edges of the town, Duardo and Minnie stood waiting, Minnie's bags at their feet. The phone call Nick had made just before they'd left his house had been to Duardo, she realized, setting up this meeting.

Duardo wore civilian clothes still, but he had his jacket folded up and tucked under his arm. From the way he carried it, Calli knew he had a gun inside the folds.

Without word or greeting, he threw Minnie's bags into the back of the jeep with Calli's. He hoisted Minnie up into the back, too, and Nick showed Calli how to unfold the two small jump seats there. She climbed into the back with Minnie, while Duardo settled behind the wheel of the jeep and Nick moved over to the passenger seat. Their unspoken coordination made it look like they read each other's minds.

The sensation was eerie. Calli knew she watched two men well-trained in military arts going about their grim business. Because they were so well grounded in their work, no communication was needed.

Duardo put the jeep into gear and took off, wheels spinning. Calli grabbed at the rails surrounding the back of the jeep. Minnie gripped her other hand, and held on as the jeep roared and rocketed down hills towards the coast.

They turned onto sealed road after ten minutes, and ten minutes after that Calli saw the striped boom gates that marked the entrance to the army base. Duardo's base.

Duardo pulled up right next to the boom gates, the red and white timber almost brushing Nick's shirt sleeve. There came a shout from the gatehouse, and a soldier wearing fatigues and a machine gun slung over his shoulder ran over to lean on the boom gate and lift it up.

Nick got out of the jeep and moved up to Calli's side.

"Minnie, come to the front," Duardo said.

Nick glanced around, checking for observers. With an acute disappointment, she realized that there would be no kiss goodbye, no soft words that would linger and give her comfort later.

"Go," she said. "There's no need to say anything."

His hand, hidden by his body, rested over hers on the edge of the jeep. "I would have it otherwise. I would have asked for more time."

She took a breath and swallowed, pushing back the childish wail building in her. "Really?" she breathed.

His eyes locked onto hers, holding her gaze. "Really," he said softly.

"*Señor,*" Duardo said quietly. A warning.

Nick dropped his hand from hers. "Duardo is a very good driver, and he knows the road to the city well. He will get you back to the city. Stay there. If the fighting continues, then you must leave the country as soon as you can. Promise me you will do this, if it comes."

"I promise."

He nodded, and turned away. The soldier with the machine gun escorted him down the access road. Another jeep, this one painted in camouflage greens, waited with two soldiers in the front. The little back door hung open and waiting for Nick. The engine turned over.

He didn't look back.

Calli took another deep, controlled breath to fill the corners of her lungs and clenched her jaw.

"Do up your seatbelt," Duardo said quietly to Minnie, who buckled her belt immediately. Duardo turned his head towards Calli. "You must hold tight, yes?"

"Yes," she said, her voice thick with unshed tears.

He nodded, and dropped the jeep into gear and drove off, accelerating hard.

The wind whipped her hair into her eyes and gave a legitimate reason for the tears that spilled down her cheeks.

* * * * *

Duardo pulled up at the apartment as the sun slid low on the horizon, and they climbed from the jeep stiffly. Everything sounded muffled, for the wind and the roar of the jeep engine had desensitized Calli's hearing. Duardo had not been content to sit behind slower traffic for longer than necessary and at times had slipped between the vehicle he was overtaking and oncoming cars with only inches to spare. He was very familiar with the road and knew exactly how much he could risk.

Once, he braked hard and stayed behind a wagon pulled by a 50s vintage Oldsmobile, even though the road ahead seemed clear. He'd shaken his head. "Too much traffic. More than usual. The news has scared them."

A few seconds later she saw why he had not tried to pass the wagon. The road turned into a very sharp left turn, moving further down the valley, even though the terrain continued to slope smoothly along the cliff side, deceiving the eye. As soon as they had made the turn, he dropped the jeep into a lower gear and passed the truck with a snarl of the engine.

That had been one of the few times he had spoken, and the only time he had shared his thoughts.

Now he carried Minnie's luggage into the apartment, pausing while Calli unlocked the door. Minnie stayed at the jeep. Inside, Beryl stuggled to her feet from the sofa, her eyes widening when she saw Duardo. He merely nodded at her and went back to the jeep.

Calli followed him. "You're going back to Pascuallita?"

"Yes."

"You're not fit yet," Minnie said, but she said it in a way that told Calli she knew that her argument would not sway him.

He shrugged. "I will be needed, anyway."

"I know." She sighed.

He pulled Minnie to him, his hand in her hair, and Calli looked away, moved and embarrassed by the tenderness on his face as he looked down at her. She walked away a little, until she could no longer hear the words in their whispers. When the jeep engine started up again, she turned back.

Minnie stood with her arms wrapped around herself, as if she were cold, watching as Duardo turned the jeep around. He waved, and drove away and as he turned the bend down the road, he waved again.

Then he was gone.

Minnie dropped her head, and Calli moved to put her arm around her shoulders, knowing she wanted comfort. But she did not cry, and she didn't seem sad. She looked at Calli with a crooked smile. "He's off to be a soldier. That's what Duardo is. And I love him for it."

* * * * *

Three hours later, Joshua arrived home, dusty and wrinkled, but calm. He took a moment to assure Beryl he was unharmed, as she fluttered around him. "They got us off the island first. Then they went back to help the Vistarians," he said. "Escobedo said no harm would come to Americans, but I never thought they would sacrifice their own countrymen in order to live up to that promise."

"Sacrifice?" Beryl said sharply.

"Two died in the first attack," he said. "And two others, later. They were civilians, working the trucks. Hell, I knew one of them." And he sighed.

Calli thought of Duardo, itching to get back to base, but detouring by more than six hours to make sure he got her and Minnie home safely. And Nick, whose first thought and first action had been to arrange that safe return. "Vistarians are an honorable race. They have a strength of character you don't see very often these days."

"No, by God," Joshua agreed. He plucked at his sweaty shirt. "I need a shower, and then we must make plans and phone calls."

* * * * *

For the next twenty-four hours, they all remained in the apartment, with the television on the government station. The only other commercial Vistarian channel had abruptly gone off the air at midnight, with no announcement or warning. The government channel faithfully reported the news as it developed, the anchorwoman speaking in subdued, sedate tones. Joshua, whose Spanish was stronger than anyone's, translated when asked, but mostly he sat staring at the screen, his brow wrinkled, deep in thought.

They tried CNN, available on cable, but the States had not yet taken any notice of events in Vistaria, and the major headlines focused on the President's tour of a Detroit automobile factory. The Acapulco station merely mentioned that there had been a riot at the Garrido silver mine in Vistaria, but spent twice the air time reporting on José Escobedo's daughter, Carmen, vacationing in Acapulco for the summer holidays, energetically celebrating her graduation from Yale law school with various American and Mexican celebrities who gravitated to the seaside resort every summer.

Joshua, when he was not watching the television, kept them busy.

"You have to pack three ways," he explained. "Until we know if this is the start of a full out revolution, or just a fart in a bottle, we have to assume the worse. So you pack one small bag with every essential you can't live without if you're crossing national borders — passport and other ID, money, Tampax."

"Dad!" Minnie gasped, genuinely shocked.

He shook his finger at her. "I mean it, Minerva. When you're on the run, you won't be able to stop at the nearest 7-11 for that sort of stuff if you need it. So take it with you.

But pack as lightly as you can because you're going to be carrying it with you all the way. The second packing is a second pack or a suitcase that you can carry with less essential stuff. Clothes, toiletries, anything that you could live without if you and the suitcase part ways."

"And the third pack?" Calli asked.

"Everything else," he said simply. "Suitcases, boxes and crates, ready to ship. It may never leave Vistaria, but we should be ready if the opportunity occurs."

* * * * *

On the second night they went to bed early, all of them tired from packing and worrying. Calli hoped she would sleep well. She had a feeling that sleep would be in short supply for a while.

The fighting at the silver mine had ceased at sunset, and the rebels had receded back into the forest and disappeared. The army had combed the island and established that the raid had been launched from boats in the channel, and the rebels had made their escape that way, too. They had gone back to their mountain hideouts.

That evening the government station had shown footage of the president visiting the silver mine, and the families of the victims of the raid. José Escobedo had reassured Vistarians repeatedly that the raid could not possibly presage further violence, because the rebels had achieved their apparent aim — the mine was shut down. In addition, the Americans had fled the main island and now considered leaving the country. Joshua had translated the rest with a sour look. *The loss of American know-how would mean the end of the mine, and the doom of Vistaria's prosperity for the near future. When Vistarians felt the pinch of a tight economy once more they would do well to remember this sad day...*

"Politicians," he said, making it sound like a curse. "Even Escobedo cannot resist scoring points from this thing."

But Calli's attention was skewered by the grainy outside-broadcast images on the screen. Nicolás Escobedo had also been on the island and walked amongst the small crowd of people that followed the president about the island. She watched as the camera panned past him, as he turned to speak to someone by his shoulder.

Her heart stirred, almost painfully. She forced herself to look away from the television. Minnie watched her but said nothing.

Joshua turned the television off after that. "I think it might be all right," he declared, rubbing his hand through his hair, scrubbing at it. "I think it was a one-off thing, like the president said. Nothing else has happened for over twenty-four hours. We might be okay."

"You mean I packed for no reason?" Minnie protested.

"No. Leave everything packed. From now on, we operate under yellow alert. You girls grew up watching Star Trek so you know what I mean. Assume the worst, prepare for the worst, but don't fire the guns off just yet. Speaking of which...do either of you have pistols at all?"

"Oh my," Beryl murmured.

"I hadn't thought about that sort of stuff," Minnie said slowly. "I know Duardo had one, but..."

Calli shook her head. "No. Neither of us have guns," she told Joshua.

"Good. Now listen hard to this. Do *not* even think about acquiring arms. Of any sort. Not even for self-protection. This is *not* the States, and I'm damn sure that the rebels are not outfitted with uniforms or even quasi-military clothes. Which means that if you are found with a gun in your possession you instantly stop being a civilian and become a rebel. Calli, you've been in prison, so you know that justice here isn't like you'd get back home. Do you think they're going to throw you in jail and give you a trial if you're found with guns on you?"

Calli shivered. "You've made your point," she said quietly.

"Good. Minnie, promise me."

"I promise," she said, subdued.

Not long after that they went to bed, their moods pensive. No one felt like talking or watching vapid entertainment. The Vistarian commercial station still broadcast static.

Calli climbed into bed and hugged herself, wishing it were Nick's arms around her. Wishing he would whisper reassurances into her ear—that his deep voice would croon soothingly that everything would be all right, that of course the rebels would not try anything while he were there, and he would protect her if they did...

But Nick was busy working to preserve his country, and if he thought of her at all, it was probably with a small, reminiscing smile for a risky indulgence.

With a deep sigh she closed her eyes and tried to sleep, knowing sleep would come no easier to her than it had on other nights in Vistaria...and she was awoken by frantic banging on her bedroom door, and sat up, blinking away sleep. It was daylight.

"What is it?" she called.

"The door is locked! Calli!" Minnie's voice.

Calli crawled out of bed and unlocked the door, and Minnie pushed into the room waving a newspaper. "Calli...omigod, Calli." She gripped Calli's wrist and shook it, waving the paper at her. Her eyes were wide, her face pale.

"What?" Calli asked, her heart skittering. War? Assassination? Nick!

She grabbed the paper and held it out so she could look at the front page. It had to be a front page headline.

It was.

Calli sat down suddenly on the office chair that Joshua had never got around to moving out of the room, her knees draining of strength. She let the paper fall on her knees, staring at the headlines, and the terrible picture beneath.

The headline was in fifty point font. Screaming.

The picture. Her gaze was pulled back to the picture. It was grainy—a telephoto lens at the least, and the actual picture enlarged to enhance the details. The black and white didn't help either. She had seen dozens of "candid" shots like this on the covers of cheap tabloids at supermarket checkouts.

She'd just never expected to see herself in one of them.

It was her and Nick, at the pond, laying on the rock together. His hand rested on her breast, and he was leaning over her, his features quite clear. Her hair, the long blonde hair, fanned out over the edge of the rock, smoothed out by the water. Her leg, the one closest to the camera, was bent, hiding more than it revealed—a minor mercy, all in all.

Minnie crouched next to her. "Calli, my God, they'll crucify Nick," she whispered.

Calli swallowed hard. She couldn't cry, she couldn't feel anything. The enormity of the disaster was too much to take in all at once. Any vestige of shame she might have felt at being plastered across a national newspaper buck naked was swept away by the weight of the consequences to come.

"Calli?" Minnie prompted.

She looked at the headline. *¡Escobedo ama Americanos más!*

"*¿Ama?*" she asked Minnie.

"Um…love. Loves."

"Escobedo loves Americans more," Calli translated and sighed. "They've already crucified him."

"Calli. Page two," Minnie prompted.

Calli turned the page. Inside, they had another photo; a bad copy of her passport photo. Perhaps even a photocopy taken at the station that first night? But they had her name, *Callida Munro*, emblazoned below the photo in bold, perfectly clear Times Roman.

"Oh God," she whispered.

Minnie squeezed her wrist. "I think you need to leave Vistaria," she said, very gently.

She shut the paper, to look at the front page again. The photo. She sighed.

"My geeky cousin Calli…the sultry seductress. Who'd have thought?"

"It's not funny," Calli said tiredly.

"No, not at all. In fact I could easily feel a little envious, even," Minnie confessed. She pointed to the photo. "I look at that and see blazing passion, even love. The body language." She shook her head. "I always knew Nicolás Escobedo wanted you very much. I just hadn't realized..."

"What?"

"You match each other," she said simply.

Calli folded up the newspaper and gave it to Minnie. "Thanks, but the rest of Vistaria is only going to see that their trusted president's brother is out screwing American women...so how trustworthy are the Escobedos going to look to them now?" She got up.

"What are you going to do?"

"I'm going to get dressed."

"You're not going to phone him?"

"Hell, no." Calli gave a little laugh. "I'm going to stay as far away from Nick as geography lets me. I think...you're right. I need to leave Vistaria as soon as I can."

"I'll let Dad know. You're going to have to sneak into the airport." Minnie left, shutting the door behind her.

Calli threw on jeans and a tee shirt, the same clothing she had worn when she landed here. It seemed fitting she would leave that way. She had already packed, thanks to Joshua's insistence, and the two small packs sat next to her bed.

"*Calli! Get down here!*" Joshua yelled at the top of his lungs.

Calli flew down the three steps to the living room proper and hurried over to where he stood in front of the television, another copy of the newspaper in his fist. He turned up the volume.

Minnie sat on the sofa behind him, chewing her lip.

The screen showed the circular iron fencing around the legislative building, the big fountain in the foreground and just off to one side. The cameraman had to be standing with one foot in the water, because the camera was elevated over the back of the heads of the crowd of people standing before the closed gates. They were shouting, waving newspapers, chanting, brandishing their fists. There was screaming and people were shaking the ironwork on the gates.

Behind the barrier, five soldiers stood, their machine guns slung over their shoulders and held down by their sides — non-threatening, but there to be used if needed. Their faces were inscrutable. They wore hard helmets and jungle fatigues.

The voice-over narration was fast, breathy. Almost panicked.

"This is *serious*," Minnie said as Calli sat on the sofa next to her.

"What are they saying, Josh?" Calli asked.

"No military action has taken place yet. But it's making the crowds more frantic. And the size of the crowd is growing. There are more people coming onto the avenue all the time."

The picture changed, showing a view taken from a moving vehicle of the Avenue of Nations. The many people there jostled each other off the pavements onto the road itself. They looked angry.

"They're talking about you," Joshua said softly, and cocked his head to listen more carefully. "And Americans in general."

Abruptly, he turned the television off.

"What...?" Minnie said.

Joshua sat on the other sofa next to his wife and took her hand. "This is the government station, but they're asking the same damn fool questions as the crappy newspaper. Why are Americans influencing the government? Why is it allowed to happen?"

Calli hugged her knees to her chest. "Nick isn't the government," she said softly, hopelessly.

"And you're just an excuse," Joshua shot back. "A damned good one as it happens. But that's all they ever needed, Calli. One lousy excuse." He pushed his hand through his hair. "Well, they have that now."

She hid her face against her knees. "I have to leave the country," she said.

"Good idea, but with civil disturbances, the first things that get shut down are the transport systems. They won't let you out." Joshua smiled grimly. "You have to stay and face the music, my girl."

"I wasn't running away for my sake," she said swiftly.

"I know. But they won't see it that way."

"Who won't?"

"The rebels. The people. Vistarians. If this rioting keeps up then the rebels will have a ready-made army at their disposal. It will take very little to turn these angry, roused civilian Vistarians to the rebels' cause now." He shook his finger at her. "So you are going to stay put on that sofa and not make a squeak, and we'll hold our breath and hope this passes too." He grimaced. "And let's hope we don't wake up to worse news tomorrow."

Calli shuddered. "It could hardly get any worse."

Chapter Fifteen

At eight o'clock that night, the news did turn worse. The television station, which had been broadcasting re-runs all day, broke into an X-Files episode and cut to a studio, where an anchorman began speaking swiftly, holding a sheet of notes in his hand. The paper visibly trembled.

"*Jesus Maria*," Calli breathed. The Spanish was too fast for her to pick up more than the odd word.

Minnie sucked in a quick breath. "Pascuallita! They're talking about Pascuallita."

Calli bounced off the sofa and ran to knock on Joshua's door.

He came out, wrapping a gown around him, barefoot and wild of hair, and went straight to the television and sat on the sofa.

Minnie had her hand to her mouth, her eyes wide. She looked at her father, stricken.

He began to nod. "Fighting in the mountains. Just south of Pascuallita. Many rebels. Some deaths. The army is there…" He looked at Calli. "This is it," he added softly. "The army has engaged the rebels in combat. This is the birth of a revolution."

Minnie gave a choked sound. Tears streamed down her face.

Joshua patted her knee. "I'm sure he'll be okay, your captain," he said awkwardly. Then he groped for the remote control. "Wait. They just said something."

He changed the channel to the local commercial station. Surprisingly, it was on the air. A woman sat behind a panel, speaking into the camera, and even without a translator, Calli had no trouble interpreting the intent of her message. She radiated fierce joy—fervor, even. "That's why the station went off the air until now," she said. "They've sold out to the rebels."

Joshua nodded. "Yes, it would seem so. We'll get nothing but propaganda from them." He listened for a moment. "They've coordinated their announcement with the rebel action, it appears. She is claiming a grand victory for the rebels in Pascuallita. They've taken over the town, she says, and will march towards the capital, drawing true Vistarians to their ranks as they go." He grimaced and changed channels. "It reminds me far too much of the Communist crap I had to listen to in Vietnam."

Calli sat on the arm of the sofa, and rubbed Minnie's shoulder. Minnie sat very still, big tears rolling down her cheeks. She made no move to wipe them away.

"They've taken Pascuallita," she whispered.

Joshua looked at her sharply, his eyes narrowing. "It's bullshit, honey. Pure bullshit. The TV station doesn't have any more idea about what's happening up there than the government station, and the government station certainly isn't saying the army took a beating."

He listened for a while to the government channel, and his face grew grave. Finally, he shut the TV off with a snap and threw the remote onto the coffee table. "Ah, truth is always in short supply in wartime anyway," he said, and got to his feet. "We can't do anything tonight. But tomorrow, we have to figure out a way to leave the country. Steal a boat, if we have to. It's only a few hours to

Acapulco from here." He ruffled his hair again. "Get some sleep," he advised.

When his bedroom door had shut, Minnie reached for the remote and turned the TV back on again. Calli sat beside her, and stared at the television, wishing she could understand Spanish better.

For most of the night they stayed on the sofa, Minnie picking out as much of the Spanish as she could, and Calli trying hard to pick up words. Names. Gradually, after much repetition, the events began to take shape in her mind.

The attack on the silver mine had been a ruse. A way to scare the Americans and force the government's strongest ally to take cover. It also had been a means of drawing army personnel to the south of the main island, away from Pascuallita, where the first main attack had always been planned to take place.

The attack, when it came, appeared to have been somewhat hasty. The announcers and the experts they interviewed speculated that the rebels had not anticipated the riots in the city, but had taken advantage of the government's distraction. Their attack had been, so far, merciless and strong. The army had scurried to meet the challenge, moving through the mountains with less speed and agility than the rebels who had trained and lived there for months.

"They *are* taking a beating," Minnie whispered.

Calli fell into a light doze somewhere in the small hours of the morning, unable to concentrate any more on the endless run of Spanish, when her heart was so heavy and she was so afraid of what the day ahead might bring. She jerked awake when a hand tapped her shoulder. She sat up from her sprawl across the arm of the sofa and blinked up at Joshua. Through the window behind him she saw the lightening sky. The day approached.

"Where's Minnie?" he asked.

She looked around. The sofa was empty.

"Her bed hasn't been slept in," Joshua said.

A chilled clamped her chest. Wordlessly she hurried into Minnie's bedroom and looked for the pack of essentials Minnie had prepared. It was gone.

"What are you looking for?" Joshua asked, from the door.

"Her pack has gone. So have her hiking boots." A flat black Vistarian hat sat on the bed—Minnie had brought it back from Pascuallita.

"Pascuallita," Calli said, and turned to Joshua. "I think...she's gone to Pascuallita."

He opened his mouth a little. "The car!" he said, and whirled away.

Calli followed him out to the front door of the apartment where he stood looking at the empty spread of cement where the little car normally sat.

"*Why*?" he said at last.

"Duardo's there."

"Yes, but why *now*? Why not last night when the rebellion started? Why not yesterday? What made her do it now?"

Calli went back to the television and sat down again. "Something must have happened," she said softly as Joshua sat next to her.

She didn't try to translate for herself—she knew she was too tired to manage it. The last time she had looked at the clock before she had fallen asleep it had been about three-thirty in the morning. Now the clock said four-forty, so she had dozed for less than an hour. Whatever had pushed Minnie out the door would still be fresh, would still be news.

"Oh, hell," Joshua said. "Pascuallita has fallen."

"So fast?"

"The rebels are fresh, this was planned, and Pascuallita was not prepared. Not braced for it. Now the rebels have a stronghold they can operate from. Of course, that would have been their plan from the beginning." He dropped his head into his hands like a man broken. "Minnie is driving straight into their headquarters."

Calli stood up.

"Where are you going?"

"I don't...I don't know. I have to stop her somehow. Head her off."

"How?" Joshua said, but the tiniest thread of hope colored in his voice.

She hesitated, knowing she couldn't tell Joshua the idea that had struck her.

"You can't go to Nicolás Escobedo," Joshua said. "I hope you're not thinking of it."

"He knows Duardo's family. He knows the area. No one else I know has that advantage."

"You're an American. Worse. You're *that* American woman, Calli. They'll tear you to pieces out there." But the hope flared stronger in his voice. He *wanted* her to convince him she could do this.

Calli rested her hand on his shoulder. "It's not quite dawn yet. The streets will be quiet. I just have to make it to the legislative building. That will be enough, I think."

"And if he's not in the city?"

"I don't know, Uncle Josh! All I can do is try, right? Hell, maybe I'll steal a car instead of a boat and drive up there myself."

"No, you mustn't do that!" he said quickly, which was the reaction she had anticipated.

"So, I'll try the legislative building instead," she said, knowing it would sound the more reasonable of the two.

Josh dropped his head back into his hands. "Okay. Okay," he said, his voice hoarse.

Calli patted his shoulder again and went and changed. Black trousers, which would meld into what remained of the night, a white tee shirt and a waist-length dark green windbreaker. Then she braided her hair tightly, dropped the end of the braid inside the jacket and put on the flat black hat that had been sitting on Minnie's bed. She suspected it was Duardo's, perhaps a gift to her, because it was much too large even for Calli's head. Her thick braid kept it firmly on her head and low over her eyes.

Josh's brows rose when she emerged from the bedroom carrying her backpack.

"From a distance they may take me for a Vistarian. At least I won't be identified as that American woman straight away, and that will be all the time I need, I think." She glanced out the window. "It's getting lighter. I must go."

He stood up. "If I were thirty years younger…"

"But you're not. Don't flay yourself with guilt, Uncle Josh. Minnie will be okay. I said I'd watch out for her, didn't I? And you must take care of Beryl."

"I won't try to leave today. We'll stay here, so you've got somewhere to head back to when you find her."

"All right." Calli hesitated, then added, "If we don't arrive back here by tomorrow, you should go. We'll find our own way over to Mexico."

He hugged her tightly. "You've surprised me a number of times since you arrived here, Calli, but never more so than just now. You've got more strength in you than I have and for that I'm grateful."

"Let's hope it's enough," she said with a smile and patted his cheek. "Because right now, I'm terrified."

"Running helps," he said, without a glimmer of a smile. He nodded towards the door. "Go."

Calli left, shutting the door quietly so that no one would be wakened and ducked in between the walls into the little alleyway of stairs—a short cut for pedestrians. The stairs plunged straight down the hill rather than following the painful hairpin bends of the road. Her heart raced and her legs trembled—she was very afraid of what she must do now. After a couple of minutes of climbing down the steps, the trembling in her legs disappeared as the muscles warmed up, but her heart continued to flutter unhappily.

When she reached the flatter street at the bottom of the hill she looked to the left, north, where the heart of the city and the main street that connected with the Avenue of Nations lay. The street was deserted, dusty.

Running helps, Joshua had said.

She broke into a slow jog, heading for the city, her backpack bouncing against her back, the fresh morning air bathing her face. After a few minutes she realized her uncle was right. Her fear had evaporated, the unsteady beat of her heart settling into a steady, strong rhythm in response to her body's need for oxygen. And jogging ate up the distance quickly. Soon she had reached the densely populated inner city core.

Many more people had appeared, gathering in small groups, whispering together. She dropped down to a swift walk, not willing to draw attention to herself. Ahead she could see the big main square, the same square she had been watching those long hours when she had been held in the cell. Now she knew the square was the center of the city, and the Avenue of Nations ran off the square, heading west towards the mountains.

She turned into the wide avenue and hurried along the sidewalk, keeping a watchful eye on the people around her and trying to gaze ahead towards the fountain to see how many lingered there, but she could not see it yet.

There were more people on the avenue, but still they did not seem to be very threatening. Perhaps the outbreak of rebellion in the north had stolen the rioters' thunder and they had given up. The small hope buoyed her somewhat as she climbed the short slope to the top of the avenue and saw for the first time the fountain there. If any rioters remained, they would surely be in front of the gates.

There were people sleeping there.

That was her first surprise. They lay on the concrete about the base of the fountain, their belongings beside them. They were homeless, perhaps refugees from Pascuallita or the new little township that had sprung up around the Garrido mine. The government had not had time to organize refugee camps yet.

It occurred to her with a start that these people were as scared about the outbreak of war in the north as she and Minnie had been, sitting on the sofa together last night, whispering their speculations to each other.

They hadn't spilled out onto the road, yet, so Calli stepped out onto the tarmac, heading straight for the gate. She wondered if she would draw attention to herself by doing so, but there was no other way to reach the gates without stepping over bodies and pushing through groups, and she would most certainly be recognized if she did that.

The road ran straight to the entrance. Calli moved around a couple of groups there, up to the closed gates, and gripped the iron bars with a small sense of relief. Soldiers still stood at parade rest behind the gates. Five of them, machine guns still hanging at their sides. She peered at all of them through the ironwork, hoping she might recognize one of them, but they were all strangers.

She recalled the phrases she had been rehearsing, and called to them, her voice low.

"*¡Oye, los Soldados! ¿Cualquiera de usted sabe a Capitán Peña Y Santos?*"

Not a flicker of reaction. Well, they had no idea who she was, after all. They'd want convincing that she knew Duardo, too. So she dredged up more shaky Spanish. "*El está basado en Pascuallita. ¿Sabe usted Duardo Peña Y Santos?*"

This time one of the soldiers looked at her, although he didn't move his head to do so. His gaze slid sideways, but he gave no other indication that he had heard her.

Encouraged, she moved further along the gate to stand directly in front of him.

"*Debo hablar con su capitán. Por favor dejame entrar,*" she pleaded.

She heard a babble of Spanish behind her, close behind, and she carefully turned her head to look over her shoulder, hiding as much of her features with her shoulder as she could. A couple of men, unshaved, dirty, bleary-eyed, watched her.

She turned back to the fence, shook it a little and nodded her head towards the men behind her, hoping the soldier had seen them, too.

"*¡Ella no es Vistariana!*" came the cry from behind her. She had been spotted as a foreigner.

She looked directly at the soldier in front of her. "*¿Conoce usted el leopardo rojo?*" she said quickly.

A hand came down on her shoulder and yanked at her, to make her turn around. She clung to the iron with a desperate grip. "*¿Ha oído usted de la dama fuerte? ¡Déjame entrar por favor! ¡Déjame entrar!*"

"You, American!" The angry cry came from behind her. Another hand grabbed her arm. She couldn't afford to look behind her and let them see her fair features. And she couldn't let go of the fence, or they would pull her into the middle of the crowd her gut told her was forming behind her. There were more mutters and murmurs around her now. She tried to keep her gaze locked on the soldier's eyes, even as her grip on the fence began to weaken and her fingers uncurl.

Someone knocked the hat off her head, and her blonde hair was revealed.

"*¡Ella no es Vistariana! ¡Ella no es Vistariana!*" The angry cry echoed along the street. Taken up by one, then another, then another, it became a chant, a rally cry.

Callie swallowed and her throat clicked, completely dry. The fury in their chant...they were ready to boil over into violence.

The soldier next to the one she had been addressing took his machine gun in hand and cocked it. Abruptly, so did the other four soldiers, his action prompting them. The sound of cold metal slapping into place quelled the crowd around her, just as her strength failed and her fingers pulled away from the fence.

The hands on her shoulders and arms dropped away.

"*¡Márchese del portón!*" the soldier at the end of the row shouted.

Calli looked around. The men surrounding her sidled backwards, easing away from the gate as ordered. As soon as they had backed up six feet, all of them, one of the soldiers moved forward and slid the bar out of the gate, his machine gun still at the ready, and cracked the gate open a few inches.

"Come," he said, waving to her. "Come."

She picked up her hat, put it back on and slipped through the opening. The gate slammed shut behind her and the bar dropped back in. The soldier pulled her forward, between the other four guards. He hurried her over to the gatehouse, up the steps, inside the small glass enclosed building. There was a counter there and an officer standing at the window, watching the drama at the gate.

He turned as the soldier hustled her in. The soldier rattled off a stream of explanation, and he studied her, then said something quiet.

The soldier tugged a little at her backpack. "Show," he said.

She pulled off the backpack, unzipped it, and spread it wide so they could see inside. Then, obeying an instinct, she stepped back from the pack, giving them free access.

The officer and the soldier dug through the pack. The officer flipped through her passport and studied her, comparing her to the photo. She took off the hat again, giving him a better view. Finally, he spoke to the soldier, a quick word. The soldier saluted and ran back to the gate, where he took up his position once more. The other four had gone back to parade rest.

The officer examined her very carefully.

"You have reached a superior officer, as you requested, Miss Munro. Now what do you want?"

"You speak English. Great," she said. "Please, you must tell me. Is Nicolás Escobedo in the city? I must speak to him."

"Why must you speak to this person?"

"Look, I know you have no idea who I am, well, perhaps you may think you know —"

"I know exactly who you are, Miss Munro. After yesterday's paper, most of Vistaria knows who you are."

She winced. "Well, if that's what it takes to convince you I have no evil purpose here, fine, I'll own up. Yes, that was me. And normally I wouldn't come within a hundred miles of Nick after all this, but it's about one of his...friends, an officer, Duardo Peña, in Pascuallita, well, not him exactly —"

He held up a hand, signaling she should stop.

She fell silent.

"What did you call him?"

"Duardo?"

"That is not a Vistarian name," he said.

"*Eduardo*," she amended. "But he hates that. No one ever calls him that."

"Except his superior officers," the man replied. "Come here," he demanded, beckoning with his finger.

She stepped closer to the counter. He leaned over and pushed aside her jacket with one hand, peering inside it. Then he smiled and picked up the telephone on the counter, dialed and spoke into it. After a moment he put the phone down. "Someone will be with you in a moment. They will take you to another place. A more secure place. *¿Comprende?*"

"Yes," she said. She looked down inside her jacket, puzzled. And saw the St. Christopher's medallion lying against her tee shirt. She looked up at him.

"You know Nicolás, don't you?"

"Yes, Miss Munro. He and I went through officer training together."

"*Gracias*," she told him.

"*De nada*." He pointed to the door. "Your escort."

Another soldier, this one without a machine gun, held open the door for her. She zipped up her backpack and followed him across the tarmac towards the legislative building. He took her around the back, slipping under the covered walkway and into the drive-through tunnel at the base of the building. The walls on either side of the tunnel were pierced by double doors, and light spilled from them.

The soldier opened the right hand door and waved her inside. Stairs ran up and down from the small foyer. He indicated she should go down the stairs on the right. The corridor at the bottom was lined with anonymous doors with frosted glass panes. The floor was dark green linoleum, the walls a somber gray. The basement felt like all the government buildings Calli had ever visited in Montana. That reassured her immensely.

The soldier opened a door to one of the rooms, showing her a wooden table surrounded by four folding chairs. The wall on the right was broken by a large expanse of mirrored window. The one-way kind, she assumed. There was no other furniture, and the floor was that same dark green linoleum. The room was as soulless as a tax interview office. Almost cheerful, Calli sat on the table and dropped her backpack down beside her. It was the first time she had felt truly safe for several hours now.

Two hours later, she still felt safe...and bored. And very tired. No one had looked in on her, and when she looked out along the passageway she saw no one else. She had been tempted to go looking for people, in case she had been forgotten, but then she remembered the officer in the gatehouse, his recognition of the St. Christopher medallion, and knew that she would not be ignored or forgotten.

Forty minutes later Calli heard people in the passage outside and saw a shadow on the glass panel in the door.

She held her breath, her nerves prickling to the alert.

The door opened and Nick stepped into the room. He shut the door behind him, and stood looking at her.

"Nick, I'm sorry—I wouldn't have come here if I'd had any other choice. I'd have stayed away forever. It's Minnie, Nick. She's gone to find Duardo—"

He crossed to the table and she braced herself, wondering if he would vent his anger in closer quarters.

But his arms went around her and crushed her against. He kissed her...thoroughly, deeply, until all her thoughts scattered and her body began to tingle with thick, warm arousal.

She groaned beneath his lips, then gave a small cry as his hand found her breasts beneath the jacket. He pushed her hat off and held her head in his hand and rained kisses on every inch of her face, and finally her lips again.

"Sweet," he said, his lips against hers.

"Nick—"

He made a small sound. "I dreamed of you whispering my name last night," he said, his voice rough. "Just as you did then."

Her heart gave a tiny leap. She had expected Nick to be angry when she finally stood before him. She had braced herself for it, even while in her heart, deeply buried, was the tiny hope that he would be pleased to see her. But she had not expected this—she had not dared hope he might speak of missing her, even indirectly.

Before she could speak he kissed her again, while his hands roamed over her body. It was as though his passion was reaching out and wrapping itself around her, and she let herself be surrounded, held. Her worries, the sick guilt, slid from her.

This was Nick. He would make everything all right. Strong, capable Nick.

His hands tugged at her tee shirt, and she slipped off the jacket, giving him access. She held her breath as he pulled up the tee shirt, exposing her breasts. She anticipated his touch, and her body tightened, ready to welcome the sharp spike of pleasure from it.

He groaned and lowered his head to take a nipple in his mouth, his hand hard against her back, bringing her to him.

The tugging and stroking at her nipple sent a sharp shock slithering down to her clitoris, and she gasped. He transferred his attention to the other nipple, sliding his tongue over the tip, lapping at the breast and nipple together, while his hot fingers spread across her abdomen, keeping her steady. The moist caress loosened her knees, spreading a weakening fire through her belly, her clitoris, and pushing her cares far from her mind. Her head fell back, her eyes closing.

Take me now. Please, she pleaded silently. The need to have him inside her, hot and thick and hard against her, was as powerful and compulsive as the need to breathe. While that need went unmet, she could think of little else.

And she knew, now, that Nick wanted her as badly as she needed him. Her soul soared joyfully.

Boldly, she reached for his belt and slipped it undone in two quick movements. Then the button beneath, which eased undone without resistance. She found the zipper and was about to slide it down, when Nick's hand grasped her wrist in a painfully tight grip.

He lifted his head from her breasts, and looked at her with eyes that seemed to peer deep inside her.

He straightened and moved away, and Calli opened her mouth a little, almost voicing a protest. The ache to feel him inside her, that first hard thrust...it throbbed throughout her body. But for whatever reason Nick had pulled back, reined in his passion. It was not to be.

Calli climbed stiffly to the floor, pulling down her tee shirt as Nick moved toward the door.

Well, at least she knew he still wanted her. Even if he had the strength, the discipline, to rise above that need for a higher purpose, she could cling to the knowledge. It brought her small comfort—Nick had been touched, even a little, by their two days together.

Her pulse leapt when he turned the old fashioned key lock with a soft click. He watched her, probably reading every emotion on her face. His eyes were dark, the lids lowered.

She dared not breathe for fear that it would break the spell of the moment.

Nick came towards her, moving slowly, almost as if he didn't want to startle her and scare her away. "I dream of you still," he said in the same low gravelly voice she recalled from her own dreams, from the first night they'd met, from every moment she had known him when he spoke of something close to his heart, that stirred his emotions.

The sound of his voice now sent a shiver through her. She had not thought she would ever hear it again.

He stepped around her a little, and when she tried to turn towards him, his arms came around her, turning her back to face the table. He stood behind her now. When she looked into the mirrored window, Nick's dark gaze watched her from over her shoulder.

His hands moved restlessly on her hips. "I dreamed of you and woke to drenched sheets and a throbbing body."

His voice rumbled right by her ear. "Two mornings now, I have woken in my lonely bed and cursed myself for wasting all the moments I did have with you. I craved with an addict's need for just one moment more. Just a single moment."

In the mirror she saw him studying her shoulder, and he bent his head to kiss the nape of her neck. His lips were hot and moist, and she shut her eyes momentarily, swallowing, for her heart seemed to be lodged there, beating hard and fast. Even though Nick spoke the words, she felt that at any second something would happen to make him pause, recant them. It seemed impossible that he should be saying such things.

Impossible…but almost inevitable.

The hope that she had buried so deep in her heart had been created because she had recognized that Nick ended their liaison with deep reluctance. She had pushed the hope away because the reasons for ending it were overwhelming.

Both of them wanted one more moment.

Why not?

"You have your moment, now," she whispered.

He looked at her in the mirror and shook his head a little. "It is not enough," he declared. "Not nearly enough."

She watched in the mirror as he pulled at her tee shirt, sliding it up her torso, up over the full roundness of her breasts, gathering it to rest across the upper slope of her breasts. "The room behind the mirror…there's no one there, right?"

"Would it bother you if there were? Would you care?"

"Well…" she began.

But Nick cupped her breasts, bringing his strong thumbs up to stroke the distended nipples. He watched her reaction in the mirror, and as she caught her breath, gasping at the rush of electric heat that pushed through her, his eyes narrowed down to glittering slits.

He continued to toy with her breasts, stroking them, rolling the nipples between his fingers. The dual caresses were relentless. Did he know how much his touch excited her? There was a direct connection between her breasts and her clitoris. She could feel each stroke, the delicious rubbing, in her clit. Her excitement was building. Her breath became ragged. She was close to climaxing, just from the touch of his hands on her breasts.

He ran his fingers along the sensitive undersides, round to the upper slopes, slid the fingers down across her nipples, tugging at them as each finger passed...until the pulsing, thrilling excitement overwhelmed her senses. Her head fell back, her eyes closed, as she concentrated on the feel of his hands, and the aching throb of her clitoris.

"Look," he breathed, his voice husky.

Calli looked at the mirror, at the reflection of his hands on her breasts, at the image of a woman she barely recognized, leaning back against him, far gone in ecstasy, her body taut and on offer.

Nick's hands slid down her long torso to the button on her black trousers, which flicked open with a single little tug. He unzipped the trousers, and they sagged around her hips.

She watched, fascinated, as his hands slide inside the loosened trousers. The reflection in the mirror of the half-naked woman being undressed and seduced sent a wicked thrill through her. In such a work-a-day room, the passion seemed more intense.

Nick's fingers slipped beneath her panties, down to curve over her mons. She closed her eyes so that she could concentrate on his touch. She shifted her legs, spreading them, giving him room, and she could feel the slickness of her arousal. She was desperately eager to have his hands on her clit, to feel his fingers inside her. Her clit gave a heavy throb at the thought.

His fingers felt thick, as they slipped between her legs and into her pussy.

"Ah, so good," she said, her voice a whisper without strength or body.

"Then it was not just me who wished for more."

She shook her head a little and licked her dry lips. "More," she added, and pushed against his hand.

The small pressure drove the heel of his hand against her mound, and a finger slipped against her clitoris. The swift friction sent a bolt of pleasure through her. It grabbed the air from her lungs and tightened her throat, forcing out a low groan. She was astonished to hear herself make such an uninhibited sound.

Nick responded with a low growl of his own. His hand tightened possessively around her, then withdrew from her clothing.

"No!" she said, her voice choked. "Don't stop. Nick...please."

"Peace," he murmured, and she realized he was bunching the band of her trousers in each hand, pulling them down. And as he slipped the fabric over her hips, he snagged her panties and pulled them down with the trousers, down to her calves. His hands trailed up along her legs, smoothing their way over her knees, up the front of her thighs, to push between her legs again. This time, freed of binding cloth, his fingers slipped deep inside her.

"Ah, such heat, *mi rubia fuerte…*!" he purred, his tone one of deep satisfaction.

Nick's thumb stroked her clitoris, and she gave a small cry, her pelvis thrusting against him. She began to shudder with the torrid excitement pouring through her.

His lips were on her neck, his teeth nipping.

"Nick, please…!" she groaned.

"Yes, by God!" He released her for a moment. Cloth rustled softly. A zipper slid undone.

He cupped her breasts again, and tugged at her nipples, while she watched his hands in the mirror. He lifted his hands up higher, to her shoulders and pushed them, bending her over. "Lean on the table," he said. His voice was thick, distorted, and the sound of it sent a shiver of delight through her. He wanted her. She was doing this to him.

She propped herself on the table, exposing herself, and trembled. His hands rested on her hips, and she felt his cock push against her from behind. She caught her breath, in anticipation of that first penetrating thrust…and he pushed into her, thick and hard, and so hot. The contact seared all the way along her vagina.

Calli gave a choked groan. Nick was big and hard inside her — deep inside her. She felt stretched. Filled. Only two days had passed since the last time she had felt him, but it seemed longer.

Nick paused for a brief moment, as if he, too, savored the moment — savored her, as he had insisted such moments should be respected. Then he began to thrust in and out, at first with a leisurely, hedonistic slowness that made her belly ripple with waves of contractions, but the motion quickly grew swifter, longer, and his breathing ragged. The tense sounds he made told her he was struggling to control the pace. He was losing the battle, she realized with a deep, feminine satisfaction.

But then his fingers slid up against her clitoris and began a knowing, delicate stroking. She clenched against him, shuddering under his touch, already close to orgasm. Her awareness narrowed down to the touch of his fingers, and the thrust of his cock inside her…and the waves of pleasure building, building…

She lifted her head up with a small cry as her climax slammed through her in waves that made every muscle clamp like a fist. Even as her climax throbbed, she felt Nick give a final hard thrust, the last one, that buried him deep inside her, his hands on her hips holding her against him. She could feel him pulsing against her, shuddering, and heard her name—a whispered groan. "Ca-lli!"

His body folded over her, and Calli closed her eyes again, hearing her heart thundering in her ears. Her thighs trembled, barely holding her up.

Nick picked himself up, pulled away from her, and helped her to stand. She heard him dressing. She straightened her tee shirt again, but when she went to fasten her trousers, Nick pulled her hands away and did it for her. "I insist," he said with a small smile. "As I was the one to put your clothes in such disarray in the first place."

She gave a small smile of her own. "I don't remember protesting."

He kissed her gently on the lips. "Wanton," he teased. Then he pulled her against him again and held her. "I'm sorry, Calli…I gave you very little choice, didn't I? But I couldn't think of anything except the need to have you again. Now. And until I had filled that need, I do not think I could have thought of anything else. Seeing you here, when I did not expect to ever see you again…I am weak, when it comes to you, Calli."

She smiled. "Nicolás Escobedo and 'weak' are mutually exclusive," she teased. "You just know what you want, that's all."

His arms tightened about her in response.

With her cheek against the soft cashmere of his dark sweater, she felt the beat of his heart and heard his breathing, a little rushed, a little uneven. She remained still, and let her heart recover, and his unique, masculine scent wash over her.

He let her go at last and stepped back a little, enough to look down at her face. He smiled a little. "I certainly didn't think I would see you again, with all this." He pushed a stray wisp of her hair off her face

"It's a horrible disaster, Nick. It almost hurts to watch it all happening. And it's all because of—"

"No!" He said it quickly, and put his finger against her lips. "Don't ever say it," he said. "Not ever. What has happened, happened, and what will happen, will be. No regrets, no guilt. That's what we agreed, remember?"

She nodded a little.

"Tell me about Minnie. Duardo. What has happened?"

Calli told him quickly. Just the facts. She knew he would figure out the rest for himself. "You phoned him, Nick. You have the number. I thought I could see if she made it that far. It must have been his family's house you phoned. That's where she'd head, I think. If I could talk to her, arrange a place to meet her, and pick her up, then…"

"Pascuallita has fallen, Calli. It's in the hands of the rebels. And any resistance there is being swiftly dealt with. We can't go in."

"Then Minnie could not either," Calli said softly. "What will happen to her?"

"She will be forced to abandon the car because traffic out of Pascuallita will be too heavy. If she tries to go further on foot she will have to fight her way through refugees. And if she continues she will run into the fragments of the army, making its way south, running under the guns of the rebels. The army has been broken there, and the base abandoned. They're on the run."

"Is there nothing I can do?"

"You?" Nick said gently, with small smile. "You would take on two armies by yourself?"

"There is no one else."

He was silent, simply looking at her.

"Do you have a car I could use, Nick?" she said at last. "Minnie took my uncle's car, and I can follow her up the coast, see if I can find her that way."

"You wouldn't have lasted five minutes outside the gates here once the people realized who you were. Do you think you would have an easier time of it with people who are on the run from their homes, from violence?"

"Damn it, Nick, I have to do something!"

He touched her cheek. "I know. But I would not have you running heedlessly into the same boiling cauldron as Minnie did."

His cell phone rang, and he gave a small curse and reached for his back pocket. "Only the most critical people have this number," he said. "I can't ignore it."

"It's okay," she assured him tiredly, as he opened the phone.

"¿Sí?" He listened, then looked at her sharply. "Duardo, where are you?" he said into the phone.

Calli sat up straight.

Nick listened for a long time. "Wait a moment," he said into the phone, and looked at her. "I must speak Spanish. It's quicker for us, okay?"

She nodded.

Nick began to speak, rapidly, with little pause. Then he looked at her again. "Do you know for certain that Minnie would go to Duardo's house in Pascuallita?"

Calli shook her head. "Minnie already knew Pascuallita had fallen. That was why she left. She went to find Duardo. I think she would go to the base, or try to."

He nodded and spoke to Duardo again. Then he snapped the phone shut and tucked it in his back pocket. "Come with me," he said briskly.

Chapter Sixteen

Calli scrambled to keep up with Nick as he hurried up the long passage. "Where was Duardo?"

"I'll tell you all of it in a while," Nick promised. "First, we must hurry." He took her up the same stairs she had come down, and back to the gatehouse, where the same officer stood watching. He straightened to attention when Nick entered.

"Fernando," Nick acknowledged. He spoke quickly.

Fernando nodded and responded, also tersely.

Nick raised his hand. "*Gracias,*" he finished. He turned and strode outside again, and Calli trailed after him, puzzled and feeling completely useless.

"Where now?"

"Behind the palace," Nick said shortly. He angled for the covered walkway.

"Why there?"

"That's where we'll find transport to Pascuallita."

"*We?*" Calli repeated.

He glanced at her. "You don't think I would let you go there alone, do you?"

"Nick, this isn't your problem. Don't you think you've got enough of your own to worry about?"

He stopped suddenly, and she almost ran into him. He caught her arms to steady her. "No one gets to choose what to worry about, have you noticed? Besides, I have made promises, both spoken and unspoken, and if I do not do everything in my power to help Duardo and retrieve Minnie for you, I would not be living up to those promises."

"Well, okay. As long as you're not doing it for me."

He smiled and kissed her, quickly, and started walking again. "That's exactly why I'm doing it," he said over his shoulder.

Five breathless minutes later Calli found herself on the other side of the palace. They had hurried through the building, catching glimpses of stairs, empty rooms, elegant foyers, before emerging through French doors into bright daylight. It was not quite noon.

A patio extended for twenty feet or so, edged by thick balustrades identical to those on the second floor of the building, the balustrades she had climbed and sat upon, only a few short nights ago. Nick strode toward a set of stairs in the middle. She paused on the top step, her eyes widening. An expanse of concrete stretched out below, and on it sat a neat row of cars and trucks in front of a couple of helicopters.

Nick reached the concrete and headed towards the cars and Calli quickly followed him down the stairs. A soldier stood at parade rest at the end of the row of cars, and as Nick approached him, a second soldier emerged from a metal door set into the foundations of the balcony and saluted to Nick.

Nick held up his hand, and the soldier threw something metallic and shining. Keys. Nick caught them with a downward flick of his wrist and turned on his heel, just as Calli reached the end of the row of cars. "Which one?" she asked.

"That one," he said, nodding over the top of the cars. He threaded his way between two of them...right past them and over towards the smaller helicopter.

Her heart jumped a little, and she hurried to catch up with him again. "The *helicopter*?" she called.

"There's nothing else that can get us there faster today." He opened the rounded glass door of the helicopter, and indicated that she should do the same.

"You can fly these?"

"I thought I'd just wing it," he said, settling into the seat.

Even as her jaw dropped, she realized he was teasing. She scowled at him, and sat in the other seat. There was a bench seat behind them, quite narrow, but clearly designed to carry two more people, or perhaps even three at a pinch. There was room for Minnie and Duardo.

"Strap in. This will be a rough trip," Nick said, buckling the H-style belt over his chest.

While her heart skittered along, coping with the series of little surprises Nick had handed out in the last few minutes, she fought with the belts and finally got the buckle fastened. Out of the corner of her eye she saw Nick insert the key into something that looked suspiciously like the ignition slot on a domestic car, and turn the key. Nothing happened.

"Flat battery?" she asked sweetly.

He grinned, and prodded a green button, and she heard the engine grind and start to rev up. Shadows moving overhead caught her attention. The extended bubble of glass let her see the sky above and the rotors slowly starting to turn as the engine cranked.

Nick tapped her knee and held out a pair of headphones. They were attached to the console by a curly lead. He already wore a similar pair. She slipped them on, and immediately the noise of the engine muffled down to almost nothing.

"Can you hear me?" Nick's voice sounded in her ear.

"Yes." She adjusted the microphone so it was closer to her mouth.

Very quickly, the blades above became a blur, and she could feel the helicopter move a little beneath her.

Nick had his hands on the controls and listened, watching his readouts. He adjusted the stick between his knees and played with the pedals under his feet, and just like that, they were airborne. The ground dropped away from them quickly. She watched the lawn recede from beneath her feet — the glass curved right over the nose and stopped about four inches from where her feet rested.

With another small adjustment of the controls, Nick turned the helicopter slowly around to face the north. It settled motionless in midair for a moment, then he pushed the controls forward.

She caught her breath, alarm seizing her, as the nose of the craft dipped sharply, and the tail came up. They slid through the air, the already-muffled *thwock-thwock* of the blades dimming further under the rush of wind.

"You'll get used to it," Nick assured her, his voice issuing softly in her ear. It was like a whisper.

She looked down at the view in front of her feet. *Las Colinas* looked very small, and already she could see the outskirts ahead, and green tree canopy beyond that. "How fast are we going?"

"One hundred and fifty knots."

She wrinkled her forehead, trying to remember what knots meant. "Can you put that in terms I can relate to? How long will it take us to get there? And where *is* there, anyway? Are we going to pick up Duardo? How did he get to phone you? I thought he was with his unit somewhere, fighting the rebels."

Nick held up his hand. "Enough. I promised you an explanation. I had not forgotten. Now I have time to spare—a little, anyway. We're heading for a place southeast of the Pascuallita base, which is where the front line is estimated to be. We should reach there in just over ninety minutes. And yes, we're going to pick up Duardo. With luck, Minnie, too."

"How? How did he get through to your cell?"

Nick shrugged a little. "He phoned. How else?" He seemed puzzled.

"I thought the army were scattered, on the run. He carries a cell phone with him?"

"They're scattered, yes. But not entirely on the run. They will try to regroup into units, to find each other, and build guerilla bands to impede the progress of the rebels until they can make contact with the proper chain of command and receive fresh orders."

"That was what Duardo was doing? Where was he?"

"On the coast. There's a fair number of seaside villages that are relatively untouched. He simply found a working phone and called headquarters. And because you had specifically named Duardo in your efforts to enter the building, the information, and your presence there, got passed along to him for feedback, and he was transferred to my cell."

"So what did you tell him? Is he all right?"

"He's cut off from his unit, but he's fine. He's almost directly south of the base, which puts him in an ideal position to quarter the area around the coast road. He will be able to find Minnie's car and track her from there. Southwest of the base, where we're heading, there's a campground—it's not used much because the jaguars like the area, too—but Duardo knows it, and it has an open, flat area I can get this beast into and still maneuver."

"And that's where we're meeting him? It'll take him hours!"

"Duardo knows his limits. He estimated he was only twenty minutes away from the campground. That gives him ninety minutes to look for Minnie before he has to make for the camp."

"But she could be anywhere!"

Nick shook his head. "It might seem that way to you, but there's a very limited number of places Minnie could safely move to. She'll be sent back towards the city if she tries to go north or west into the mountains, and the easiest route south, the route she will be forced to take, is the road she drove there on. And she'll have to go by foot. If Duardo finds her car, he will find her shortly after that. He's an excellent tracker."

Calli sat back in her seat, feeling a huge swell of relief. "Are all your officers so...useful?"

"Duardo is a good sample," Nick said judiciously. "He will do well."

She rubbed her forehead, and let her eyes close. They were gritty with lack of sleep.

"It may not be as straightforward as that, though," Nick added.

"Why?" she demanded, opening her eyes.

"There are rebels throughout the hills in that area, and Duardo is wearing a uniform. If he is seen, he will have to fight his way out of it."

"But if Minnie is with him…"

"Then she will be fair game too."

She closed her eyes again, ill with fear, and felt Nick's hand on her knee. "Now you know why I tried so hard to avoid this outcome, Calli. Politicians do not count the innocent amongst their victims."

"But we will have to, won't we?"

He didn't answer her and Calli felt a heavy, dark weight settle in her heart and mind.

* * * * *

Nick held a steady course north, following the spinal mountain chain for another hour. Then carefully, he adjusted their course for a northeasterly direction, and the mountains fell away to their left. For the first time Calli saw evidence of war: black smoke spiraled up into the air to the north of them and spread into a gray haze across the sky. As they got closer, she could see tiny orange lights flickering.

"Fire," Nick said, pointing to them.

"Oh God…" she breathed.

He pointed again, this time toward the coast ahead of them. "The coast road."

She could just make out a thin smooth line, merely an indentation in the tree line, running parallel with the coastline. "I can't see people on it."

"Too far away. Keep watching," he said.

Abruptly, he yanked on the controls, and the helicopter tipped sideways, as if a giant hand had pulled an invisible rug out from under them.

Calli gasped and gripped the sides of her chair, looking over her shoulder at the ground that seemed to be sloping up towards her. "What's happening?" she yelled.

"Tracers!"

"*What?*"

Nick pulled back on the stick, slowed the helicopter, but they still slid down that invisible chute towards the ground. The engine made a peculiar whining noise, clearly overtaxed. He tugged at the controls again, throwing all his weight into it. The helicopter jigged sideways, and was suddenly climbing up into the air. Calli took a deep breath as her stomach flipped and dug her fingers into the upholstery.

Slowly their ascent smoothed out again, and she saw mountains directly in front of her. Somehow they had got completely turned around. But the 180-degree turn meant that this time she saw what had alarmed Nick the first time. From the forest at the foot of the mountain came a flashing, and a line of white dashes that reached out through the sky towards them.

"Ohmigod, that's gunfire. They're shooting at us!"

Nick wrenched on the controls again, and the helicopter again slid down the sharp slope in the sky, only this time the forest rolled past Nick's shoulder. She swallowed hard, not sure whether fear or the aerobatics that made her stomach cartwheel, and hung on grimly.

"I'm going to get down lower, use the trees as cover," Nick said. His voice was calm, remote. He might have been discussing using milk instead of cream in his coffee.

He eased them level and pushed the nose down to increase their forward speed. "We're almost there."

He guided the craft along the treetops, and it seemed like she could lean down and snag leaves in her hand, they looked so close. It gave her stationary objects to measure their speed against — they were going very fast.

Ahead, she could see the coast road again, and this time they were close enough that she could see a long row of vehicles and a thick stream of people alongside them.

Refugees.

The helicopter turned again, and the road slipped underneath her and out of her view. They were heading northwest, but Nick eased the controls a little and they began to bank in a curve to the left. He looked out past Calli's shoulder.

"That's the campground down there," he said.

She looked. There was a bald spot amongst the treetops — pale green intersected by a thin strip she assumed was a road. "Do you have to circle to let Duardo know you're here?"

"No need. He'll hear the helicopter for miles. If he's here, he'll make sure we spot him."

"But you're circling anyway?"

"I'm not going to land unless I have to. I'd be a sitting duck down there, and I've got far too valuable a cargo to take such a risk."

It took her a moment to realize he was referring to her, and she felt her cheeks bloom with an unusual heat. She could think of no suitable response, and anyway, her silence had already extended far too long to make a snappy answer possible. Finally, she looked away to her left and down to the ground, scanning the visible area of the campsite.

"There," Nick said, pointing to the northern edge of the site.

Calli peered. She could see nothing.

But Nick was already bringing the helicopter around, bringing it lower, towards the campsite.

Then she saw a small dot, moving out from the rim of the trees, and realized her perspective had been skewed: she had been looking for something much larger; there had been nothing to give her a sense of scale. The small dot must be Duardo, which made the campsite larger than she had thought. They were higher than she had guessed too.

The helicopter dropped almost vertically now, turning just a little on its axis, and she lost sight of Duardo's figure. She leaned forward to watch past Nick's chest for Duardo to come back into sight as they swiveled full circle, and then she saw him. They were at treetop height now, and Duardo waved towards the trees behind him. He wore jungle fatigue pants and a black sleeveless stretch tee shirt that didn't look anything like army issue. In his right hand he held an automatic pistol, down by his side, while he waved with his left.

And from between two trees, Minnie appeared, dressed in jeans and a torn tee shirt, running for her life. Calli caught her breath as relief, shock and fear speared her chest.

Duardo let Minnie pass him, then began to run behind her, a slow lope that covered the ground as quickly as Minnie's all-out sprint.

"There's trouble," Nick said, very quietly. He put the helicopter down on the ground, but she could tell by the way he juggled the pedals with his feet that he was keeping it poised for immediate take off. "Open your door and get in the back. Quickly."

She obeyed, fumbling with the awkward catch on the door, then shucking off her safety harness and headset and squeezing through the two seats into the cramped back area. By the time she turned around, Minnie was almost to the helicopter. Her small face was white, and her eyes wide, her mouth open. She held out her hand, almost leaning towards them as she ran.

Behind her, Duardo looked over his shoulder every few steps.

Trouble chasing them.

Minnie was at the door now, scrambling to get up the awkward step into the cabin. She gasped for breath, and as she miss-stepped and her shin hit the edge of the doorsill, she gave a breathless little whimper. Calli held out her hand, intending to boost her up and through into the back seat, to make way for Duardo.

He reached the door and held it open, out of Minnie's way. His head was turned back, watching.

From the edge of the trees, three armed men rushed out into the open. As they lifted their rifles up, Nick shouted, "*Down!*"

Minnie threw herself across the front seat, and Calli felt Nick's hand on her shoulder, pushing her down. Out of the way. There was no arguing with the force he used. She folded without resistance, dropping into the tiny space between the bench seat and the back of the chair she had been sitting in. She could just see over the windowsill.

But Duardo merely turned, his gun raised, and fired off three shots.

The men at the other end of the empty field flinched a little, but they must have known his pistol couldn't reach them for all but one of them kept running.

Minnie tried to clamber into the back seat.

"Minnie, no. Stay down," Nick said sharply.

Duardo glanced at her, looked back over his shoulder again.

The third man had halted and raised his rifle to his shoulder. Even Calli, who knew nothing about weapons, sensed that this man was a marksman from the way he held the rifle, sighting along it with care.

Duardo took a step, swinging around to face the open doorway, his back to the rifleman, and at the same moment Calli heard the rifle fire, like a small thunderclap, complete with echo.

Duardo jerked forward, his shoulder hitting the doorframe. He made a small grunting sound and fell over the seat, almost on top of Minnie.

Nick let go of the controls, picked Minnie up around the waist and almost threw her into the back. Then he grabbed Duardo, a hand under each arm, and hauled him into the seat. He lunged over the top of him and snagged the door and shut it.

Duardo moved slowly, sitting himself up in the seat.

"*Stay down!*" Nick roared—to whom, Calli wasn't sure, but she stayed down anyway and pulled Minnie down too.

The helicopter was already lifting. Almost straight away Nick pushed the stick forward, dropping the nose and shooting them up and forward at a great speed. The engine screamed.

She heard a quiet *crack!* and saw a small neat hole appear in the screen just in front of Nick. *Bullet hole,* her dazed mind identified. Nick did not even flinch. The steep ascent continued.

"Calli!" he said.

"What?"

"Pull off your tee shirt. Get it behind him, put pressure on it. Hurry!"

She struggled back onto the bench seat. She didn't understand why he had given her such a strange order, but hurried to obey anyway.

"NO! *Duardo!*" Minnie screamed, and tried to push past Callie into the front.

Calli froze for a second as the truth slammed into her. "Ohmigod," she whispered. Then she ripped off her jacket with trembling, thick-fingered hands, then her tee shirt, and wadded it into a ball. Minnie was in her way. She pulled her petite cousin back with a force that almost rammed her into the back wall. "I have to get to him," she said.

She pushed through the seats, leaning on the console in the middle, her legs still dangling in the back and reached for Duardo.

He was slumped in the seat, his chin on his chest, his eyes closed. Her heart tightened and a watery, weak rush of adrenaline surged through her. "Duardo!" she called, and tugged at his arm.

No response.

She grabbed a fistful of his tee shirt and hauled on it. She had to get him leaned forward, so she could reach his back. But his hand reached up to snag her wrist, pulling her fingers from his shirt. He lifted his chin and looked at her and very gently shook his head. A little drop of blood escaped the corner of his mouth.

The surge of adrenaline swirled into a sickly panic.

"No!" she shouted at him. "No!"

"Minnie," he said softly, and swallowed.

Nick's hand dropped onto her shoulder. "Let Minnie through," he said.

She gritted her teeth, shook her head. "No. I get the pad on, we get him somewhere."

"Calli," Duardo said.

She looked at him, ready to battle it out with him, too, if necessary. They *would* get him somewhere. Things *would* be okay. This was real life. Not the eleven o'clock news. He would be just fine, goddammit.

But Duardo smiled a little. "*La dama fuerte*," he said. "Thank you for not letting go."

She couldn't breathe. Couldn't speak. There was something building up inside her that was jamming up everything.

Nick's hand was on her arm, pulling her up, pushing her back through to the back seat. She fell onto the cushion, still clutching her balled up tee shirt, her limbs as useless as a stringless marionette's. Her hand hurt with the force of her clenching, but she didn't let go of it.

Minnie had squirmed through the opening in the seats and half lay across Duardo's lap. She smoothed his brow, kissed him, patted his shoulder, and all the while her throat worked, as if she couldn't speak the words building there. Her eyes were wide, their focus on him fierce.

Duardo ruffled her hair. "I regret..." He closed his eyes, took a slow, struggling breath. "English...agh," he whispered. Then, "Nick?"

Nick stared straight ahead, his face a mask. "*¿Sí, Duardo?*"

"*Dígala yo estaba equivocado...Sí yo no había insistido a hacer mi deber entonces yo habría tenido la alegría de es su esposo. Aún un solo día...yo habría sido orgulloso.*"

Minnie's face crumpled, and she began to weep silently, showing that she had understood part of it. Enough of it.

Nick took a breathe, and Calli saw him swallow. "Minnie, he said, 'Tell her I was wrong. If I had not insisted on doing my duty then I would have had the joy of being her husband—'"

Minnie gave a little choked cry as Duardo's head rolled loosely to one side.

"'...Even a single day...I would have been proud,'" Nick finished, his voice a flat rasp.

Minnie buried her head against Duardo's chest, holding him.

Calli watched, too numb with shock to comfort her.

Beside the silent pair, Nick reached up and thumped the doorframe with the side of his fist. Once. Twice. And a third time that traveled through the metal and made the craft shiver.

Chapter Seventeen

They landed back on the same square of concrete they had taken off from that morning, and only then the horrible silence in the cockpit broke.

Nick half dragged, half lifted Minnie away from Duardo's body, as soldiers raced across the concrete and opened the door on that side. Two of them had a stretcher and eased Duardo out of the seat and lay him on the canvas.

Nick held Minnie against him. She seemed limp in his arms and did not protest as the soldiers carried the stretcher away. Nor did she resist when he opened his door and lifted her out onto the concrete beside him.

He looked at Calli then, his expression bleak. "Come."

She carefully maneuvered her cramped body to the concrete, surprised she could move at all and was capable of standing. She tugged at her crumpled tee shirt, finally having the elbowroom to straighten it up. She didn't bother tucking it back into her trousers. Somewhere in the last few hours, the elastic holding her braid had snapped or been pulled off, and her hair had unraveled. The ends brushed her elbows, and she pushed it back tiredly.

Nick took her arm, and Minnie's too, then led them over to the row of cars. "*¿Quiero uno con poder y manejo bueno?*" he called out.

"*¡El sedán de BMW, señor!*" a soldier answered.

"Keys?" Nick asked. "*¿Las llaves?*" he added.

"*¡Sí, señor!*" The soldier turned and ran.

Nick directed them to the dark blue BMW the soldier had recommended for its power and good handling, the two qualities Nick had specified. "Get in," he told them. "I'll get you back to the apartment and then off the island. It's no longer safe for you here."

Calli slid into the front passenger seat, and Nick helped Minnie into the back before walking around and settling behind the wheel. He was handed the keys as he shut the door, and he started the car and backed it out.

Minnie had curled up into a ball on the back seat and shut her eyes. Shutting out the world?

Rather than direct the car towards the front gates, Nick drove across the concrete to a gravel path that skirted the southern wing of the palace. Beyond the building the manicured lawns quickly turned to wild grasses, then the road slipped between trees and emerged onto a narrow and deserted neighborhood street, a good mile away from the palace. He turned sharply left and headed for the downtown area.

As soon as they turned onto a major road Nick braked sharply. People moved along the street itself. Nearly all of them carried, pulled or pushed belongings in sacks, carts, trolleys, whatever had been to hand. They hurried along, fear the common expression on their faces. Most of them headed east.

"Where are they going?" Calli breathed.

"The coast. Off island. It's almost a hereditary instinct in Vistarians to flee the island when bad trouble strikes." He changed gears, and let the car drop into a crawl. "We'll have to use side roads. There's a route over the back of the hill that will get us to your apartment."

"What trouble are they running from? The rebels are north."

Nick glanced at her. "Not for long. If the people are fleeing the city, it means they expect the fighting to break out here at any moment. Word will have passed." He nudged the car through the people, easing it towards the right. Once he could steer into a side street, he picked up speed, for the street was nearly deserted.

No businesses were open, and no one not running for the coast was out on the streets. It reminded Calli of news footage she had seen of cities that were the focus of war — empty streets, bombed-out cars, silence, and everywhere the dust and rubble of disaster.

"How could this happen so fast?" she asked. "Yesterday, *Las Colinas* was a normal city. Even this morning I did not see this sort of..." She was at a loss to categorize what she saw.

"Exodus," Nick supplied. "What it comes down to is that I was caught napping. Worse. I was caught by my own complacency. I thought we had time, José and I, to fix this." He did not say the words with any emphasis.

Calli touched his shoulder. "You can't take on all the guilt. There are others who are also responsible for Vistaria."

He glanced at her, and his expression was stony, unforgiving. "The others didn't fuck up as badly as I did."

He said it gently, but he might have slapped her and achieved the same impact. She snatched her hand back and folded her arms across her stomach, feeling sick.

They made the rest of the trip in silence, and Calli made no attempt to cross the soundless barrier between them. When Nick pulled up at the apartment, she opened the door herself and then opened Minnie's. She tugged on Minnie's hand and coaxed her to get out.

Nick did not linger to watch. He moved ahead, to the front door. He knocked, a hard rap, and when Joshua opened it, he shepherded him inside.

Calli walked Minnie into the apartment, and turned her to face her. She stroked her cheek. "Did you lose your pack of essentials?" she asked gently.

"Everything is in my pockets," Minnie said, her voice ethereal. Distant.

In the lounge room, Calli could hear Nick talking to Joshua. Low, controlled. The leader was back in charge again.

"I think we're going to leave again very soon. Do you have anything else you want to take?"

Minnie roused a little. "I don't want to leave at all," she said, quite calmly.

"We have to. The fighting is going to break out in the city very soon. We have to go over to Mexico. Foreign nationals here, especially Americans…they won't be treated well. This is their war, Minnie. Not ours."

Minnie seemed to take a moment to process this, then she nodded and sighed, and the sigh seemed to vent any resistance in her. "Yes," she said softly. "I suppose we must leave then."

* * * * *

A little less than an hour later they piled back into the car. This time Joshua and Beryl were with them. The plan was simple; they would drive to the yacht club on the coast and use Nick's boat to cross over to Acapulco.

Nick sat behind the wheel again, Joshua in the passenger seat. Between Beryl and Calli in the back seat, Minnie sat like a statue. She had withdrawn into herself again.

Her remoteness worried Calli, but she didn't know what to do about it. She mentally listed it as something she must take care of when they reached the boat. She couldn't deal with it now. She knew the drive to the yacht club would not be as breezy as Joshua made it out to be.

Nick had an encyclopedic knowledge of back roads and side streets. As a result, they avoided crowded main thoroughfares nearly altogether. When they drew closer to the eastern outskirts of the city, Nick sat up straighter, showing more alertness than before.

"What is it?" Joshua asked.

"We have to use the main road for a few miles. It's the only one until we get to a turnoff, about five miles away."

"Oh well," Joshua said philosophically.

The car climbed over a raised lip and bumped onto a wide, sealed road. They turned right, heading east. The sun sat low behind them, sending their long shadow down the road.

There was a lot of traffic, moving slowly. Cars, buses, mini-vans, rusted out hulks blowing blue smoke, even horse-drawn carts. Along both sides of the road a long, strung-out line of people headed east, too, carrying their burdens, shepherding children, goats. This far from the city, they had settled into a rhythm and uniform speed. None of the panic Calli had seen in the city showed here, just a stoicism that told her more clearly than words could just how used to fleeing and hiding Vistarians were. As

Nick had said, it was in their blood, part of every page of their history.

She felt a sadness for the pretty country and the happy people. Their resistance to outsiders, to Americans, hadn't just been whipped up overnight. The rebels had tapped into a deep-rooted foundation of fear built by generations of abuse. And her sadness was tinged with indignation, too. How could a people be treated this way? How could anyone watch it and not want to take up their cause?

Nick had taken up that cause. And now he would look upon these refugees and tell himself he had failed to save them from this misery.

She moved forward to sit on the edge of the seat and reach through the front seats to lay her hand on his chest. Although she could not see him because of the headrest, she said very quietly by his ear, "Don't look at them and tell yourself it's finished, Nick. This doesn't have to be the end. Not until you decide it's over."

Silence. But she knew he listened, for he had stopped breathing. His chest did not rise or fall under her hand.

"Yes, they're taking a beating, and you've made a mistake," she added. "But it was just a mistake, and it doesn't have to be fatal. Look at them, Nick. They're sturdy, determined. All they need is you to find a way for them to get back what they've lost."

She felt him breathe again. A deep breath. He picked up her hand, and she felt his lips against the backs of her fingers.

Satisfied, she sat back again and saw that Joshua had turned to study her. She gave him a little smile, but could only manage to curl up one corner of her mouth. After a moment, he turned back to watch the road again.

Thirty minutes later, after climbing up and down undulating hills, they turned off the main road without meeting any trouble, nosing their way through the pedestrians with agonizing slowness. The new road was sandy — they drew closer to the coast now — but it was firm enough for Nick to pick up speed.

The trees closed in around them, crowding right up to the edges of the road. At times, small branches would actually swipe across the windows as they went by. After a mile or so the hard dirt road swung left, heading toward the northwest, and a tiny track branched off to the right.

Nick turned right, but he did not slow his speed, and now the bushes scraped along the sides constantly. The dirt grew softer. Boggy.

They turned a long, curving bend in the road, Nick working at the wheel to keep the car in the deep ruts, as it leaned sideways. As the curve straightened, two things happened at once — the windscreen directly in front of Nick blossomed with three stars that radiated out across the glass, and Joshua threw up his hands with a dismayed, "Oh, holy shit!"

Nick stamped on the brakes and the car slewed to a halt, the back of it fishtailing a little in the loose sand as he fought the wheel to keep the skid under control until they had halted.

Calli leaned forward to look between the seats. On the road ahead of them, she could see the outline of two men standing with their legs spread. A third stood off to the side, and he lowered a gun that he had been aiming at the car.

Joshua whistled. "Bulletproof glass?" he asked Nick.

Nick nodded.

"You are one lucky son of a bitch," Joshua declared.

It confirmed what Calli had thought—the stars on the windscreen were bullet marks.

"Everyone stay very still, and nobody say a word, no matter what they say. Understood?" Nick said in an undertone.

"Who are they?" Calli breathed.

"I think we're about to meet our first official rebels."

The smaller of the pair standing on the road waved them forward. The man with the pistol ran down to stand level with the car and Joshua's open window. "*¡Fuera! Salga del coche.*"

"What did he say?" Beryl whispered.

"*¡Ponga las manos arriba!*" he screamed.

Joshua shot his hands up into the air. "All right, already," he said. "I'm getting out."

"All of you!" the man said with a heavy accent. "All. Out."

Nick switched off the engine, pulled out the keys and got out of the car. Calli followed his example and tugged Minnie into following her.

The man with the gun herded them towards the other two. A fourth man stepped out of the trees, pointing a rifle with a long, curved magazine at them. Calli caught her breath and tried not to show any reaction. The fourth man was Harry, the congenial guitar player she had met in the truck on the way to the party. He did not look so young or easy-going now.

They were surrounded. Calli kept Beryl and Minnie beside her and in the center of the ring where Nick, Joshua and she would offer a little protection if the men began firing.

The smaller of the two men standing in the middle of the road appeared to be unarmed, but the other held a large revolver, cradling it in the crook of his other arm, his finger resting against the barrel. All of them were unshaven and dirty, and none wore anything that resembled a uniform. Harry wore the jeans and tee shirt she had seen him in at the party

The small man smiled as Nick stopped in front of him and spread his hands in welcome. "*La mirada lo que yo me agarré hoy…Señor Nicolás Escobedo.*" He seemed to be gloating.

"Pablo Santos," Nick drawled. "I'm surprised to find you on the other side."

Pablo laughed a little. It was not a pleasant sound. "When Serrano told me to watch this dirty road, I thought he had sent me away, but he was right. He said that rich *bastardos* would try to get to their big boats and run away. But I do not think even he thought someone like you would run away, *el leopardo.*"

Nick simply looked at him.

"*¡Oye, Pablo!*" It was Harry, speaking softly. "*La alta rubia allí. Esa es la dama fuerte.*"

In amongst the Spanish, Calli focused on words she recognized. *La dama fuerte.* Her skin crawled. Harry was talking about her.

Pablo stepped forward a little, trying to move past Joshua so he could see her. "*¿La mujer de Escobedo?*" he asked with an evil smile, and reached behind his back.

The motion seemed to trigger Nick into action. He took two big strides towards Calli, pushing Beryl out of the way as he did so. A shout went up from the rebels surrounding them, panic clear in their voices. Nick threw his left arm around Calli and at the same time he spun her around a little. Calli felt his right hand tug something between them. His hand shot out to point at Pablo...and his gun was in it.

Beryl screamed a little, and Minnie dropped to the ground, her hands over her ears.

At the same time Pablo pulled his hand out from behind his back and brought up a revolver and cocked it, pointing it straight at Nick.

And both of them grew still, their guns aimed directly at each other.

Nick had pulled her around so she would be out of the line of fire. Calli began to tremble when she realized that Pablo had either intended to shoot her out of hand, or else use her to force Nick to comply with whatever he wanted. Thank God Nick had guessed his intentions.

Pablo smiled a little. "But shoot me, and Harry will kill everyone here. Including you."

"But you'll be dead," Nick responded, his voice low and even.

Pablo considered it a moment. Then, with a quick movement he lifted his revolver up in the air, taking his finger off the trigger. "You see?" he said. "This will get us nowhere."

Nick didn't lower his gun, and from the corner of her eye Calli could see that none of the other men had, either.

Pablo shrugged and let the gun hang from his hand. "We have more to offer you, *Señor* Escobedo, than a bullet."

"Recruitment?" Nick said, his voice dry. "What makes you think I would sell out as easily as you?"

Pablo's face flushed, but he shook his head, shaking it off. "How long is it since you heard a status report, Nicolás? Three hours? More?"

Nick didn't answer.

"The army has laid down its weapons. The people have emerged from their homes to show support for the revolution. Serrano is on his way to the palace. And your brother José will be escorted from the grounds before midnight tonight. We have won, a great victory that will be forever known as the fastest revolution in history."

"I don't believe you," Nick said evenly.

Pablo shrugged. "Believe me. Or not. It doesn't matter. I can see from your face that you know the end is near, even if it has not happened already. We could use your skills, *el leopardo rojo*. We could use your expertise."

Nick shook his head a little.

"Think about it," Pablo encouraged. "You have worked your whole life to make Vistaria a good country. Serrano is simply offering you a second chance to continue that work. He would be a fool to not acknowledge your skills. And he knows, and you know, Nicolás, that after today, after this revolution is over, there will be much rebuilding. Much more work to do."

"Why would I consider such an offer when you and your associates have already wiped out all the work I have done to this day?" Nick demanded.

Pablo pointed to Harry, on the other side of the irregular circle surrounding them. "Because if you do not agree, Harry will shoot you all."

"I see. Work for Vistaria, or die. Is that it? And if I agree, you let the rest of them go?"

José took a moment to answer. "I have my orders," he said.

Nick's slowly lowered his gun. Calli wanted to protest, to cry out her disappointment, but how could Nick resist such an offer?

She felt his arm loosen from around her shoulders and stepped back a little. He lifted up her chin to make her look at him, turning to face her properly. "I have to accept," he said simply.

"I know." She held back the torrent of words, the warnings her instincts yelled at her.

He kissed her, but it was a dry, passionless touch of the lips, and she knew then that she had lost whatever hold she had on him. Nick had long gone from her. The man that kissed her now had no thought for her. His mind was elsewhere, already turned to the task of rebuilding a country. He had no use for the American woman who had begun the conflagration that had ruined that country in the first place.

His hand was on her shoulder and moved around to plant itself in the middle of her chest. "Go away," he said firmly, and gave her a mighty shove. It sent her tumbling backwards, to land almost flat on her back in the dirt. She grunted as all her breath was knocked out of her.

She lifted her head, stunned, just in time to see Nick spin on his heel 180 degrees, the gun coming up. He fired one shot, and Harry dropped to the ground, the lethal-looking rifle clattering down with him.

"Down!" Nick said.

Joshua dropped to the ground, bringing Beryl with him, the old soldiering reactions barely blunted. Minnie remained a condensed ball on the ground.

Nick spun again, another half circle, to face Pablo. The revolutionary was just bringing his revolver up to aim, an expression of anger and shock building on his face. Nick shot him directly between the eyes then instantly leapt towards the crumpling body. At that moment, the man who had stayed standing in the middle of the road fired his own pistol at the place where Nick had been a second before.

Nick caught and held Pablo's body against him and shot at the man with the revolver. Calli saw a small red rose bloom on the man's forehead as his knees gave way and he folded into the dirt.

The fourth man was between Nick and the car. He had just brought his gun up to aim, shock slowing his movements. Nick spun to face him, bringing Pablo's body around as a shield. He pulled the trigger for a fourth time.

The man fired anyway, and the bullet thudded into the sand at Nick's feet. The man fell over and lay still.

It was suddenly very quiet.

"Stay down," Nick said, his voice flat. He turned, his gun still at the ready, checking all three of the rebels. His face was an expressionless mask, his eyes narrowed in concentration. Then he straightened and let Pablo's body drop to the ground, then put another bullet in the man's temple. He walked around to the other three rebels and did the same to each.

Finally, he moved to crouch next to Joshua where the older man lay on one elbow, his arm around Beryl, who had her face buried against his shoulder. "We're okay," Joshua said quietly.

Nick nodded and moved to Minnie. "Minnie?" He laid his hand on her shoulder.

She pointed to Harry, and her hand trembled. "He was the one. He was the guy at the party."

"I know," Nick said soothingly. "I remembered his face."

"It was he who nearly got Duardo killed—" She stopped abruptly, and lowered her hand. Wrapped her arms around her knees. "I'm okay," she said hollowly. Nick patted her shoulder and rose and came over to where Calli lay propped on her elbows. He crouched next to her and put the gun on the ground, then helped her sit up.

"Did I hurt you?" he asked. "When I pushed?"

"My pride, for a moment. God, Nick, I thought you were going to join them!"

"That's what I wanted them to think. It's the only way I could get them to relax and drop their guard—just enough to give me the time I needed against four of them."

"I still can't believe you pulled it off."

He dropped his gaze, as if he was suddenly ashamed. "I was tempted," he confessed, his voice low. "For a moment I considered it."

"That's natural," she said gently. "He offered you the one thing in your life that has meaning."

"But the price was giving up the only other thing in my life with meaning," Nick said, lifting his head again to look at her. "Pablo's orders were to kill anyone trying to leave the country. He knew I had guessed it right. I could see it in his eyes." He got to his feet and helped her to hers.

But Calli was still trying to process his first statement. "What could possibly mean as much to you as Vistaria?" she asked, trying to quench the hope soaring in her.

He smiled a little. "You, of course." He turned to look at Minnie. "At the end, Duardo understood it better than I did. Don't sacrifice love, for there is no greater cause, and you never get the time back if you let it slip away."

Minnie smiled a little, but her cheeks were wet with tears.

Nick picked up Calli's hand. "I won't allow Duardo's sacrifice to be meaningless." He kissed her hand. Then he took her in his arms and kissed her properly, but briefly, then let her go. "We must go. Now. I have to get you to the boat."

✳ ✳ ✳ ✳ ✳

Twenty minutes later they clattered onto a long dock, running like crazy for a long sloop tied up at the end of the wooden pier, their bags and packs slapping against their legs and backs. Although they had not been challenged again, Nick took no more chances. He grabbed the rail of the boat and vaulted over the side onto the decking. "Joshua, come with me!" he called as he pushed aside a pair of doors. He climbed down into the cabin.

Calli helped the other two on board and went below, to see what else needed doing. She found both her uncle and Nick standing at a radio, listening. Nick had the microphone in his hands, as if he had been speaking shortly before.

Nothing but harsh buzzing and static.

"What's happening?" she asked.

"Shhh…" Joshua told her, and shook his head a little, glancing at Nick.

The radio crackled to life, suddenly, and a tinny, distant voice sounded.

"*Soy arrepentido, Nicolás. Ha sido confirmado. José murió hace veinte minutos. Sobre.*"

"Ah, dammit…" Joshua breathed.

Nick grimaced and looked down at his feet. Then, after a second, he lifted the mike. "*¿Cómo?*"

The response lagged a bit. "*El fuego enemigo… No vuelva a la ciudad, Nicolás. Ellos estarán en el Palacio antes de interrupción de día…Usted tendrá que encontrar otra manera. ¿Oye usted? Sobre.*"

Nick looked at Joshua, and it seemed they exchange a silent communication, for he sighed and said into the mike, "*Sí, oigo. Sobre y fuera.*" He threw the mike onto the shelf beside the slim radio set and turned the radio off.

"I didn't get the last part," Joshua said apologetically.

"I didn't get any of it," Calli added.

Nick leaned against the shelf with his elbow, running his hand over his face. "José is dead," he said. "He died twenty minutes ago. Enemy fire, they tell me, along with a hard warning not to go back to the city. They estimate the palace will be taken over by the revolutionaries by dawn."

"I'm sorry, Nick," she said softly.

"With José dead, you can't go back," Joshua said quietly. "You have to come to Mexico with us. Regroup there, get your bearings. And Carmen is there, too. She must be told."

Nick shut his eyes for a moment. "The fastest revolution in history," he said.

"It's not over until you say it is," Calli said. "As long as you don't quit fighting, it's not finished."

He looked at her and gave her a small smile, but it was almost a grimace. "Thank you," he said softly.

Chapter Eighteen

The unnatural motion of the mattress beneath her woke Minnie from the shallow sleep she had achieved. She rolled onto her back and stared up at the bottom of the bunk above her. Scattered light off waves played on the painted wood, reflected through the porthole next to her. While she watched, the aching hurt and sadness came back, slipping over her like a pall.

"Duardo," she whispered to the dark.

She deliberately recalled the last moments again, trying to acquaint herself with the fact, for it still did not seem real—as if someone would arrive very soon and explain that it was all a terrible mistake, so sorry, speak to our lawyers. So she lay there and remembered his words. Nick's voice, as he translated them. The feel of Duardo beneath her as she lay against him for the few moments she'd had before they had taken him away—

Abruptly, she sat up in the bunk, and her head slammed into the bunk above. She held her forehead and rolled her eyes, trying to clear her mind and her sight, as a potent mix of excitement and horror burst through her. Mindful of her parents, who slept the sleep of the truly exhausted beside her, she whispered the astonishing fact just to herself, trying it aloud to see if it sounded as hopeful as it seemed in her stressed-out mind.

"He was still warm...!"

* * * * *

Just after midnight they crossed into international waters, the graceful yacht skimming the waves with the spinnaker billowed out full, spraying iridescent foam aside with each crest of water.

Calli emerged from belowdecks where she had been checking on the family of three sleeping in peaceful berths. She was armed with hot coffee and wore a sweater she had found in a cupboard. Nick sat at the wheel, but rested only one hand on it. She handed him the coffee, and he thanked her distantly. He seemed pre-occupied.

"We'll be in Mexico some time tomorrow," he said, taking a sip and dropping the cup into the swinging holder hanging from the console.

"What's wrong?" she said softly. "Is it what Pablo said? You're not running away, Nick. You're just...regrouping. We both know you won't leave Vistaria to fend for itself for long."

He shook his head. "That wasn't what I was thinking at all," he said.

"Then...?"

He glanced at her, and she recognized discomfort in his expression.

"What?" she asked, a spurt of fear touching her.

"*La dama fuerte*," he said softly. "I never asked you if you wanted this. If you wanted...me."

"Oh," she said inadequately.

"Calli, you're never going to have a normal life with me. I can't offer you a damned thing. Not even a nation to reside in. It's just me. And I'm..." He took a breath, let it out. "I'm afraid it won't be enough. I've done nothing but push you away, I know that. I've put you through...well, a war. But I want you to say yes. I want you to stay with me. Always."

She considered this for a moment.

"The lady stays silent," Nick murmured to himself, but she could hear the note of worry in his voice.

She gave a little laugh. "You'd better start teaching me Spanish, Nick. It seems to be the one thing I can't teach myself out of a book."

He plucked her from the deck, put her on his lap and wrapped his arms around her. Before she could gasp her surprise, he kissed her, and this time it was not a brief one. When he let her draw a full breath again, she said, "The wheel!"

"I am watching it," he assured her, his voice low, deep, the way she remembered it from the first time they had met.

"Always, Nick?" she asked softly, not quite able to believe he wanted her to stay with him forever.

"Until the end, whenever that may be." He cleared his throat. "Duardo said it best. Even if the end was tomorrow, and we only have this day in which I call you mine, I'll take that. I will grab it with both hands, and be proud...and very grateful that you stayed."

About the author:

Tracy Cooper-Posey is a national award-winning writer. An Australian, she brought her family with her to Edmonton, Alberta, Canada in 1996 to marry. Tracy is a "net citizen": She met and courted her husband on the Internet, and has coordinated discussion groups and teaching on-line. She also wrote and maintains her own web site. She teaches creative writing both on-line and at college, and entertains students and the public with anecdotes and insights into one the most antisocial professions in the world, and the peculiar industry it drives.

Tracy also writes as Anastasia Black.

Tracey Cooper-Posey welcomes mail from readers. You can write to her c/o Ellora's Cave Publishing at P.O. Box 787, Hudson, Ohio 44236-0787.

Also by TRACY COOPER-POSEY:

- Winter Warriors – with Denise A. Agnew &
  Rosemary Laurey

Writing as ANASTASIA BLACK:

- Forbidden

Why an electronic book?

We live in the Information Age—an exciting time in the history of human civilization in which technology rules supreme and continues to progress in leaps and bounds every minute of every hour of every day. For a multitude of reasons, more and more avid literary fans are opting to purchase e-books instead of paperbacks. The question to those not yet initiated to the world of electronic reading is simply: *why?*

1. *Price.* An electronic title at Ellora's Cave Publishing runs anywhere from 40-75% less than the cover price of the <u>exact same title</u> in paperback format. Why? Cold mathematics. It is less expensive to publish an e-book than it is to publish a paperback, so the savings are passed along to the consumer.

2. *Space.* Running out of room to house your paperback books? That is one worry you will never have with electronic novels. For a low one-time cost, you can purchase a handheld computer designed specifically for e-reading purposes. Many e-readers are larger than the average handheld, giving you plenty of screen room. Better yet, hundreds of titles can be stored within your new library—a single microchip. (Please note that Ellora's Cave does not endorse any specific brands. You can check our website at www.ellorascave.com for customer recommendations we make available to new consumers.)

3. *Mobility.* Because your new library now consists of only a microchip, your entire cache of books can be taken with you wherever you go.

4. *Personal preferences are accounted for.* Are the words you are currently reading too small? Too large? Too...ANNOYING? Paperback books cannot be modified according to personal preferences, but e-books can.

5. *Innovation.* The way you read a book is not the only advancement the Information Age has gifted the literary community with. There is also the factor of what you can read. Ellora's Cave Publishing will be introducing a new line of interactive titles that are available in e-book format only.

6. *Instant gratification.* Is it the middle of the night and all the bookstores are closed? Are you tired of waiting days—sometimes weeks—for online and offline bookstores to ship the novels you bought? Ellora's Cave Publishing sells instantaneous downloads 24 hours a day, 7 days a week, 365 days a year. Our e-book delivery system is 100% automated, meaning your order is filled as soon as you pay for it.

Those are a few of the top reasons why electronic novels are displacing paperbacks for many an avid reader. As always, Ellora's Cave Publishing welcomes your questions and comments. We invite you to email us at service@ellorascave.com or write to us directly at: P.O. Box 787, Hudson, Ohio 44236-0787.

Printed in the United States
22981LVS00003B/49-144

9 781843 607472